CUMBRIA LIBRARIES

3800304705353 5

KT-407-994

THE PROPERTY OF LIES

THE PROPERTY OF LIES

A Herbert Reardon historical mystery

Marjorie Eccles

This first world edition published 2017
in Great Britain and the USA by
SEVERN HOUSE PUBLISHERS LTD of
19 Cedar Road, Sutton, Surrey, England, SM2 5DA.
Trade paperback edition first published
in Great Britain and the USA 2017 by
SEVERN HOUSE PUBLISHERS LTD

Copyright © 2017 by Marjorie Eccles.

All rights reserved including the right of
reproduction in whole or in part in any form.
The moral right of the author has been asserted.

British Library Cataloguing in Publication Data
A CIP catalogue record for this title is available from the British Library.

ISBN-13: 978-0-7278-8720-7 (cased)
ISBN-13: 978-1-84751-827-9 (trade paper)
ISBN-13: 978-1-78010-895-7 (e-book)

This is a work of fiction. Names, characters, places and incidents
are either the product of the author's imagination or are used fictitiously.
Except where actual historical events and characters are being described
for the storyline of this novel, all situations in this publication are
fictitious and any resemblance to actual persons, living or dead,
business establishments, events or locales is purely coincidental.

All Severn House titles are printed on acid-free paper.

Severn House Publishers support the Forest Stewardship Council™ [FSC™],
the leading international forest certification organisation.
All our titles that are printed on FSC certified paper carry the FSC logo.

Typeset by Palimpsest Book Production Ltd.,
Falkirk, Stirlingshire, Scotland.
Printed and bound in Great Britain by
TJ International, Padstow, Cornwall.

PROLOGUE

She hadn't meant to come back here – not ever. The people. The place itself. What it has come to mean . . . Don't go, every instinct had screamed when she got the note. But she has been drawn, totally against her will. The note wouldn't have been sent without purpose – would it? And yet, that inner voice won't go away, repeating itself over and over, like a gramophone record with the needle stuck in the groove, scratchy and insistent, setting her teeth on edge. Run, get away, go, go . . .

It is a wild night, intermittent rain, scudding clouds driven across a gibbous moon, the wind roaring, protesting trees moaning and waving demented, shaken heads. Buffeted and unsteady, she picks her way gingerly among the rubble on the ground, through the whipped-up storm of grit, dust and builders' detritus, towards the half-demolished structure that rears up in front of her. It's different, now that more of the ancient building has been knocked down. And very confusing. As she enters, the wind howls down the tall chimneys and whistles through glassless windows and along empty passages. Outside, a tarpaulin, caught by the wind, cracks like a pistol shot.

Eventually she locates the staircase. A rope is stretched across the foot, meaning the way ahead is forbidden, and perhaps dangerous. Her heart is going like a pump engine, but she ignores the warning. The passages upstairs creak and groan with every footstep. It's really dark up here and her torch when she switches it on gives out only the weakest of glimmers. Stupid, stupid mistake! In her frantic hurry to leave, it had never occurred to her to check the battery. It flickers once or twice then goes out.

She thrusts the useless thing into her pocket, but there is no turning back now, having come so far. It can only be a matter of time until she finds her night vision and her eyes adjust to the dim outlines around her. She pushes on, each footstep echoing. She stops. *Was* that an echo? No, just the scrabble of a mouse, or some other night creature. Still disorientated without her torch, she stumbles on, and crashes into a heavy ladder propped against a wall, painfully barking her shins and bringing her to a full stop. A minute to steady herself, before edging past it and moving a cautious few steps forward, trying to regain her sense of direction. Then she hears the sound again and this time she is certain the footsteps behind are real.

'At last! I thought you weren't coming.'

There is no reassuring answer. Panic strikes. But her eyes are becoming more adapted to the dark and she recognizes where she is now – trapped in a narrow corridor with only one exit, the outlines of a door dimly visible at the end. Another rustle behind her, and she runs headlong towards it, wrenches at the knob and sobs with relief as it turns. It opens on to nothing but yawning pitch-blackness.

For a second or two she teeters, blind with terror, her hand scrabbling for purchase on the rough wood of the doorframe, struggling for balance. Before she finds it she feels hands safely grasping her upper arms. Then a mighty shove forward.

She pitches out and the night swallows her scream.

PART ONE

ONE

June 1930

The sign is large, still newish and shiny: MAXSTEAD COURT SCHOOL FOR GIRLS, it says, gold on dark green. It looks more welcoming than the deserted old lodge situated at the side, or the large, wrought-iron gates, which have a slightly forbidding look, and are indeed shut tight, if not locked. Ellen gets out of the car and tries them, but they won't budge. She mutters, having no desire to make any attempt at manhandling them open, but then she notices a smaller gate to one side, also of wrought iron, presumably for the convenience of people on foot, and tries it. At least that's open.

She goes back to her car, where there's plenty of room to park on the grass verge on the opposite side of the narrow country road, leaves it among the cow parsley and buttercups, and admits herself into the school grounds through the smaller gate. It probably isn't the best idea for the prospective French teacher to arrive at the doors in a smart little car anyway. The new, bull-nosed Morris is supposedly a shared convenience for both herself and her husband, although she knows it's really an inducement not to attempt solo-riding his big BSA motorcycle again. As if she ever would. The one and only time she'd attempted that, a journey into Shropshire she'd known was foolhardy by the time she was halfway there, makes her go hot and cold whenever she thinks about it.

She begins the walk towards the school. Trees line the long drive and give welcome shade on a day that promises to be hot. It has been a freak month or so, high winds and rain, bitterly cold spells alternated with periods of near heat waves, but that's English weather for you. Maybe last night's thunderstorm and today's rising temperature heralds a real change now that June is here.

Halfway down the drive she looks at her watch and sees she is ten minutes early for the appointment. She has a feeling that

Miss Hillyard will be a stickler for punctuality, meaning neither too late nor too early an arrival, so she has time to take in the view of what she hopes might soon become very familiar to her.

At this point the drive begins to dip and the whole of Maxstead Court is visible. The building is new as a school, though ancient as the ancestral home of the Scroope family, who had owned it for generations before increasing taxes, death duties and a general lack of funds for maintenance had forced them to sell. It still looks rather grim, to tell the truth, even on this beautiful day. Grey and square, it rises like a fortress against the dark background of Maxstead Forest. That, too, had once belonged to the Scroopes, as had the hundreds of surrounding acres, and the village of Maxstead itself, come to that, until it was all sold off. The house – what is now the school – stands at one end of grounds that stretch out to its side. The large gardens have been retained, both ornamental and kitchen; new tennis and netball courts installed, and a playing field provided. A tidy sum it must have cost, to turn the large, draughty rooms of the ancient pile into suitable classrooms, dormitories and so on for the privileged young ladies who are boarders at the school, but the eye-watering fees are surely large enough to compensate. And presumably they'll bring in a profit, in time. The school hasn't been open long and scaffolding – just visible at one end of the building – is evidence that structural work is still going on. As yet, as Ellen was told at her first interview with the principal, it does not have its full complement of pupils; only about seventy girls in all, ranging in age from twelve to nearly seventeen.

Ellen is eagerly looking forward to taking up her career again, at last able to follow the work she was trained for and loves, though marriage and teaching don't go hand in hand, at least not for women. It's a ruling she considers outrageous and outmoded, but it's one that still applies, though it was conveniently waived when women were needed to step into the breach during the war and fill the gaps left, with so many male teachers away in the army. Women who now at last have the vote and have equal rights, in theory, with men. But this is a school run by a woman who once fought for women's rights and was later driving ambulances on the front line in France, and since she also owns the school, she is at liberty to scorn such views. Ellen smiles, looks at her watch and then continues her walk down the drive, feeling free at last from what she considers her long years of servitude, only able to use her skills for work as a private tutor or translating for a publisher – when she could get either. It's a long time since she has felt that everything is so well with the world.

But when eventually she comes to where the drive emerges on to the gravelled forecourt, a parterre with lozenge-shaped beds filled with a blaze of bedding plants, she sees that all is far from well with the world. Or not with the world of the man and woman who face each other angrily at the foot of the steps, not bothering to lower their voices.

The row appears to have been going on for some time and, even as Ellen registers what's happening, Edith Hillyard, that calm and dignified figure who had interviewed her a week ago, raises her arm and delivers a swingeing blow to the man's face. He is a well-built man, but she is almost as tall as he is and is no lightweight herself, and he rocks on his feet when it connects. Ellen, brought stock-still in her tracks, and feeling distinctly de trop by now, expects him to retaliate and gets ready to intervene – although what she, five foot in her stockinged feet, can do against such a pair is not immediately clear. Fortunately, there seems to be no need for her to do anything. The man simply stands there while Miss Hillyard turns contemptuously away and walks back up the steps and into the school.

He stares after her for a moment, then spins round and begins striding furiously up the drive. There is no way for him to avoid meeting Ellen, unless she darts away to find undignified shelter under the trees, but she doesn't see why she needs to do this. His quarrel isn't with her. All the same, as he passes her, scarcely taking in the fact that she's there at all, his face still contorted with self-absorbed rage, she feels an instinctive shrinking. Edith Hillyard may have won the fight, but Ellen doesn't think she has by any means won the battle.

She lingers as long as she can before reaching the door and ringing the bell, so as to give the headmistress time to pull herself together and regain her composure. She need not have bothered. Miss Hillyard, tall and stately, comes unruffled into the small room where Ellen has been asked to wait, with her hair freshly combed and perhaps a trace of powder on her calm face. 'Good afternoon, Mrs Reardon.' She smiles and offers a steady hand (the one which had nearly felled the man). It feels firm and cool.

Ellen is led into her study next door and tea follows almost immediately, brought in by the same rather nervous young maid who had answered the doorbell. 'Thank you, Ivy, you can leave it there on the small table. It looks very nice,' Miss Hillyard adds, smiling approval at the starched, lace-edged white tray-cloth, the shining silver teapot, pretty cups and saucers all nicely set out. Ivy blushes and departs.

'She's new, still learning,' explains Miss Hillyard, pouring tea and offering digestive biscuits.

Ellen is glad to see the headmistress is a woman who recognizes the value of encouragement. Despite what she has just witnessed outside, she feels her original judgement of her as a pleasant, even-tempered woman, firm but kind, wasn't entirely misplaced. She is distinguished and middle-aged, with a host of qualifications behind her. Her thick dark brown hair, drawn unfashionably back into a bun low on her neck, shows no signs of grey. She is brisk and businesslike, and when they have drunk their tea, she immediately begins a discussion of the details and conditions of Ellen's employment that were put forward at the preliminary interview. Now that Ellen has had time to consider and has agreed to them, Miss Hillyard says she would like her to start immediately, although it's mid-term. She will be working here three days a week – with occasional extra duties, perhaps, when called for?

Ellen hadn't really needed time to consider the terms offered – she'd jumped at the opportunity to work here – though she doesn't tell Miss Hillyard that; and the salary which has been offered is generous enough for her to comply with the request for extra duties, though not so eagerly that she doesn't stipulate certain limits and conditions of her own. One of which is that she might be allowed, on very odd occasions, to bring her dog with her. 'My neighbour's delighted to look after him while I'm here, but in case there happens to be a time when it's not convenient for Mr Levett to have him . . . If there's somewhere he can be accommodated, that is?'

'Of course,' says Miss Hillyard smoothly, after only the slightest hesitation. 'I dare say the domestic staff will be delighted to do the honours.'

A glance at the headmistress's liquid-eyed cocker spaniel bitch, sitting quietly obedient in a basket by the fireplace, causes Ellen a slight qualm, wondering how this pretty little dog, whose name is Goldie, will respond to an exuberant Jack Russell, but there has been no suggestion of the two fraternizing, which is just as well, although Tolly has learnt a few manners and rules since his ownership was transferred to Ellen.

But Miss Hillyard has evidently felt it expedient not to object to the request. 'Of course, I understand, you have your private life to consider.' She refills their cups. 'Your husband is a policeman, I believe?' she asks after a pause, looking thoughtful.

'A detective inspector. That's what brought us to Folbury. They've recently opened a dedicated detective branch here and he's in charge. It's still quite small.' Consisting, to be precise, of Herbert Reardon himself, Detective Sergeant Joe Gilmour and two newly fledged detective constables. Neither a detective superintendent nor a detective chief inspector has so far been deemed necessary. Ellen hopes, against present evidence to the contrary, that this might soon prove to have been a mistake that will be rectified, confident that her husband is more than able to fit the bill for either position. If that happens, and with her job here, and the lovely little house they now have near the town centre, with a garden sloping towards a view of the River Fol, she can ask for no more.

'Well, I'm very glad you did come to live here, and that Mrs Ramsey remembered you. I can't be without a French teacher any longer. A *reliable* teacher,' the headmistress adds.

'Mademoiselle Blanchard was French, I understand?'

'Precisely,' says Miss Hillyard.

French, and therefore untrustworthy, is the implication. Not at all what Ellen had intended to suggest. But Miss Hillyard is evidently still smarting at the abrupt departure of Mademoiselle Blanchard. If she had been the sort of woman who sniffs, she would certainly have done so.

'I meant that a Frenchwoman might be a hard act to follow.'

'I can understand you might feel that, of course, and Mademoiselle was excellent as a teacher of French,' she admits, 'but I have no fears about your own abilities, Mrs Reardon, and Mrs Ramsey speaks highly of you. It was fortunate she could recommend you, and that you could come at such short notice.'

'Kate and I go back a long way. We taught together for some time.'

'So she told me. I've known Kate a long while, too.'

A bell rings and there are sounds of the school emerging from its classrooms. Miss Hillyard stands up to terminate the interview. 'I'm extremely glad you have decided to accept the position, Mrs Reardon. I'm sure you will be happy with us. I'll introduce you to the other teachers now, and then, if you wish, perhaps a quick tour round to familiarize you with everything? There wasn't enough time for either when we last spoke to each other, but since it's break now, I'm free for a while.' Although her reserved manner prevents her from showing it, it's evident she can't wait to show off her school.

Ellen says she would be delighted, but before they can set out there is a quick double knock on the door. At Miss Hillyard's invitation to enter, an athletically built woman bounces into the room, a whistle on a ribbon round her neck. She has thick, curly hair and is wearing a square-necked white blouse under a tunic similar to the ones the girls wear, navy blue serge with three box pleats back and front from a yoke, with a belt of the same material. It's short enough to reveal her knees and an inch of muscular thigh clad in beige lisle stockings. She stops short at the sight of Ellen. 'Oh, I'm sorry, I didn't realize . . .'

The head introduces Ellen and explains, somewhat unnecessarily in view of the gymslip, evidently the woman's working garb, that Miss Cash teaches games and physical training.

'Daphne,' adds Miss Cash, responding to Ellen's outstretched hand with a strong grasp and a brief nod. They exchange pleasantries for a few minutes and then Miss Cash says, 'I came to tell you there's been another incident, Miss Hillyard. Gym knickers missing from Antonia Freeman's locker.'

'Well, that should narrow the list of suspects. There aren't many needing them that size,' says Miss Hillyard, evidently not bereft of humour, although she does not allow herself to smile. 'It's probably a joke – and Antonia shouldn't have left them in her locker. I'll look into it later.'

'Very well, Miss Hillyard.' The other woman doesn't look satisfied, but as Miss Hillyard has spoken dismissively, she has no option but to bounce off again, giving Ellen another casual, but not unfriendly nod. Miss Hillyard doesn't explain the reference to 'another incident'.

They have just emerged into the small anteroom where Ellen had waited when the telephone in Miss Hillyard's study rings. She hesitates. 'Oh dear, I rather think that may be a call I'm expecting, so if you'll excuse me, I must answer it. Do sit down and make yourself comfortable. I shouldn't be long.'

The anteroom is pleasant, with a couple of easy chairs and a small sofa where visitors can wait – and presumably girls too, before being admitted to see the head – which must be rather more reassuring for them than the traditional wait standing in the corridor, stomach churning at what is to come. Ellen strolls to the open window and looks out over the green lawns and paths where girls have appeared. Unlike Miss Cash, they are wearing their summer uniform of green print dresses with white collars and cuffs, an enlightened innovation, though it hasn't yet gone as far as dispensing with the universally hated black woollen stockings.

The window, which looks out over the stretch of grounds to the side of the house, is wide open, and Ellen perches on the cushioned window seat. The extensive lawn has just been cut and the sweet scent of mown grass drifts into the room. In the distance she can see the figure of a man pushing a mower back and forth over the playing field. Girls are moving around in pairs, arm-in-arm, or gathering in groups. One is lying on the grass just under the window, chin propped on her elbows, reading intently. Older girls perch on the low stone walls that run around several raised flower beds, giggling and gossiping, while younger ones toss a ball or simply chase about running off surplus energy. High-pitched chatter and shrill laughter fills the air. Why is it that any group of women, whatever their age, sound like a gaggle of geese, Ellen wonders, at the same time feeling a surge of contentment at being back in her own environment. She lets her imagination picture a day when her little goddaughter, Ellie, Sergeant Joe Gilmour's daughter, might well be a pupil here. Then she recalls the fees, laughs at the idea and puts the picture from her mind.

A short, stocky woman clad, despite the warmth of the day, in a tweed costume, plus tie, and a green Tyrolean hat, approaches the girl who is reading, and although she walks with the aid of a stick, it doesn't hinder her from moving briskly. The girl is so absorbed in her book that she hears nothing, and starts when the teacher prods her with the stick, none too lightly. A clipped, donnish voice comes clearly through the window. 'Get up at once, Catherine. Don't you realize how damp the grass is?'

The girl raises a vivid face, still eager and animated from what she has been reading. The animation fades as she sees the severe teacher and she scrambles up, finger in the book to keep its place. 'Oh, sorry, Miss Elliott, I didn't notice.'

'You'll notice soon enough if you get rheumatism,' Miss Elliott replies sourly. 'Everything's soaking after last night's storm, you silly girl. What's wrong with the library, if you want to read?' She frowns. 'What's that you have there?'

Catherine holds out her book and Miss Elliott gives it a quick glance, but evidently can't find anything unsuitable about it to criticize and returns it without comment. 'Get yourself tidied up before your next lesson, you look a disgrace.' She stumps away, but Catherine doesn't immediately follow. She doesn't look chastened, but her expression is hard to read. She is a tall, graceful girl of about fourteen, who looks as though she might normally present a neat appearance. At the moment, however, Miss Elliott is right: the damp has creased the front of her dress from lying on it, and her straight, fair hair is a mess where she has evidently run her fingers through it.

'I'm sorry to have kept you waiting so long,' says Miss Hillyard behind Ellen. 'That's Miss Elliott, by the way,' she adds with a rather wry expression, indicating the tweed-clad teacher, who has now halted a noisy group of juniors, presumably in the hope of dampening their high spirits. 'Maths. A bit of a martinet, you'll find, but I was fortunate she was available to come here when we started. She was principal of another school but her increasing lameness has forced her to take up a rather less taxing position. I think you'll find her an interesting person when you get to know her.' Her gaze transfers approvingly to the girl, now walking away unhurriedly, the book under her arm. 'And that's Catherine Leyland, one of our two scholarship girls.' Her face shines with pride. 'Our most able pupil – though not, perhaps, a star at maths, which doesn't make her a favourite with Miss Elliott, I'm afraid. Oh dear, there goes the bell.' She looks vexed. 'What a nuisance! That call took much longer than I expected, and I shortly have the sixth form for Latin. I'm so sorry. I can get someone else to show you round, though. Miss Draper has a free period and I'm sure she would be delighted. Unless, of course, you want to be on your way home?'

'No, no. Not in the least. I'm dying to see the school.'

She has given the correct response and Miss Hillyard looks pleased. 'Come along then.'

The staff room is comfortable and relaxing, furnished with chintz-covered armchairs, small tables, well-filled bookshelves and some nice watercolours on the walls. It's tidier than most staff rooms, but perhaps the newness hasn't worn off yet.

Sitting at a table is Miss Eve Draper, the deputy headmistress, who teaches English, a bespectacled, plump and untidy woman with a quantity of soft, light brown hair which seems intent on escaping from its pins, but who is evidently as proud of the school as the headmistress is; her face lights up when the request is conveyed to her. 'Oh gosh, yes, delighted. Give me a minute or two while I sort myself out. Take a pew.'

Miss Hillyard, with another apology for abandoning Ellen, leaves while the other woman endeavours, without much success, to stack into a neat pile the slippery-backed exercise books she has been correcting. Abandoning the attempt, she scoops them up and shoves them anyhow into a cupboard, slams the door on them and beams. '4B can wait there for a while.'

She proves to be good-natured and talkative. In the intervals as they make their tour, they exchange information and learn that she and Ellen's friend Kate Ramsey (the one who recommended her for this position) had trained, a few years apart, at the Agatha Dean Teacher Training College, as had Miss Hillyard.

'Imagine that, her being at Agatha's as well!' Miss Draper says, beaming, as if this is evidence of a bond, though it's not all that surprising. There are only so many teacher-training colleges, after all. Ellen has frequently met up with fellow alumni in the course of her work. But she doesn't point this out.

Miss Draper seems a likeable woman, quick to make friends, and Ellen detects a definite case of heroine-worship as she rattles on about how much Miss Hillyard has achieved since the school opened. 'Lady Maude, who used to live here, couldn't believe the transformation when she was invited to look round and see what's been done. It was a dreadful wrench for the old lady to leave the house, but it couldn't be kept up, you know; the Scroopes had to sell. She now lives in The Bothy – oh, sorry, the Dower House,' she corrects herself, waving vaguely towards chimneys which can just be seen beyond what is now the playing field. 'I believe she was apprehensive that her home would have been institutionalized, but she was very happy to see it isn't at all like that. The head's frightfully clever at that sort of thing.'

Ellen duly admires the alterations that have taken place, and with genuine approval. The grey stone building itself is somewhat grim, despite the softening effect of cheerful flower beds and smooth green lawns, grim enough to strike despair into the heart of any little girl snatched away from her parents for the first time. Yet the transformation from what could only have been a rather barn-like atmosphere in such an old house has certainly been well done. Such places are invariably chilly, and though the thick walls provide a coolness welcome on a hot day like this, she's pleased to note the generous provision of radiators for the winter months.

'I'm sure the girls love being here.'

'Oh, absolutely!'

Since the classrooms are now in use for lessons, it precludes their inspection, but Ellen's respect for Miss Hillyard's venture grows as they visit the other parts of the school – the dining room in which staff and pupils take their meals together, and the girls' dormitories, although the older girls share study-bedrooms, three to a room. A rather different aspect is revealed when a peep into the gloomy and unwelcoming library reveals that it has been left in its original wood-panelled state, with its no doubt unreadable tomes stacked on the shelves and stiff chairs around a long, central oak table. Not a place to encourage girls to curl up and read, or even to browse. Miss Draper wastes no time there and quickly moves on.

'And that's about it,' she says as they emerge, 'apart from the art room, along there.' She looks a little uncertain about viewing it, but as she remembers there is no class on at the moment, her face clears. 'It used to be known as the garden room, and it's only being used for art as a temporary measure. But it serves very well for the time being because there are big windows for the light. We hope to have something better shortly.' She pushes open the door.

'Oh! Oh, not empty after all! Miss Keith is here.'

She looks about to withdraw, but then stands her ground. A woman is standing with her back to them, occupied in front of an easel. She lifts a languid hand to acknowledge their presence, but continues with what she is doing, still with her back to them. Miss Draper rolls her eyes, but they wait and eventually Jocasta Keith does turn around.

Ellen immediately feels acutely aware of her own shiny nose, the short bob which her hairdresser describes as serviceable, and regrets her entirely unglamorous blouse and skirt. She feels almost on a par with Miss Draper, who seems to have lost more of her hairpins and looks as though she has grabbed the first available garments when she woke up that morning – or even perhaps slept in them. Miss Keith, on the other hand, is immaculately made up, and although she is wearing a three-quarter-length loose smock to protect the clothes underneath, it's short enough to show the lower half of a navy blue skirt with fashionable godets, flesh-coloured silk stockings and rather enviable shoes. The make-up is entirely unnecessary. Perhaps not precisely beautiful, she is still a striking woman by any standards. She has a pale and flawless skin, brown, almond-shaped eyes and classical features. Her vivid lipstick outlines a full, rather sensuous mouth and her dark hair is beautifully arranged. She does not look like anyone's idea of a schoolmistress.

And certainly not one in a small, as yet undistinguished school on the outskirts of a village, whose only amenity is

Folbury, a market town several miles away. What is such an exotic specimen doing, teaching here?

'Sorry, I can't shake hands,' she says, spreading out paint-stained fingers, not looking, or even sounding remotely regretful, but actually rather scornful. She is clearly impatient of the interruption and throws sideways glances back to the canvas on the easel – which is as colourful as her appearance, and seems to be an abstract with a good deal of angry reds and purples in it. Ellen has no knowledge on which to base judgement, but it isn't the sort of thing she would want to encounter on her living-room wall before breakfast.

'I hope you're going to be more accommodating than the last French teacher,' Miss Keith says ungraciously when she learns that Ellen will be replacing Mademoiselle Blanchard.

'Well,' says Miss Draper, 'I'm sure I don't know what you mean by that, Miss Keith. Mam'selle was easy to get on with.'

'Depends who you are, I suppose. At any rate, Mrs Reardon, you'll have relieved Miss Draper of a burden.'

Miss Draper reddens and says rather abruptly, 'It was no burden. I wasn't trained to teach French but I've been happy to stand in.' She attempts, unsuccessfully, to secure some errant hair with a hairpin. A short silence ensues. 'Well then, we'll leave you to it, Miss Keith.'

When the door has closed behind them and they have walked silently back along the corridor, she eventually says, 'I'm afraid I'm frightfully ignorant about modern art, but I do believe Miss Keith is regarded as rather good by those who know more than I do.'

Ellen feels this comment is more than generous, considering Miss Keith's attitude, but Eve Draper evidently has a nicer nature than she herself has. 'Well, you've seen the best part,' she goes on more cheerfully, Miss Keith commendably forgotten (or ignored), 'now for the worst.'

What she means by this is evident as they stop to look out of a large ground-floor window which gives a view of the rear of the school. The house, solidly regular from the front, unexpectedly proves to throw out two wings of unequal length to the back, neither of which as yet forms a habitable part of the school. Miss Draper explains that the west, longer wing, its interior almost finished, is intended for a science lab, a new art room and not least a gymnasium, freeing the assembly hall from gym equipment and enabling it to be used for its proper purposes. Miss Hillyard is apparently keen on her girls eventually being taught chemistry, physics and biology.

The truncated look of the much older, east wing, on the other hand, is explained by its half-demolished state and its enclosure in scaffolding, part of which Ellen had noticed from the drive. Miss Draper explains. This is the original house, dating from the fifteenth century, of more recent times used as domestic quarters: a laundry, stables and coach houses with servants' rooms above. It has in fact been unused and uninhabited for more years than anyone cares to remember, and although it's basically sound, the inside is presently in such disrepair that the question hovers as to whether it's really worth saving at all. 'There's talk of it also providing a library and common room for the girls – and perhaps even a domestic science department.' She looks rather embarrassed at this last, and Ellen senses controversy. Not everyone is willing to admit that aspects of life, post-war, are rapidly changing, but look at what has happened to Maxstead Court and its owners. At the moment, girls whose parents can afford the fees here are unlikely ever to have to cook a family dinner or make their own clothes, yet there could come a time when even they might be glad they had learnt to cook and sew.

In fact, part of the ancient wing has already disappeared, razed to the ground. The stables and coach houses have gone. What is left is an oddly sheared-off arm looking forlornly like those pictures of houses in the Flanders battlefields, ruined by bombs and shells, leaving their insides, doors and staircases nakedly exposed.

'I'm afraid the builders have left things in rather a mess, haven't they?' comments Miss Draper.

This is only too obvious, looking at the forlorn evidence of abandoned activity all around. The two wings and the main building together form a roughly three-sided courtyard, destined when finished, she says, to make a quadrangle (it's already known as the Quad) of the present rubbish-strewn space, with perhaps a fountain and flower beds at the centre, but at present this needs some effort of the imagination. Ellen, who has recently had all too many experiences of the unaccountable appearances and disappearances of tradesmen in the overhaul of the house she and her husband have recently bought, sympathizes. 'They'll be back when it suits them, I expect.'

'It's not quite as simple as that – and for a very good reason, I'm afraid.' Miss Draper's kindly face clouds.

'Projects like this are expensive,' Ellen hazards.

'Oh, it's not that. Or not so much. I'm afraid something frightfully shocking and sad happened, and the builder who was doing the work is no longer available.'

It is an all too familiar story that Ellen now hears. Sometimes it seems as though the unrest and desire for change which has come over the world since the war is to blame for everything, particularly for the current depression. Britain's first-ever Labour government and the Prime Minister, Ramsay MacDonald, aren't doing very much for the unemployment figures. Jobs are hard to find, businesses have regularly gone to the wall. In this case, as Miss Draper explains, the small firm who had been doing the work here had been declared bankrupt, and the owner, shattered by the disgrace of it, had driven his car into a tree while drunk, killing himself in the process.

'So shocking, and such a dreadful pity, although he luckily left no family. He did *such* a good job on the rest of the school, nothing but the best was good enough for him. But I believe Miss Hillyard is hoping his assistant will take over the work and that he's keen to do so. It might give him the opportunity to start up his own business, even as things are now, seeing that the firm had an excellent reputation and a backlist of very satisfied customers. Michael Deegan is another of the same stamp, though better at business, let's hope, than poor dear Mr Broderick. It takes time to sort these things out, of course. But meanwhile,' she frowns, 'no one seems to know what to do about clearing this mess up.'

Grass and weeds are growing between the old, cracked paving stones, passage across them made more hazardous by the rubble left scattered around. Wheelbarrows, a cement mixer, planks, buckets, ladders and piles of bricks have apparently been left where they stand, creating more potential risks.

'It's quite dangerous and strictly out of bounds for the girls of course,' Miss Draper goes on, 'but now the builders aren't here, I'm afraid they sometimes use it as a short cut to the tennis courts if they are short of time, rather than go round by the other way. *And* for larking about and so on,' she adds disapprovingly. 'For some reason that old ruin does seem to exert a sort of fascination.'

'Because it's forbidden?' suggests Ellen.

Miss Draper laughs. 'Very likely. But with all this rubbish strewn around, they could easily have an accident.' She cranes her neck to peer short-sightedly across the sunlit space towards a shapeless, dark bundle of something, yet more rubbish, that lies next to a tarpaulin which seems to have been blown aside.

Ellen, with sharper eyesight, follows the direction of her gaze. After a moment or two she says, 'I'm afraid, Miss Draper, it looks very much as though the accident might already have happened. We'd better get across there, quick.' Miss Draper gasps and then, with one accord, they run.

Having got there first and taken one horrified look at what has been revealed by the blown-away tarpaulin, Ellen pulls it gently back again. She hears the other woman's ragged breath as she comes up behind her. 'Don't look, Miss Draper.'

But Miss Draper has already seen. It appears she might be going to faint, or be sick, or worse. She is a strange colour. Her breathing becomes even heavier and her hand presses on her chest. 'It's Mam'selle,' she whispers, 'Mam'selle Blanchard. I – I suppose we must get the doctor.'

But Mam'selle – even to Miss Draper's myopic eyes – is far beyond that, and they both know it.

TWO

Viewing the dead was a sombre fact of life in Dr Kay Dysart's profession, and not least when wearing her police doctor hat, when it was all too often gruesome. But the dead she saw, even in those circumstances, hadn't usually reached this stage of decomposition. Rodents had been here before her, blowflies and other insects had all helped to reduce what had once been the body of a woman to a thing of putrefaction. The stench made her gag, though it was less over-powering now than it would have been had the body been discovered earlier. 'She's been here for some time,' she announced. Stating the patently obvious in order to concentrate on not actually being sick and disgracing herself, because even experienced doctors can feel nauseated at times. 'A month or six weeks, maybe?'

The woman's body lay across a rough, sprawling heap of jagged masonry, mortar, plaster and wrenched-up floorboards pierced with long rusty nails, tossed there like another piece of tawdry detritus. Detective Inspector Reardon and his detective sergeant, Joe Gilmour, had retreated to one side, having already seen more than they wanted to see. After a necessary quick inspection, the whiff of decay had been enough grounds for retreat into the shade cast by the long shadows which lay across the light-filled space between the school proper and this scaffolding-caged wing. They were joined by the cameraman and his assistant, who were waiting to photo-graph the body from all angles, before it should be borne away on a stretcher. Reardon in particular saw himself as having a strong stomach, but even he felt no need to prolong the agony, and both men had been happy to leave the doctor, a competent professional, to her task. He swallowed down bile, and with it the sadness he always felt when a young, vital life had been so summarily terminated, subdued as always in the presence of untimely death. He didn't often dwell on the transient nature of life, but at times like this it was forcibly brought home to you.

The late afternoon sun as it moved towards evening had lost none of its power as yet. He wiped the sweat from his brow while Gilmour, not one for standing still at the best of times, jacket off and hooked over his shoulder, began mooching around among the rubbish.

There was plenty of it. They'd been told the work on this part of the school was a project temporarily in abeyance. Abandoned, more like it. With no attempt to tidy it up a bit before leaving, either. Builders' equipment was strewn around anyhow: a cement mixer, planks, ladders, stacks of bricks shrouded in canvas, and even a few spades and picks, all scattered amid a wasteland of uncleared debris and muddy puddles dried up by the sun after last night's storm. The last days of Pompeii without the volcanic ash. The *Marie Celeste*.

The rubbish providing the body's last resting place was a rough, sloping pile which had been shovelled against the end wall of the partly demolished wing while awaiting removal. Originally an internal wall, this now presented a bare, blank face – blank except for still visible traces of what had once been a staircase, leading to a door at what must be the first floor, which even so meant it was at a fair old height. But the whole of Maxstead Court was a house of high ceilings and several storeys, as Reardon well remembered.

This wasn't his first visit here. Three years ago, when a body had been discovered on the edges of Maxstead Forest, he'd been called in from Headquarters in Dudley where he then worked to assist the uniformed police at Folbury, who didn't yet have their own detectives. That was before the estate and the house itself had been sold, when the formidable Lady Maude had been the chatelaine, before it was ever thought of as a school.

He turned his attention back to the wall, squinting up to the point where the staircase would have finished. A door, for God's sake! A door left in situ when it surely should have been removed and the space at least temporarily bricked up in the interests of safety. An act of criminal negligence by the builders, if ever there was one. An accident waiting to happen. He estimated the trajectory of a body catapulting from it. It would hardly have failed to hit that lethal accumulation of rubbish directly below. Yet people could, and did, survive very much higher falls than that.

'Don't give it a thought,' said the doctor who, having now ensured that the body had been removed with due care and attention, had picked her way over to where he was standing, following his glance and shrewdly interpreting what he'd been thinking. 'She couldn't have survived a fall like that – not with those injuries. Amongst other things, her neck was broken, and it would be a miracle if the spinal cord wasn't damaged.' She glanced again at the wall and the track of the staircase. 'If she *did* fall.'

Reardon had come across Kay Dysart several times previously in the course of both their duties, and respected her opinions. She was short and dark-haired, with a quick, clipped way of speaking; not one to waste time or mince words. She was sharp and it was no surprise that she'd interpreted the situation immediately. There might – conceivably – be circumstances when you could open a door such as that one, unaware, and step out into space, but you could hardly close it behind you, nor cover your own body with the tarpaulin which had hidden it until now. It was still held down at one corner by several large stones but, in last night's unexpected storm, the wind had whipped under the edges and lifted most of it clear of the other chunks of masonry which had weighted it down.

'Nasty. But she would have died pretty well instantaneously,' the doctor assured him, seeing the expression on his face. 'Landed face downwards if I'm any judge, then toppled over. Do you know who she is yet?'

'Yes. Her name's Blanchard, Isabelle Blanchard. She was a teacher here at the school. French.' The teacher his wife was replacing. Ellen who, along with another member of the staff, had found the body, a circumstance he did not find reassuring. Despite the horrific injuries, time, the depredations of predators and the insect infestation which had rendered the dead woman's features unrecognizable, her fellow teacher had instantly identified her by her clothes and what must once have been glorious red-gold hair. A Frenchwoman with red hair? Not an unknown or impossible combination, obviously, though for some reason Reardon always imagined Frenchwomen as being dark. 'Apparently, she left several weeks ago.'

'So what was she doing back here?' asked Gilmour, joining them. 'And what the heck was she doing in a dangerous building like that, anyway? Death trap, whichever way you look at it, isn't it, sir?'

Gilmour only called him 'sir' on duty – and when he remembered. They were good friends, and off duty it was different. Their wives had become friends, too, and not only because they were aligned in sympathy at the way police work intruded on their private lives. Despite being two such oddly assorted women on the surface, Ellen as a professional woman and Maisie, who had started out her working life as a maid-of-all-work and had progressed to becoming a trusted employee, running the home of a respectable Folbury family before marrying Joe Gilmour.

'Well, that's a problem I'll leave with you,' Dysart said. 'I'm off now. The pathologist will be able to tell you more than I can after the autopsy, and give you an estimate of how long she's been dead.' The name of the pathologist in question was Donald Rossiter. He was in fact her recently married husband, but marrying him seemed to have made her oddly self-conscious about saying his name. She kept her maiden name for professional reasons. Sketching a salute she left, clearly not sorry to be doing so, having completed what she was there for, the mandatory task of pronouncing life extinct, even in the patently dead.

Gilmour looked after her briskly departing figure. 'Not a nice job for – for her.' Maisie had trained him to know better than to say 'for a woman', but that was clearly what he meant. He was young and go-ahead, but more conventional than he liked to imagine; he still found the idea of a woman undertaking this sort of job hard to stomach. He had a candid, open face and russet hair – not as red as the dead woman's, but the bane of his life as a detective, since it was the first thing anyone remembered about him.

Reardon said, 'We'll need to speak to Miss Hillyard and the staff, but let's have a look in here first.' He gestured towards the cheerless edifice whose grey stones reared up behind them.

Fixing an overall view of the scene in the mind was always a first priority, that and the urgent need to follow up what had happened in the first hours after the crime was committed. There was no extreme rush for that in this case. The trail was long cold. When the pathologist was able to give a more accurate indication of how long she'd been dead, then would be the time to concentrate their enquiries and narrow down the investigation within the timescale given. All the same, the usual adrenalin surge was pushing Reardon on, the need to fit the death within the bigger picture as soon as possible, starting with the place from which Isabelle Blanchard's body had fallen. 'I reckon we're going to need a torch, Joe.'

'There's one in the car.' Gilmour sloped off to fetch it and Reardon ducked beneath the scaffolding. Behind it, the grey stone façade of the centuries-old building seemed solid and capable of standing sturdily on its ancient foundations for several more, despite the fact that it was being demolished. He twisted the circular iron ring set in the heavy, studded oak that would lift the latch. The door didn't yield. It was either irremovably stuck, or locked. He stood back and looked for another entrance.

'Bolted inside. You want to get in there, round the back's the easiest way,' said a voice behind him.

I knew this room would have to be my study as soon as I saw it. It's a corner room, flooded with light, with windows on two sides, the main one overlooking the gravelled parterre and the ugly geometric beds at the front, presently planted with the glaring bedding plants Heaviside loves. Not next year. Next year there will be roses, like the ones in the bed under the other window. Roses. I can never have enough of them. A long stretch of grass runs from that bed, either side of which are the herbaceous borders of the old walled garden. It runs up to the playing field beyond and, in the distance, the forest. A calm, measured view, hallowed by centuries, and one that as yet still astonishes me, that I should own it – Edith Hillyard, who had seemed destined to be the caring, spinster daughter, whose only reward would be in Heaven.

There is no breeze today and each tree and flower is limned with the late afternoon light, looking still and taut, as if manifesting the tension that's gripping the whole school after the horror that's happened here.

Lessons have been suspended for today, but Eve Draper, dear Eve, the living exception to the rule that an untidy personal appearance must proclaim inefficiency, has taken everything in hand. This despite the shock, for a woman with such a weak heart, of finding the body of Mam'selle. To contain the ferment and speculation that's bubbling like a cauldron, she has seen the girls corralled into the assembly hall under the watchful eye of Matron, while she and the rest of my teachers are waiting in the staff room as requested by the police. Including the new French mistress, who has stumbled into all this, poor woman, even before she has even started work here. Detective Inspector Reardon, now in charge of what has happened, is her husband. How is that for irony?

So this is where it has all been leading. To catastrophe, for me and for my school. My school. A fantastic achievement – it would be false modesty to deny it. Twenty-five years ago, I had only just left school myself, and the idea of being headmistress of my own private boarding school for girls had never at that stage entered even the wildest of the dreams no one ever even suspected I had: dreams that one day we might have money, that my mother need not have to get a few shillings by making buttons, hour after hour, as an outworker for the factory round the corner. That my father would miraculously be returned to us.

There are occasions, more frequent of late, when I have to struggle with the sense that I don't deserve my present circumstances. I manage to overcome this by reminding myself that my success has happened through a combination of my own brains and determination, and above all hard work and persistence. Luck, perhaps. Yes, that played a part, but others shared in that same good fortune and haven't ended up nearly so well.

This edifice I've been so careful to build up around myself ever since then, can it possibly be about to be demolished? All I've striven for, and accomplished, is it going to be snatched out of my grasp? The peace of mind so long sought, and finally – almost – achieved; is that, too, to be taken from me?

I could pour myself a stiff drink to calm my nerves, but I've always despised the use of alcohol as a crutch. Especially in the duty I must face shortly. I must address the assembled school and calmly explain to them the tragedy that has befallen Mam'selle, order what must be done, allay the children's fears and quell any signs of hysteria that might arise. For the sake of the girls, the school has to continue to function normally, despite what has happened. I must take control of my emotions.

I'm not sure I can do that.

Of course I can, I always have. I straighten my shoulders, smooth my hair, open some paperwork and concentrate on it while I wait for the detectives to come and see me.

The voice Reardon had heard after trying the door came from somewhere in the corner, where this jutting east wing joined the front of the house. He turned and saw an elderly man standing there, watching him. Collarless flannel shirt, sleeves rolled to the elbows, baggy corduroys held up with braces, heavy working boots, horny hands. Smoking, and leaning on a heavy spade, looking like a parody of a gardener – but then, he *was* a gardener, or used to be. Reardon recognized him from his previous visits to Maxstead. Heaviside, that was his name, a joke dished out by the Almighty, considering the spareness of his wiry frame. A dour man of few words and a habitual, sardonic expression. Not really a likeable chap, if he recalled rightly.

'I know you, don't I? You worked for Lady Maude.'

'Still do. But she don't need me so much with the tiddly bit of garden she has now at the Dower House, and that don't keep me in ciggies, so I work here an' all.' A cough that seemed habitual suggested he'd be better off without them.

The Dower House once more, was it? Reardon liked that better than The Bothy, whimsically so named by the wife of Maxstead's land agent who had occupied it for a time. The garden there would be small enough for Lady Maude to tend it herself for the most part, which was good. She would not live easy in retirement otherwise. She had never been afraid of getting her hands dirty and the gardens to the big house here had been her pride and joy.

Gilmour returned, brandishing a flashlight as the old man was saying, 'You want to get in there, follow me.' He started off, not bothering to check whether they were behind him, his heavy boots making short work of any debris that got in his way as he scrunched over it. Reardon shrugged and nodded to Gilmour. They followed him to the back of the wing. Once there, he put his shoulder to another heavy oak door, assisting its reluctant opening on to a dank passageway that led them to what had at one time been the kitchen. It was ancient and unbelievably cavernous, a room still retaining its complement of stone sinks, heavy block tables, hooks from the ceiling and various sculleries and passages opening off. A great cast-iron range was built into one side of an enormous fireplace, equipped for spit-roasting anything from sides of beef and mutton to sucking pigs and poultry. It must have been a miserable and gloomy place to work in day after day, despite the great fires that would have roared constantly, since all the windows were high up, presumably to prevent kitchen maids from gazing outside when they should have had their hands and minds on the washing up, scouring pans or peeling potatoes. Gilmour found a panel with servants' bells, each labelled with the room it served, shook his head disbelievingly, and peered into a half-open hatch which revealed a hoist, where food had once been sent upstairs by means of a pulley. 'How the other half live!'

'*Lived*,' the old man corrected him. 'Not in years, the Scroopes. Lady Maude wouldn't have it. Had a better kitchen put in t'other wing.'

Reardon let Heaviside lead them towards the stairs, suspecting that this section of the house, evidently the earliest part of Maxstead Court, would be something of a rabbit warren, though it was not really dark inside. It was daylight and most of the windows had lost their glazing anyway. But despite it being eighty in the shade outside, the place had a dank, clammy feeling to it, and he wasn't wrong about it being a maze. As they went forward the silence engulfed them, the only sounds other than Heaviside's cough their footsteps on the old floorboards, the creaking timbers of an ancient house, the scuttering of small creatures behind wainscotings.

'Spooky, ain't it?' Gilmour said behind him.

Reardon grunted. He was no stranger to places where violet death had occurred. There was a reason for stories of them being haunted. Murder left a stain on the air, and vibrations behind it. Nor did it end there – it sent out ripples, its tentacles stretched out to touch everything and everyone who'd been connected with the victim in life. A cold finger touched his spine.

They progressed through what felt to be an endless labyrinth of passages and rooms, although any enquiry as to their functions was met with a shrug and a negative shake of the old man's head. At last they reached the stairs, cordoned off by a warning rope stretched across the foot.

'Thank you, we'll manage on our own now,' Reardon told him.

'Find your own way, can you? Please yourself then, you got time to waste.' As if he knew what the answer would be, without waiting for one Heaviside lifted the rope and ducked under.

Reardon could have asserted his authority and insisted, but decided it wasn't worth arguing with this stubborn old cuss. They followed him, prepared to tread warily, but these particular steps proved to be stone, and dangerous only in that their centre was worn and hollowed by the passage of time and thousands of feet.

Once upstairs, following Heaviside towards the place they were looking for, Reardon conceded he had done well not to leave them to find their own way. They might have wandered around up here until the end of time amidst those countless rooms, most of their doors closed, and passages that appeared to be dead ends. Negotiating a rabbit warren would have been a doddle compared with this place! There, at last, the old man indicated what they sought. It was at the end of a narrow, windowless, perhaps ten-foot passage. Gilmour shone the torch they hadn't needed until now as they approached it cautiously. They stared at a door barred across with several lengths of floorboard nailed to the frame to prevent it being opened – on to what would be nothing but space.

Heaviside watched them silently for a moment or two before turning away and growling, 'Well, there 'tis. Can't stand here talking all day.'

'Just a minute, don't go,' Reardon said. 'Somebody's had those planks off and put them back again.'

The nails which had originally secured the timbers to the frame had evidently been prised out with some force, leaving splintered holes in the old woodwork, and then nailed back, but not quite in the same place. Some of the nails had bent when they were re-hammered in, and when Gilmour took hold of one of the boards and shook it, it threatened to come away. The door had been unbarred with malicious intent, leaving no doubt that it had been deliberately done to send Isabelle Blanchard to her death.

'Well, maybe somebody has been at 'em,' said Heaviside, 'but I don't know nothing about that. Except it weren't me.'

Folbury's fledgling detective section consisted so far only of Reardon himself, Gilmour and two detective constables. Jim Gargrave was new to the division, and Dave Pickersgill had been transferred from Inspector Waterhouse's uniforms, here in Folbury, much to Waterhouse's chagrin. The new section was a thorn in his flesh; he had been in sole charge until now, he couldn't see the need for change, and Reardon's tact was stretched to its limit to keep relations sweet.

Before the arrival of the two DCs to make a necessary, but what he reckoned – apart from the door that had been tampered with – would prove to be an almost certainly unproductive search of the empty wing, Reardon made his way to Miss Hillyard's study. Meanwhile Gilmour, at his diligent best, took himself off to interview the maids, the housekeeper, and anyone else who might provide some information they could use. Not that he expected much from it, but it was a necessary preliminary before the business of real detecting, and you never knew. Since the newly formed detective division had begun to operate, there had been no murders in their line of work – except for one, when a workman in a sweet factory had shoved a colleague into a vat of boiling sugar after an argument, in full view of six witnesses. Murder, all right, but not a case needing many detecting skills on their part. There was enough to keep them busy, God alone knew, but it was mostly to do with petty crime. This was different. He was looking forward to getting stuck in, to justifying to the top brass that the newly formed detective force hadn't been such a bad idea after all.

*   *   *

Reardon understood why his wife's first interview with Miss
Hillyard had given Ellen such a favourable impression. He felt
the same way when they began their conversation. Remaining
calm even in the face of the disaster which had befallen her
school, she had given direct answers to his questions and
didn't waste time bemoaning the shattering discovery and the
upheaval of the last few hours, nor the effect it was going to
have on her pupils, although that had to be uppermost in her
mind. She had gone so far as to say that she hoped the enquiry
would be conducted as discreetly as possible, as she was
concerned at the effect this was going to have on her girls, but
at the same time assuring him that everyone concerned would
cooperate fully in discovering how this dreadful accident could
have happened.

Being married to Ellen meant that he'd met quite a few
teachers in his time, and Edith Hillyard was a lot less intimidating than some of the headmistresses he had encountered,
though he suspected she might show dragon's claws when the
occasion demanded. She looked so perfectly at home in her
study, a quiet, tastefully furnished room, her little dog, after
one sniff at his feet, obediently retired to curl up in its basket.
Mistress of her own domain, Miss Hillyard, quietly confident,
headmistress personified. The sort of woman you would implicitly
trust your daughters to, without any worries. A safe pair of hands,
as no doubt the politicians would have it. She was hiding her
anxieties well, and he respected her for it, though he was hardly
surprised. Never mind outward appearances, women in her
position invariably had a core of steel; it was what got them
where they were.

'We'll do all we can to help,' she reiterated.

'Thank you, I would appreciate that.'

An intelligent woman like her could not already have failed
to draw the obvious conclusions. She, too, had seen what Ellen
and Miss Draper had seen and must realize that very soon the
truth of how the Frenchwoman had died must emerge, but if
she wanted to keep up the fiction of accidental death for the
moment, he was willing to go along with it. He had sympathy
with her over that. Her school was still in the early stages of
being established and its reputation could easily be damaged

by any whiff that anything in its environment (or whatever had caused the death of the French teacher) might be dangerous. The scandal of a murder could finish it off completely.

He understood what she must be going through, but she had to be the starting point for their enquiries. 'You understand it's necessary to find out as much as we can about Mademoiselle Blanchard and her background?'

'Of course. Though I don't know that I can be much help.'

'Let's begin with how long she had worked here.'

'She joined us in January, at the beginning of the new term. I needed a good French teacher rather quickly when the person I had appointed had to give back-word because she suddenly had to have an operation – a serious one, by all accounts. She didn't know how long it would be before she could return, but fortunately she was able to recommend a temporary replacement.' Mlle Blanchard, she explained, was a Frenchwoman who had previously been teaching English in France but had recently come to England. She hesitated. 'Well, I met her, and found she spoke perfect English and indeed seemed highly suitable. As it turned out, I'd made the right decision – she proved to be an excellent teacher. You may imagine how upset I was when she decided to leave so suddenly, without giving me any notice. She said she had family problems at home, but she was vague and declined to say what they were.'

'Home being France, I suppose? Where exactly?'

Another hesitation, then she shrugged. 'I'm not quite sure.'

There was something going on here that he couldn't quite put a finger on, other than a justifiable annoyance, or anger, at the woman's desertion. 'We need to inform her family, her next of kin, Miss Hillyard,' he reminded her, surprised that she didn't know where the teacher had come from.

'I have an idea she didn't have any family, but I think she must have come from somewhere in Alsace.' She gave it a moment's thought. 'I believe the school where she taught was the Lycée Honoré de Balzac, in Metz, so I suppose they would have an address.'

'You'll have references from them?'

'Actually, no, I haven't.' She bent from her smoothly polished, uncluttered desk and spoke to the little dog, which had emerged

from its basket and was sniffing around Reardon's feet. It
responded immediately when she called, and she lifted it on to
her knee, stroking its head with a large, capable hand. After a
while, she went on, 'She promised she would write and ask for
them, and as I was desperate, I told her there was no need to
wait for a reply before starting; she could begin immediately.
I had no doubt they would be good. Yes, I do realize that sounds
most . . . unprofessional. But Mlle Blanchard was only
temporary and she had seemed like a godsend in the circumstances, and, as I said, she turned out excellently, so I didn't
bother when the references didn't come. I was hoping she would
stay on when it seemed that Miss Catherall's illness was more
serious than at first thought, and that it was unlikely she would
be returning.'

No references? This seemed to him quite an oversight, but
he let it pass. 'I take it she lived in at the school?'

'Of course.'

'It would be helpful if we could see her room.'

'You may, but I doubt it will be any use – she left nothing
behind and it was thoroughly cleaned out when she went.'
She smiled. 'We won't be needing it, of course, now that your
wife will be teaching here. May I say how delighted I am?
I'm sure she will fit in well with us.'

'I'm sure she will. Ellen is very adaptable.' But he wasn't to
be deflected. 'You say Mademoiselle Blanchard was already
living in England when you offered her the post?'

'That's right. She may have been staying with her friend
Miss Catherall, the teacher who was taken ill and recommended
her, but I don't know for certain.'

'Was that the forwarding address she left when she went?'

'She didn't leave one, and I didn't ask.' She sighed and again
began the rhythmic strokes on the golden fur of the little dog.
If it had been a cat it would have purred; as it was, he – or she
– emitted little snuffling noises to show its ecstasy. When Miss
Hillyard spoke again he noticed her slightly heightened colour.
'I'm afraid our last meeting was somewhat acrimonious. She
left without notice at the beginning of the Easter holidays.
Leaving me in the lurch, Inspector Reardon. Her excuses were
feeble and, frankly, I wasn't inclined to be sympathetic to her.

She showed me a side to her character I hadn't suspected; she was offhand and really rather rude. I won't tolerate that sort of attitude from anyone – girls or staff. I wrote her a cheque for the salary she was owed and I have to say I was glad to see the back of her.'

It occurred to him that he would not like to be on the receiving end of it if he had crossed Miss Hillyard, especially if she felt she had right on her side. 'In that case,' he said, 'we may have to trouble the lady she replaced, since she obviously knew her – Miss . . . Catherall, I think you said?'

She stood up and fetched a manila folder from a filing cabinet. 'Phoebe Catherall. She lives with her mother, I believe.' She wrote down an address in the Moseley district of Birmingham, and passed it over. 'You can try, of course, but it's doubtful if she'll be well enough.'

'Thank you. If not, the mother might know something. But I'll speak to the other teachers first. Maybe they'll remember more about Miss Blanchard and we won't have to trouble either of them.'

Miss Hillyard allowed herself a small, relieved smile. 'Maybe they will. They had slightly more to do with her on an everyday basis than I did.' Pushing back her chair, she placed the little dog on the floor and made as if to rise, her smile indicating termination of the interview, but Reardon wasn't finished yet.

'The puzzle is, of course, why she came back to the school if she left it under unpleasant circumstances. And of course why she was in that empty part at all.' Or indeed, he thought, if she had ever gone away at all, but had lain there, under that tarpaulin, all that time.

'Yes, that question had occurred to me, too.'

'Can you give me the precise date she left?'

That, too, she could supply. 'Of course.' She produced the necessary information, all neatly docketed in the manila folder. The date Isabelle Blanchard had started, the date she had left. Details of her salary. Everything except her past.

'And when exactly did the building work on the school finish?'

He made a note of the date she gave, the first week in April. Before the dead woman had left. So at what point after that

had her body landed on the pile of rubble and been left to rot,
hidden under the tarpaulin?

He then learnt the story of how the builder, a Mr Frank
Broderick, had died, leaving not only the restoration work
unfinished, but his affairs in disorder. The untidy state of the
site was accounted for when she told him how his team of
workmen, with wages still owed to them and no prospect
of payment, had downed tools and walked out. It was all taking
time to sort out, but she was in touch with the young fellow
who had been Broderick's assistant, and who was hopeful of
restarting the business. He was, in fact, due to come here for
a meeting with her the following day.

'Good. I'm anxious to have a word with him in any case,
but it can wait until then. We shall need to speak to the pupils,
too, the older ones at least.'

Of a sudden, she was a tigress, ready to defend her young.
'Is that really necessary? How can they possibly know anything
about this unfortunate occurrence?'

'I'm afraid it will be necessary. It's surprising what information turns up, even in the unlikeliest of situations, even from
children. Sometimes especially from children.' He gave her his
most reassuring smile. 'And we're not ogres.'

'Of course not.' She sighed. 'Very well. But please remember,
they are vulnerable young girls. I won't have them upset in any
way.'

'I'm afraid we'll have to be nosing around here for some
time, but we'll try not to be a nuisance and we won't disrupt
your school routine, or your pupils.' He had tried to assuage
her misgivings, but hoped he had got the message through to
her that they weren't here for a joyride.

She eyed him steadily. 'What I said applies to my staff, too
– all of whom I can vouch for, I might say. I was very careful
when choosing them. I'd known them all previously, one way
or another, apart from Daphne Cash, the games mistress, who
came in response to an advert.'

'Small world. It must have been an advantage, knowing those
who applied.'

She smiled again. 'It didn't happen like that. I invited them
to join me.'

THREE

Talking to the rest of the staff hadn't taken long, mainly because none of the teachers could throw any more light on Mam'selle's circumstances than Miss Hillyard had been able to do. Reardon had given the nod to Gilmour, letting him do the talking while he himself listened, watched and tried to sum the speakers up. It had soon become evident that Gilmour wouldn't be required to do much talking. All of them were well accustomed to taking the floor, expressing themselves and explaining facts to others, but in the end there was nothing more to be gained, apart from the fact that Mlle Blanchard had evidently been at some pains to keep her previous life hidden, had not in fact allowed herself to become close enough to anyone for them to have inadvertently discovered what she didn't want to reveal.

It had been a cold, calculated and brutal way of killing anyone, and Reardon soon came to the conclusion that it was not one he could readily associate with any of the women they'd just listened to. The main feeling he came away with was that they were all pretty much what they seemed on the whole; intelligent and well adjusted, as far as he could tell so far, their lives fulfilled by using their brains on something other than simply being housewives and mothers, if only by teaching sometimes reluctant schoolgirls.

He didn't lose sight, however, of the fact that there were bound to be tensions among any group of women living so closely together, though they were not evident here on the surface. But who knew? One of them might have known Isabelle Blanchard previously and have borne her a grudge. A lingering grudge, enough to lure her back to get rid of her permanently? It was possible, anything was possible, and sooner or later, they would all have to be seen separately, but it wasn't yet a priority.

The one who didn't seem to fit in with the group was the art mistress, Jocasta Keith. Saying little, sitting aloof and smoking constantly – this last to the disapproval of Miss Elliott at least, the oldest of the other teachers. He decided he should talk to her alone quite soon. She might be more forthcoming away from the other women. The discontent he sensed in her didn't fit in with his theories about these women being happy in their chosen sphere. In fact, her impatience with the whole situation was obvious, holding herself aloof as she did, as if the whole matter was of no concern to her, and not troubling to hide her feelings.

'We shouldn't have too long to wait for the PM result,' remarked Gilmour. 'Rossiter usually gets a move on.'

He and Reardon were on their way home, the car bowling along the deserted country roads leading from Maxstead – when it wasn't chugging up the many hills along the route, some of them steep, passing scattered villages and isolated farms sleeping in the dying sun. This particular road they were on skirted its ancient forest, once the hunting preserve of kings, teeming with wildlife, roamed by herds of deer, which was now a destination for charabanc parties to view the bluebells, or picnics for those lucky enough to own a car.

Gilmour's comment received only a grunt in response, but he knew when to keep silent and said no more. It was going to be one of those investigations that would need patience – not a quality he himself possessed in great abundance, though he could summon it up when needed. He had a premonition he was going to need it this time. Meanwhile, he let himself enjoy this chance to drive.

The rural aspect was beginning to give way to the more suburban delights of Folbury, and in fact they were within sight of the Beacon, Folbury's famous landmark, that sentinel rising hundreds of feet above the rolling pasturelands, the site of warning or celebration flares from the time of the Armada to the Armistice, before Reardon asked him to pull in when he could. It seemed they weren't finished yet. 'I know we both want to get home, but we need a few minutes.'

Gilmour was to drop Reardon at the Market Street office in Folbury before parking the car in the police garage, after which he'd still have a good walk home. He sensed Reardon, too, was ready to call it a day, though Gilmour knew he had yet to prepare a report for their new chief at HQ, who was young, highly efficient, and expected the same from everyone else.

The inside of the car had been like an oven when they got in to drive home, but the heat generated by the sun on hot metal had dissipated somewhat as they had driven along with the windows open and it was more comfortable now. The sun was low in the sky and it was behind them anyway as he drew to a halt.

'Right, Joe. Here's what we'll do. I'll make an early start in the morning and get back to Maxstead. There's that builder chap to see and I don't want to miss him. You can take the car and go over to Moseley. Make it your first port of call and see if you can speak to this friend Mlle Blanchard was staying with, this Miss Catherall; find out what she can tell us about her replacement. It's a starting point. We'll take it from there.'

'Don't have much else to go on so far, do we?'

'What's new?' Reardon replied. Floundering was the name of the game at the beginning of any investigation, or that was what it usually felt like – if you let it. To admit it was to admit defeat before they'd begun, a vote of no confidence in their own abilities. But this was where it began, the disorientation, the grubbing around for facts to put together and hopefully coming up with something that would give them a firm lead in which direction to go. It didn't make it any easier, knowing so little of the victim. Not that there was any overwhelming urgency in this particular instance, but Reardon still felt charged with the need to get on with it. Gilmour, more impatient than he was, always itching to get things moving, was even keener.

This proposed visit to Moseley suited him, and he suspected Reardon had known it would. It meant he intended using his motorcycle to get out to Maxstead, but since the boss actually *preferred* that as a mode of transport, and since Gilmour dearly loved driving and the Gilmour finances didn't yet run to being able to afford to run a car of their own, much less a Wolseley Seven like this police car, he regarded the opportunity as a gift. The car was nice and roomy, with a fair turn of speed, though the built-up area from Folbury into Moseley, a suburb of Birmingham, wouldn't give him much chance to put his foot down.

He didn't, however, fancy questioning someone who might still be in hospital – might even be at death's door, if the head-mistress was to be believed. 'Didn't Miss Hillyard say she was seriously ill?'

'Her mother, then, if she's not available.' Reardon lapsed into silence again and still didn't seem anxious to move off.

'She had a purpose in going back to the school – the French teacher, I mean,' he said at last. 'And to that part of the building in particular. I know that's a statement of the obvious, but it bothers me.'

'Makes you wonder why she came back at all when she'd seemingly left for good – and what caused her to leave, anyway? Something must have happened while she was there.'

'Right. And another thing – how did she get there, or back, when she'd done what she came for, come to that? Not an easy place to get to, Maxstead. The other end of nowhere and no signs of any form of transport. Not even a bicycle.'

'Taxi? Or there's a bus service, once a flood, so they told me. Goes to the village, and like all these rural buses, it'll stop wherever you want it to. I'll put Gravy on to it tomorrow. He can talk to the taxi firms and the bus service. Right up his street.' Gilmour grinned. DC Gargrave was the youngest addition to their team, so new his feathers were still wet. He was a bit of a clever clogs, too full of himself, but he knew enough not to object to the boring jobs that inevitably fell to his lot, and to take his nickname in good part.

'Do that, but make sure he understands to keep it low key when he asks around. I don't want the press getting hold of this yet, not before we've got more facts under our belts, and I hardly think Miss Hillyard will, either.' Inevitably, the local paper would nose it out soon, and there was a keen new editor at the *Herald*, anxious to make his mark. Murder at a girls' boarding school where the parents were likely to be well known and influential and were certain to make a fuss, would be meat and drink to him, but the detrimental publicity was unlikely to be welcomed by either the parents or the school.

Reardon still wasn't ready to move, and went back to what

was evidently foremost in his mind, as well as in Gilmour's. 'So how she got there might not be all that difficult to find out . . . but leaving? She had that torch in her pocket, remember, which suggests it was night-time when she came, or would have been soon, and I don't suppose these country buses run late. Having a taxi wait for her to return doesn't sound feasible.'

'Maybe she intended to see the headmistress and just hoped she'd be allowed to stay on?'

Reardon raised an eyebrow. Gilmour spread his hands. Fair enough, it was a lame suggestion, but theories were thin on the ground at this stage.

'I can't see anything other than that she was brought here in a car,' Reardon said. 'And by the one who left after helping her to step out into space. The same one who nailed that door back afterwards.'

A drift of poppies in the field next to where they were parked made a scarlet splash against the ripe, gold corn. He was reminded of the hexagonal beds in the gravelled forecourt of the school, none of which had lost any of the bright, patriotic hues that Lady Maude had favoured when she lived there. It looked as though Heaviside was keeping the old owner's traditions alive.

Heaviside. Something about that grumpy old cove remained caught in Reardon's attention. The old gardener was a truculent character, not the sort to give help willingly, even if asked for it. Yet it had been offered in this case. He'd been prepared to show them the way up the stairs to that door. But not to give any other information, and it crossed Reardon's mind to wonder why. It didn't take much effort to believe secrecy was an innate part of his character, but it might also have been fostered by the occurrence. Had he known Miss Blanchard? How much connection, if any, was he likely to have with the teachers? More likely any interaction with staff at the school would be with the domestics, the cook and Mrs Jenkins, the housekeeper to Lady Maude, who had also continued to work at Maxstead now that the old lady no longer needed her.

'All right, let's go,' he said at last.

* * *

I don't feel I acquitted myself very well with Mrs Reardon's husband. He's sharp and I let my uncertainties show and certainly didn't feel I'd projected the image of a competent, sensible and responsible headmistress, whose concern for the girls in her care is paramount.

One way and another, it has not been a good day. I had to send for little Daisy Rawlins this morning and tell her that her father had died suddenly, that her uncle would be coming to fetch her and take her home for the funeral. She will not be coming back afterwards. Mrs Rawlins has decided already that she will take her family and go to live back in Scotland, with her own mother. Poor child.

Tragedy, even one not directly concerned with oneself, affects different people in different ways, my mother used to say, and she should know. She wore it like a heavy cloak round her shoulders, letting it drag her down, suffering it like a penitent. I have learnt through bitter experience to live for the moment, and take happiness where I can, and it usually serves me well enough, but poor Mother, she never could do that, never shake off the past. I hope Mrs Rawlins, and Daisy, will have a better future.

I was sad when my own father died, but unlike Daisy, who is thirteen, I was too young to mourn him for long, or to know how pointless his death had been. Jamie Hillyard, my father. Big, warm and loving; someone who used to catch me safely when I jumped dangerously down from the top step at the front of our house and into his arms, laughed and lifted me high above his head. Someone who sang funny little songs before bedtime, and made me laugh, who disappeared mysteriously from my life when I was five. For years, until I learnt the truth, and had to accept that he was dead, I prayed he would return.

Now, I must remember what living in the past did to my mother, and concentrate on how to get out of this situation which is none of my making. I thought I had dealt with the problem. It was hard, but right, what I did, and I have no regrets. Not even now, when it has become like playing a game of Statues, knowing those behind are creeping up to get you, but whenever you turn, they are all frozen in time.

The telephone rings and its shrill clamour makes me jump. It will be Michael Deegan, about continuing the work on the east wing. It brings me up sharply. Whatever has happened, life here must go on. I will arrange a time tomorrow for him to come and see me, brisk and businesslike. I won't tell him of what has happened here today, and that the police will want to speak to him. Time enough when he gets here.

FOUR

After supper that night, his notes for the report to the new DS in Dudley now in order, which Reardon had brought home to finish, they sat out in the garden in the cool of the evening. He watched Ellen for some time, lying back in her deck chair. 'Do you still want to work there?' he asked.

She adjusted the cushion behind her head so that she could turn to look at him properly. 'What, at Maxstead? You're suggesting I should leave – when I haven't even started?'

It was a question stupid enough to require no answer and he waved an apologetic hand. 'Perish the thought. Don't know why I asked, love. Except that it could put you in an impossible situation, you do realize that?'

'There's no fear of that,' she answered wryly. 'As soon as they knew the man in charge was my husband, they all shut up like clams. Every one of them, even Eve Draper. United we stand, because nothing must be said that would be taken as criticism of Maxstead.' She sighed. 'Well, that's understandable. Whatever happens, it's going to reflect on the school, isn't it? If parents start taking their girls away, that means their jobs are at stake. So the sooner your business there is finished, the better, as far as they're concerned. All right, I'll keep my eyes and ears open, that's what you want, isn't it? But spying on my new colleagues wouldn't be a good start to my career there.'

'Spying? That's a nasty word, and who said anything about it? On the other hand,' he added after a pause, 'we can't afford to be too nice when it's a case of murder.'

Ellen gave him the old-fashioned look that said she knew what he was up to. It wouldn't be politic to say more. He smiled and turned back to the latest Edgar Wallace, but fictional crime had no more appeal for him than it usually did. He'd already read the last three pages without taking in a word, and shifted uncomfortably on his newly bought deckchair. On the decks of ships was where they belonged, in his view. The man who invented them clearly didn't have legs as long as his. However he adjusted it, his knees were either up in the air or being caught at the back by the crossbar.

Two deckchairs, and a little table for drinks between them. Just the thing for sitting out on hot summer evenings in the garden, given suitable weather and that you ever had the time for such indulgences. A luxury he could rarely afford, though he'd grabbed the opportunity now, while the new case was still more or less in limbo, just to show willing. He'd made time tonight to please Ellen, as if that stood a chance of becoming a regular thing in this new house.

New to them, the house was, although it was old. It had been in a right state when they'd bought it – which of course was how they'd been able to afford it – but they'd both worked like Trojans and now it smelt of fresh paint and wallpaper and had a new gas cooker and bookshelves he'd almost finished putting up for the growing collection of books he and Ellen shared a passion for. And a garden. If a stretch of scrubby grass and a patch of nettles and brambles at the end could be so called. Taming it would have to be faced, sooner rather than later. He'd need to ask Joe Gilmour for some advice on how to start, because he hadn't a clue. The Black Country streets where young Bert Reardon had been brought up didn't feature gardens, only a back yard with an outdoor privy.

It was a source of rejoicing to him that Ellen was so happy in the move here. He'd been afraid it might not work. For himself, he was gradually getting used to it after Dudley, though he still felt disorientated sometimes, as if he'd been picked up and put down in the wrong place. There had been a few occasions when he'd found himself actually missing grimy old Dudley. On the other hand, there was his new job, demanding enough to keep him on his toes and his brain working, and they had exchanged their terraced house with a view of smoke stacks and chimneys for this.

It was the only old house in the short street. The others were four pairs of new, semi-detached dwellings, built on land which had once been attached to a now demolished large house. It was something of a mystery why this small house, once part of the estate, hadn't been pulled down, too. Small being the operative word. If he stood in the centre of the kitchen he could, at a stretch, touch each of the four walls. Still, the only other room downstairs was long, low-ceilinged, with a huge old fire-place and windows at either end, one of which gave on to the sloping garden, and a view which would have been the deciding factor, had they not already made the instant decision to buy the house on a love-at-first-sight basis. The crumbling wall that rose at the bottom of the garden was part of an old boundary wall that had once surrounded the ruined, moated castle that had stood for the Royalists against Parliamentary forces three hundred years ago. A good way beyond it was a glimpse of the mellow buildings, the red roofs and quadrangles, the playing fields of the King's School, an old chantry school, and beyond *that*, the green, red-earthed countryside began.

Folbury itself was unpretentious, comfortably mixed, a market town which had managed to retain the character of its medieval origins along with its progress towards modernity. Black-and-white timbering coexisted agreeably with the elegant simplicity of a few Georgian terraces. There was an ancient, timber-framed moot house, a Victorian town hall, the remains of the ruined castle, a fish and chip shop, a penny bazaar, a picture house and a Woolworth's, and enough pubs to shake a stick at. Folbury had its unlovely, industrial side, almost a separate entity that was allied more to the Black Country. Folbury was where the Black met the Green, as the locals had it.

Tolly, lying supine at Ellen's feet, temporarily stuffed by his evening meal and stupefied by the sun after the long walkies Ellen had given him, emitted a sudden snore, but settled back. He was a Jack Russell, a smart and friendly little terrier with a piratical patch over one eye. He had been totally in love with Ellen ever since she had adopted him when he was left alone in the world after his master died.

Reardon gave up trying to read, and as he closed the book he saw that Ellen was watching him, and that she had noticed him fingering his scar, the wartime scar on the side of his face, a habit he too deplored whenever he found himself doing it. He knew it gave him away, a sure sign that his thoughts were straying elsewhere. 'All right,' he said, 'tell me what you know about those teachers.'

Ellen smiled. She'd known he would come back to it, but she didn't bat an eyelid. 'Give me a chance!' she said in token protest. 'I've only just met them.'

If Reardon knew women – and his wife in particular – they could find out more about anyone after meeting them for five minutes than he with all his experience as a detective could in an hour. 'OK. I'll tell you what I know, and you fill me in with what you've picked up.' She smiled again and let him begin, ticking them off on his fingers: 'One. Miss Mildred Elliott.' She of the Tyrolean hat and masculine handshake, beneath whose tweed costume, manly tie and permanent expression of dry disapproval he could detect no softness. Terrifying. Maths, naturally. 'Bit of a martinet, I'd guess?'

'That may be to disguise that she's often in pain, poor woman. It does affect some people like that. Her arthritis, or whatever it is, meant she was forced to resign as principal of another school.'

'Was she, by Jove? Well, that explains a lot.'

'She may be a bit too outspoken, but that doesn't mean she hasn't a lot of common sense, you know.'

All right, he was willing to accede to that. Perhaps she wasn't entirely the miserable old trout he'd marked her down as. He looked again at his list. 'Next, Miss Marian Golding.' A dim woman he hardly recalled. 'Teaches history, doesn't she?'

'The Stuart period's her passion. She only comes alive when she talks of Rupert of the Rhine.'

'*Who?*'

'Prince Rupert – cousin to Charles the Second and commander of the Royalist army in the Civil War. Very dashing and glamorous, by all accounts, very good looking. The Gary Cooper of the seventeenth century. The ladies fell down before him, and Miss Golding too. She's writing a historical novel with him as its hero.'

'Who would have thought it? Hidden talents, these teachers, evidently. What about Miss Scholes, the music teacher? Is she secretly composing another *Messiah*?'

Ellen laughed. 'Nothing so interesting.' She sobered. 'It's sad, really.' Alma Scholes, who taught Geography and Music, was the youngest and prettiest member of staff. She still wore the diamond engagement ring a young captain had placed on her finger before going back to France, never to return, and, according to Miss Draper, played 'Clair de Lune' and Chopin ballades in the evening with tears in her eyes.

Next was Daphne Cash, athletic and well built, with a bust that challenged the pleats in the gym dress she wore. A garment that Reardon, who was old-fashioned enough to believe that ladies should be ladies, considered short enough to be embarrassing. Seemingly entirely wrapped up in timetables for the games and exercises she ordered for the girls, but certainly one with enough agility and strength to have pushed someone from a high door, and nailed it back again afterwards. Which, however, called for an element of premeditation that didn't quite fit in with his view of her.

And there was of course Miss Draper, the English mistress and assistant head, from whom Ellen had got all this information; the one who, with Ellen, had discovered the body.

'Yes, she's a bit of a gossip, but she's a dear, and really very able.' That confirmed the suppositions he'd already made about her. Eve Draper was untidy, wore a sloppy cardigan, and both her hair and her spectacles constantly refused to stay in place, but behind the specs was a pair of shrewd eyes, and she had pulled herself together remarkably well after the shock of that horrible discovery. He made a mental note to speak to her again.

'She's a tigress where the school's concerned. Don't be taken in by her appearance. She's a stickler for order and tidiness – in the school, at least. She has trouble with her heart – I thought she was going to collapse when we saw the body, but she didn't. Maxstead is as much her life as it is Miss Hillyard's – who can do no wrong in her eyes, incidentally. But I should think you could trust her if you want to get at the truth.' She leaned over the side of her deckchair and pulled at a stubborn dandelion growing from a crack in the crazy-paved area from the back door to the weedy grass patch. It snapped, leaving its roots where they were. 'Jocasta Keith wasn't very nice to her when we met, by the way.'

Jocasta Keith was the art mistress, she who stood out like a . . . Well, there was no way you could compare Jocasta Keith to a sore thumb, but she stood out anyway in that bunch of

women; none of whom – with the exception, perhaps, of Miss
Draper – were precisely dowdy, but who, in comparison with
her, seemed like a flock of dull, brown sparrows.

'How precisely, not very nice?'

'Oh, you know how some women can be.'

He raised his eyebrows.

'It was nothing much, I suppose, just that she was rather
disparaging about Miss Draper standing in for the other French
teacher after she left so suddenly, which was a bit unfair, seeing
that Miss Draper had consented to do it as a favour. She speaks
and understands French reasonably well, I believe, but that's
not the same as teaching it, by any means. And I don't know
how well they got on – Mam'selle and Miss Keith, I mean. I
couldn't quite make out whether she liked her or not, and she's
a bit of a misfit herself, it seems to me.' She repeated what had
been said. 'But all the other teachers say Mam'selle was nice.'

'Sounds like damning with faint praise.'

'I think that's just what it was,' she said after a moment.
'Because, you know, in spite of what they pretend, I don't think
any of them were all that much struck with her; not even Eve
Draper, who's the soul of kindness.'

Yet Reardon recalled one voice which had spoken up while
he was talking to the staff, a rather timid intervention, as if it
was daring to say that *someone* had to speak up for the dead
woman, the way things were going: 'The girls liked her.' The
sympathetic comment had come from Marian Golding, the rather
dim-looking history teacher, the one apparently in love with a
ghost, Prince Rupert. Although not entirely divorced from
reality, perhaps.

But she had soon been put down and abashed. '*Admired* her,
rather than liked her, don't you mean? Couldn't see any further
than that supposed chic. She wore *scent*,' declared the tart Miss
Elliott, who herself moved in a carbolic mist of Lifebuoy soap.

No love lost there, but there had been no dissenting voices
to what she'd said. The Frenchwoman had worked with them
as a colleague for weeks, but he guessed she had remained a
stranger to all of them. Because it was her nature to be reserved,
or because it suited her purposes not to give away anything of
herself? But Miss Golding's remark about the girls liking her

gave him an idea that, wherever the truth lay, talking to some of them, as he intended to do the following day, whatever objection Miss Hillyard might have, might help to build up a more balanced view of the dead woman.

Could anyone work alongside a group of women for any length of time and remain such an enigma as Isabelle Blanchard seemed to have been? It was a moot point. Despite all the denials, he couldn't help thinking that somebody must know more than they were admitting. And yet . . . well, he was a detective and liked to think he could recognize a lie or evasion at twenty paces – and his gut feeling told him that in this instance they could all be telling the truth, at least as they saw it.

'How has the school struck you, Ellen, in general?'

She thought for a moment. 'Miss Hillyard is absolutely dedicated to making it succeed – and I don't mean simply in terms of how many rich pupils it can attract. She's really concerned with encouraging the girls to use their minds. She's chosen *Erudio Pro Vita* – education for life – as the school motto, which can't be bad, can it?'

He thought about that for a bit. 'But is it a happy school?'

'Yes, from what I've seen of it, I'm pretty certain it is,' she said slowly. 'But I can tell you – at the moment, there's something going on there under the surface. For one thing, there's been a series of mischievous incidents. Well, practical jokes, I suppose you'd call them. I don't know what they all were, nobody seems to want to talk about them, but one involved stealing a girl's gym outfit, which, by the way, was subsequently found back in the locker room.'

'Girls will be girls, I suppose.'

'Ye-es. And, there's another thing.' She recounted the curious scene she'd witnessed when she had arrived at the school that afternoon, Edith Hillyard and the man she'd been quarrelling with. 'I don't suppose it has anything to do with what's been going on, but it was jolly queer, I thought.'

'I agree, that sort of thing hardly seems to chime with what I've seen of Miss Hillyard. Intriguing. What sort of man was he? Young or old, short or tall? Handsome, ugly? What did he look like?'

'Well, he'd just had this row with Miss Hillyard and had his face well and truly slapped, so he wasn't exactly exuding charm. He was in a furious temper and I doubt if he'd even remember passing me. He strode up the drive as if the Furies were after him.'

'He was walking up the drive? No car?'

'Not by the house, and I didn't see one near where I parked, just opposite the gates, though there was ample room.' She frowned. 'The road was empty, in front and behind, but I suppose he might have left it some way off.'

This interested him because it chimed in with that puzzling aspect of the case he'd mentioned to Gilmour – by what means had Isabelle Blanchard planned to leave? Maxstead Court was at the edge of Maxstead village, and a long way out of Folbury. This man, like Isabelle Blanchard, could scarcely have arrived at the school without any visible means of transport. Since he wasn't superhuman, and legging it from Folbury was scarcely an option, it had to be some form of wheeled transport, even if it was just a bicycle. Had Ellen simply failed to notice it, or had it been deliberately concealed? And if so, why? As a legitimate visitor to Miss Hillyard, he would surely have driven down the drive to the front doors of the school. Another thought struck him, and he made a mental note to check if there was anywhere that offered accommodation in the village, which this stranger – or even Isabelle Blanchard – had booked.

'Somebody will have to do it,' pronounced Avis Myerson.

She and three other senior girls were sitting on the grass in a distant and rather overgrown part of the school garden, almost hidden by a screen of bushes. An exclusive set who didn't encourage interruptions, still less any attempts to be included, they were objects of envy by the rest of the school, because the group was led by Avis, who was daring and exciting and therefore currently the most popular girl at Maxstead. Almost everyone wanted to be her friend and thought she should have been made head girl, but Miss Hillyard had chosen Pamela Urquhart instead, a serious and clever girl who wasn't half as much fun. Whereas Avis could be a scream, and often had them all in fits with her imitations of the teachers. When she was in the mood.

After she had made her pronouncement, the girls looked from one to the other and their collective glance came to rest on Josie Pemberton.

'Well, it's not going to be me, no fear. Not this time,' she declared with spirit. 'It's someone else's turn to do the dirty work.'

She hoped she sounded more certain than she felt. She knew she should feel suitably privileged that she'd been allowed to have Avis as her best friend. But that wasn't all nicey-nicey – she could cool very quickly if you got the wrong side of her. She was very sure of herself, almost seventeen and only biding her time for the two terms she had to endure here at Maxstead until the time arrived for her stint at finishing school in Switzerland, after which . . . Well, then her two older sisters, presently painting London town red, could look out, she told the others, who had no trouble in believing her. Avis was capable of anything, even veiled insolence to the mistresses at times.

Josie repeated now, a little defiantly, 'No, not me.' But discomfort wriggled like a worm inside her. What had started out as a great lark had later become something else entirely. Not so good, kind of wrong in a way she didn't really understand. And, since yesterday, the thought of it was sending cold shivers down her spine. 'The place will be simply swarming with police,' she objected lamely.

Avis looked at her with pity. She replied, as if talking to a very young child, 'Exactly. That's why.' Her eyes were like blue marbles, the way they went when you didn't agree with her. Sometimes she reminded Josie of the hated nanny she'd once had, who'd later been dismissed for spanking Josie's little sister. Quite often Josie, who was really the most daring of them all, and was not usually at all timid, was actually quite scared of her. Avis did her best to be outrageous, she laughed at authority and you did things you knew you ought not to do in case she laughed at you, too.

When she'd first announced the idea of getting together to form a private set, Josie, thrilled despite herself to be one of the chosen, suggested they should be called the Maxstead Secret

Society. Avis was scornful of such a feeble suggestion and instead decided they would call themselves The Elites. Josie wasn't sure what an Elite was until she'd looked it up in the dictionary, and even now she still wasn't clear why it applied. It would be a hoot, Avis had said; something to enliven the boredom of being in this prison. Maxstead didn't feel like a prison to Josie. She liked being here. Maybe it was supposed to be a joke.

Said Nancy Waring now, who would go along with anything Avis suggested, 'You're such a duffer, Josie Pemberton.'

Josie felt herself going red. She didn't like Nancy and didn't care what she thought, but she didn't want anybody to think she was stupid, or a coward.

She turned to the other member of the group who hadn't said anything yet. 'What do you think, Catherine?'

Catherine Leyland was much the youngest of them all. She had only been allowed to join them because of sharing a room with Antonia Freeman and Selina Bright, which had meant she would be bound to know what was going on and therefore couldn't be left out. They'd all three been invited to be Elites, but Antonia had rather scornfully refused, and Selina had never been that keen and only joined in when it suited her, so she didn't really count.

But, to tell the truth, the main reason Catherine had been asked was because Avis said she might have sneaked to Miss Hillyard otherwise, though Josie didn't think so.

Catherine was almost – though not quite – fifteen, but the head, who obviously thought her the bees knees because she was so clever, had already placed her well ahead of her year. Nobody liked swots, but Catherine didn't swank that she came first in practically everything – except in maths, the one chink in her armour. Miss Elliott was beastly to her sometimes, and it was obvious from the blank stare she had that she hated that, but she didn't dissolve into tears like the maths teacher's other victims, and it was Miss Elliott who usually ended up with a red face, although she always had the last word: 'Wake up, girl! You're in a world of your own!' she would say sharply, making Josie feel sorry for Catherine. Being in a world of your own must be very lonely.

'Well, what are we going to do?' Avis demanded. 'We' she said, though Josie knew it was her she meant, and she didn't see why she should do anything. A suspicion had been growing on her that she'd only been included in the Elites for the same reason they'd included Catherine – because she shared a room with Avis and Nancy – and it rankled.

She could see now that everything about their society had been wrong, really, though none of them had thought so at the time. The secrecy had been a giggle and the risk of being found out sort of thrilling at first, but now, because of what had happened, it was more like a thrill of fear. But she hadn't known how to say they should abandon being Elites, without being a spoilsport or everyone thinking she was becoming a *prig*, for Heaven's sake!

It was Catherine who answered Avis with a shrug, as if the solution was simple. 'Either you don't want to be found out and someone must clear up. Or you could just leave it.'

'But the Hill's sure to find out – or more likely Miss Draper, who'd only tittle-tattle to her – and then—' began Nancy.

Miss Hillyard finding out wasn't something any of them wanted to think about, and even Avis didn't look quite so confident for a moment. But Catherine said sharply, 'That's hardly fair to Miss Draper, is it?'

Out of surprise, nobody replied, mainly because it was true. Although Miss Draper was the nicest teacher in the school, she was the deputy head after all. If anything was wrong, she'd have to report it. But they were also astonished at Catherine, who normally kept such opinions to herself. She stood up now and brushed the grass from her skirt. 'We've talked enough. Come on, Josie. What about that algebra prep?'

Josie jumped up with alacrity. As it happened, she wasn't actually hopeless at maths herself and she'd begun – almost – to see the point of algebra last hols when Daddy had explained it was all a matter of logic, if you could try and see it that way. She'd been amazed but really pleased when *Catherine* had actually asked for her help! She'd assured Josie she wouldn't need her for long and she would soon be on top of it, and she'd been absolutely right, Josie thought admiringly. She couldn't have managed to master anything like that so quickly, nor could she imagine anyone else she knew doing it either, but Catherine wasn't like everyone else, was she? How was it nobody ever thought *she* was a prig?

Avis shrugged and pretended to look bored and Nancy, after a glance at her said, 'Well, I vote we go ahead.'

'Then count me out,' said Catherine, almost absently.

She had lovely eyes, a sort of greeny-gold, but that stare of hers when she was concentrating on something else could somehow blank you out, and Nancy reddened.

'Me, too,' Josie ventured, encouraged.

'You're only saying that because you're scared,' countered Nancy, turning on her. '*Ghosties and ghoulies and long-legged beasties and things that go bump in the night,*' she intoned, making a silly, whooing sort of noise.

'Shut up, Nancy,' Avis ordered.

Nancy's little black eyes snapped, but she answered, 'I was only going to say she'll have to be careful. And Josie's not very good at that, is she?'

'Well, we'll have to see, won't we?' Josie was scornful of somebody as stupid as Nancy. All the same, she wasn't going to let anybody think she would let the side down.

FIVE

Gilmour parked the police Wolseley neatly alongside the kerb and walked up the path to the front door of the house he sought, a brick-built semi-detached in a quiet avenue of similar houses near the park. A few feet of neatly kept garden, white lace curtains at the bay window that moved aside before the door was answered by a plump, late middle-aged woman in a flowered pinny, her face already sharp with suspicion. She looked him up and down and kept her hand on the door ready to close it. He could almost read the 'Not today, thank you,' on her lips. She probably thought he was another Hoover salesman, trying to sell her an electric vacuum cleaner.

'Mrs Catherall?'

She blinked. A moment's hesitation, then she shook her head. 'Nobody of that name here.'

'I'm sorry, I must have made a mistake.' Gilmour gave his name, but not his business. 'I was told Miss Catherall, Miss Phoebe Catherall, lived here with her mother.'

'Somebody told you wrong, then,' she answered in a broad Brummie accent. She moved the door a fraction but, before closing it in his face, hesitated again. Giving his name, and maybe his easy, disarming manner, seemed to have mollified her somewhat. 'Miss Catherall did live here, but I'm not her mother,' she admitted at last.

'She lodged with you?'

'She was a *paying guest.*'

'Oh, I see, Mrs . . .?' He smiled.

'Mrs Cooper, if that's anything to do with you.' A Brummie right enough. They were a sharp-witted lot, and not easily taken in, even by nice-looking young fellows with a pleasant manner.

'Is Miss Catherall still in hospital, then? I'm anxious to speak to her – if she's well enough, that is.'

'Hospital? What do you mean, hospital?'

Her suspicion was turning to alarm, and Joe thought it was time to show his warrant card. She inspected it but it did nothing to appease her. 'You must be looking for somebody else. Miss Catherall would never do anything wrong, if that's what you're after her for.'

'It's nothing like that at all. We're just trying to trace her in connection with something that's happened to a friend of hers.'

She looked hard at him, then up and down the street. It was deserted, but curtains might be twitching and he *was* the police. She swung the door wider and stood back. 'I reckon you'd best come in.'

He stepped into a hallway just wide enough for a narrow runner, with a six-inch surround of highly polished, parquet-patterned lino, and followed her into a small but equally gleaming front room, where three-quarters of the space was occupied by a bulbous three-piece suite in rust-coloured uncut moquette, protected by linen chair-backs embroidered with lazy daisies and crinoline ladies. He found a space to stand on the hearthrug.

'What's all this about Miss Catherall being in hospital, then? As far as I know she wasn't poorly.'

'Is that so?'

'Healthy as you or I, last I saw of her. Getting into a taxi with her two suitcases, off to this new job – Maxfield or some-where it was – and pleased as Punch over it.'

'Maxstead Court.'

'Yes, that was it. Maxstead.'

'She never got there, Mrs Cooper.'

'Oh, my God! Hospital, you said. Are you telling me she had an accident?'

'Not so far as I'm aware. It's a bit more complicated than that.'

'Something tells me I'm going to need a cup of tea.' But she had reined in her suspicions enough to add, 'Sit you down and make yourself comfortable while I get it.'

He was left to contemplate the cottage garden scenes on the chair-backs and the photographs and knick-knacks on every surface, and note that a wireless was playing somewhere in a back room, until Mrs Cooper returned with a strong brew and a plate of cake.

She looked expectant when she'd poured and handed the tea. He took the cup from her, deciding that he would fare better with his questions if he first gave her an edited explanation of why he was here. 'You must be wondering what all this is about, Mrs Cooper?'

'It might have crossed my mind.'

Gilmour accepted a square of lardy cake and began by telling her of the letter written by Miss Catherall to the headmistress at Maxstead Court, explaining that she was to have an operation, but was able to recommend another person to take her place.

'I've told you, she never said nothing about any operation to me,' she interrupted, but added doubtfully, 'She isn't one to give much away, however. I suppose she thinks it's nobody's business but hers – which it isn't. It's funny, though.'

'I'm afraid it's beginning to look like a necessary fiction, an arrangement to enable this woman to take her place.'

'What? You mean she was telling lies? That's not like her. What would she do that for?'

'We don't know yet.' He paused. 'Though in fact she might have been lucky in not taking up that post. I'm sorry to have to tell you that the other teacher – the one she recommended to replace her – has died, in rather suspicious circumstances.' She looked shocked. 'Did Miss Catherall ever mention anyone by the name of Isabelle Blanchard?'

He pronounced it in the English way, mainly because he was embarrassed at the thought of attempting the correct pronunciation – he'd been more occupied in drawing cartoons in the back of his school exercise book than learning to speak French – and partly because he thought that was how she might have been known to Mrs Cooper if ever they had met, but she looked mystified and said she'd never heard mention of that name. Then it dawned on her what he'd just said. 'What do you mean, suspicious?'

He had to tell her.

'Oh, my God!' After a minute, she admitted, 'Well, I must say, I *have* been wondering about her, Miss Catherall, I mean, since she left. We'd got used her being here, you know, and she said she'd let us know how she was getting on, but there's been no word, not even a card on Norman's birthday, which it turned out was the same as her dad's, so she wouldn't have forgot.'

'Well, she seems to have gone to ground.' He hoped she'd take that as just a figure of speech and not one with the connotations that jumped to his own mind as he said it. 'It's important we find her in view of what's happened to her friend, you do understand that?'

'I'd like to know what's happened to her for her own sake. After what you've just told me.'

'What can you tell me about her?'

The news had shaken Mrs Cooper, although now that she'd got over the shock, she seemed more inclined to believe what he was telling her about her lodger – her *paying guest.*

Phoebe Catherall had been with them for about two years, she said, but they had never got to know her intimately, not really. 'We got on all right, I won't say we didn't, but she was inclined to keep herself to herself, you know. We never came all that close, but I liked her – we both did, my hubby and me. He's an invalid and can't get out and she used to bring books from the library for him. She didn't seem to have any other interests but reading. She was a big reader and I think she was lonely. No friends, though she was nice. Quiet, but nice.'

He could still hear the wireless in the background, with Norman, presumably, listening to it. His being an invalid was probably the reason why they took in lodgers to supplement their income.

'She didn't seem to have much to go on with, but she was very well spoken, you know. What it was, I reckon, she'd come down in the world since she lost her mother and father in the war, when they all lived in France. I always thought she was a cut above what she did.'

'Teaching's not a bad profession to have,' he said, wondering what Ellen Reardon would have said to that view of her work.

'Oh, no, she wasn't a teacher. She only had a bit of a job playing at the picture house of an evening, see. The Springfield, down the Stratford Road it was; accompanists they're called, aren't they? Though she used to say she'd soon be out of a job, with all these talkies coming. And Saturday mornings she played for the dancing lessons they give in the ballroom upstairs. It wasn't much, was it? Didn't bring in much, neither. I was that pleased for her when she told me she was leaving because she'd got a job as a French teacher in that posh boarding school. I don't think she was qualified, mind you, but she once told me that though her father was English, she'd lived in France all her life and of course she spoke French like a native, so I don't suppose it mattered. Anyway, if she could teach French as well as she played the piano – neither of us is that musical, you know, but she'd play the old joanna for us, sometimes. Lovely, it was, to hear it played properly, though it did get on my Norman's nerves a bit sometimes, all that classical stuff, I mean.'

An upright piano stood squeezed into the corner, polished to perfection, the repository for a garish pottery vase of indescribable ugliness, set on a tasselled runner. Gilmour recognized the piano was only there as a handsome piece of furniture that signalled their ability to afford it. He'd have put money on it that it had never been opened since their paying guest had left.

'It's important that we find Miss Catherall, you understand. Is there anything else you can think of that might be useful?' She shook her head and he closed his notebook. 'Well, thank you for talking to me, Mrs Cooper. I'd just like to take a look at her room before I go though, if you wouldn't mind.'

'I don't mind at all, except there isn't nothing to see. When she left, it gave me a chance to spring clean and do it over, ready for my next guest. I'm a dab hand at papering, though I do say it myself.'

'I'm sure you are,' he smiled. Mrs Cooper was still spry and active and women did seem to enjoy hanging wallpaper, his Maisie included. Gilmour himself was relegated to paintbrush duties.

There didn't seem to be much point in seeing the room. He'd have bet a week's pay that house-proud Mrs Cooper wouldn't have left cupboards and drawers unemptied and unscrubbed, but he decided while he was here he might as well take a look.

'Looks nice, doesn't it?' she said proudly, pushing open the door of a good-sized upstairs room at the back of the house, still smelling of new paint and paper. Although it overlooked the back yard, it backed on to the park, and at some distance beyond the fence he could see trees and a stretch of grass, a sparkle of sunlight on water, a glimpse of greenery that made for quite a pleasant prospect.

As he'd anticipated, the spotless room was devoid of any obvious trace of its previous occupant. 'You're sure she didn't leave anything behind, then?' he persisted hopefully, in case Mrs Cooper had found something forgotten tucked in a cupboard and decided to keep it should her ex-lodger ever request it. But, sure enough, Phoebe Catherall had taken all her possessions with her when she took herself off. Clearly, she had never had any intention of returning, and Mrs Cooper must have known this. Still, she asked him as he was leaving, 'You'll let me know if you hear anything of her, won't you?'

He promised he would, but before he went he said, 'One thing I haven't asked: what about her visitors?'

'She didn't have any, that I was aware of. Except the once.'

His interest sharpened. 'When was that?'

'A month or two back, I couldn't say exactly.'

'Did she by any chance have red hair?'

'I didn't say it was a woman.'

'A man?'

'Well, it weren't a grizzly bear.'

He laughed. 'Sorry. Stupid question. What was he like?'

She shrugged. 'I didn't get much of a look. Tall, youngish, I suppose, but everybody's getting to look young to me nowadays. I let him in and called out to her she had a visitor. She asked if she could take him into the *front room*, here,' she said, stressing the words to indicate there'd been no impropriety, and adding, 'He only stopped about fifteen minutes, before I heard him leave.'

'I don't suppose he gave you his name?'

'No,' she said, 'he didn't. And I didn't ask.'

Reardon was waiting for the call which had been put through to the police at Metz, in the hopes of locating the school where Isabelle Blanchard had taught. The dubious honour had fallen to him since he was the only one at Folbury Police Station who spoke a little French. He was by no means fluent, but he had just about enough to get by, having been taught by Ellen before their marriage. It was how they had met: she the teacher, he the adult pupil.

He still approached the task with some trepidation, knowing there was every chance he might be put on to some German speaker, one who spoke French as hesitant as his own, in view of the fact that Alsace-Lorraine, with its turbulent history, had been the subject of a tug-of-war between France and Germany for centuries, annexed first by one nation, then the other. Then he reminded himself optimistically that people living there in Metz must of necessity have become used to switching from one language to the other. He pushed back his chair and waited.

Adjacent to the almost finished science lab, a room designated for eventual use as a storeroom, but not yet completely fulfilling its purposes, was where they were parking themselves for the time being. A cheerless little space it was, a room scarcely bigger than a cubbyhole, with a table and some chairs pushed in, somewhere they could talk to people away from the school's main activities in between their journeys back and forth from Folbury. But by no means to be considered an office. Miss Hillyard had, however, gone so far as to allow a temporary telephone extension to be set up. The room was adequate enough, notwithstanding that it had only a very small window with a view dominated by the scaffolded east wing and the blank space where the demolished part had once stood. From where Reardon sat with the telephone, the fatal door in the wall couldn't be seen properly, but he knew it was there and it was uppermost in his thoughts and speculations at this moment, a still unanswered question, while he waited for his connection.

In the event, when at last he was put through, he found the gods had smiled on him and he was speaking to someone who had a very fair command of English. He need not have bothered making a list of ready-translated questions; his enquiries were fully understood and soon helpfully met. There was not much he wanted to know, anyway – he simply needed to obtain a little information about the school where Isabelle Blanchard had taught, and how he could contact them.

Ten minutes later, he had hung up the receiver and was contemplating the blank space where the answers should have been.

There was no school going by the name of Lycée Honoré de Balzac in Metz, nor anywhere else in the area that the police officer knew of. The name Blanchard had likewise received no recognition. Both of which, he supposed, explained the references Miss Hillyard had failed to receive, but left him still with a big question mark, and even more frustration.

'Tell me about that door,' he said later to the man who sat facing him. 'Why it was left like that?'

Michael Deegan, the late builder's site manager, looked down at his hands. Large and well shaped but not looking used to manual labour. He didn't in fact seem like a building worker at all. Well dressed, with a head of unruly dark hair combed into part-submission, nice suit and tie, but then, he had come to Maxstead for an arranged meeting with Miss Hillyard, hoping for a future commission to continue the abandoned work on the school. He had been very shocked when he'd learnt what had been discovered on the site where the firm had recently been working, and still didn't appear to have recovered. He appeared to be going over the news in his mind and it took him some time to answer the question.

'The door?' Reardon prompted.

Deegan found his voice and, once started, gave the information readily enough. 'Due to be bricked up that day, the day Mr Broderick didn't turn up and we got news of what had happened to him. The men were upset because they'd all liked Frank, but they naturally wanted to know what was going to happen about their jobs, and of course the wages they were owed, and one fellow started to get a bit nasty about it all. O'Byrne, it was. There's always one, isn't there? But I could do nothing to help and the result was they packed the job in. Walked off. I couldn't stop them and to tell the truth I didn't blame them.' He raked his fingers through his hair, upsetting its equilibrium. 'The fact is, it hasn't been a happy job. We Irish, you know, we're a superstitious lot. Things were found and rumour got around that the job was unlucky.'

He didn't look particularly Irish, any more than he looked like a builder, though given his name it was hardly surprising. No accent, well-modulated English public school, rather. Not handsome, but pleasant looking with an open face. Pale complexioned, and smoke grey eyes that lit up when he smiled. A crooked smile he used often, and a charming manner. He was tall and looked fit. The sort of chap that always seemed to set the ladies' hearts beating, even – or perhaps especially – this group of spinsters? They couldn't encounter many like him in the course of their day. He was older than Reardon had at first thought. There were laughter lines at his eye corners and a slight fullness under the chin. His thick hair might well conceal a few threads of grey.

'You found things? What sort of things?'

'A child's shoe, a broken rosary, a bunch of ancient keys. It's not unusual on a job like this. You'd be amazed what you come across, and not only the bits of old glass and pottery, coins and suchlike that you might expect. This lot had all been there for God knows how many years, but it was the rosary that did it.' He pointed through the window to where a number of old stone slabs of varying shapes and sizes were leaning against one of the walls. 'The half we've already pulled down was one of the oldest parts of the house, older than the rest of the wing by a couple of hundred years maybe, but it was stone-flagged like all the downstairs rooms. It's good stone, and it's intended for paving the courtyard here when – if – we finish off. But none of the stuff we found meant anything; you find similar bits and pieces in any project of this nature, in these very old buildings. The rosary was found somewhere under those pavers, been there for centuries, more than likely. I think the chaps were afraid of coming across a skeleton, but of course we never did.'

'The men walking off – was that the reason the door wasn't bricked up, as intended?'

'The section adjoining it had only gone down a day or two before, yes – but I had fastened the door up securely myself.'

'You mean you nailed it up? Are you sure?'

'I'd hardly forget a thing like that.' Deegan looked indignant.

'I don't suppose you would,' Reardon said appeasingly. 'You can't be too careful, I dare say, this being a school.'

'True, although those little girls weren't supposed to come near here.'

Some of them not so little, Reardon thought. And in his

experience even little girls could be as adventurous, not to say as disobedient, as boys, given the opportunity.

'This whole thing's been a bit of a nightmare to be honest,' Deegan said suddenly. 'Frank dying like that, I mean, but in the end we've managed to salvage enough to pay the men what they were owed. When he died, he owned nothing but his house and his car. Not a penny in the bank. He had no family, poor old Frank. I believe his wife died early in their marriage and there were no children. His house was sold to pay off the creditors, the car was a write-off.' He swallowed and fell silent, looking away, as if struggling not to let his emotion be seen. His boss had evidently meant more to him than he was saying. Reardon waited to let him get over it and it didn't take long. Deegan was clearly one who didn't like silences and soon went on to fill this one, answering most of the questions Reardon had prepared before he could ask them.

'I was very fond of Frank. He'd been very good to me, you know, and he was talking of taking me into partnership. Since he died, I've been struggling hard to get money together to buy what stock there was – including all that stuff out there, which I left because I'm hoping Miss Hillyard will let me finish the job – finishing the inside of this wing for the art and science rooms, and then on to whatever she decides to do with the rest of it. It will give a good boost to starting up my own business if she does. There's a lot of goodwill out there – Frank had worked up a good reputation.' He bit his lip. 'If only.'

Two of the saddest words in the world.

'Forgive me, Mr Deegan, but you seem like an educated man—'

'So what am I doing working on a building site?' He shrugged. 'I trained as an architect – partly trained, that is, until the war machine got me.' He didn't explain more and Reardon didn't ask. There were scars from the war, unlike his own, which didn't show. But sometimes they did, even in smiling Irish eyes.

'So money was a problem?'

'Not on this job. With other customers, yes. But Miss Hillyard was never late with coming up with the necessary. When money was due at certain stages, it was always there.'

The Maxstead Court that Reardon had known before, when

it was still owned by the family who'd occupied it since the
Dark Ages, hadn't exactly been falling down, but it had been
in severe difficulties regarding repairs to its structure, and its
upkeep. Death duties after the decease of Sir Lancelot Scroope,
rising taxes and the general state of the British economy had
in the end been the nail in the coffin which had forced the
family out of their ancestral home. They had been lucky to find
a buyer for it. Reardon thought he would be very interested to
find out where the money had come from to fund such extensive
refurbishment and repair. Edith Hillyard was said to own the
school personally. Either she was a very rich woman in her own
right, or she had a backer.

'You've been working here for some time. You must have
got to know the staff.'

'We're on nodding acquaintance, that's all.'

'Did you know Mlle Blanchard?'

'Isabelle Blanchard? I spoke to her once or twice, that's all.

A flicker of some emotion that Reardon couldn't read crossed
his face. Policemen have nasty suspicious minds, and for a
moment his antennae quivered. The man could be lying, for
any amount of reasons. Perhaps there was more to Michael
Deegan than showed on the surface. A man like him, doubtless
attractive to women, and he'd known the dead woman well
enough to know her first name.

'What it was, she was concerned about the girls using what
they're calling the Quad as a short cut to the tennis courts.
Not that they were in any real danger, but it wasn't the place
for them, and we had enough to do anyway without silly little
girls who wouldn't do as they were told. It wasn't our job to
keep an eye on them.' He sounded slightly defensive all the
same. He took a quick look at his watch.

He was clearly anxious not be late for his appointment with
Miss Hillyard, and Reardon had no wish to keep him from it,
so he wound things up with a few more questions. Nothing
significant emerged and Deegan left. Reardon felt he rather
liked what he'd seen of the man. In fact, it had come as a bit
of a relief to speak man to man after so much feminine input.
He wasn't by any means a misogynist, far from it, he liked
women, and respected them, but he'd long ago admitted that

questioning them when they might well be under suspicion wasn't precisely his forte. Even Gilmour was far better at it than he was. For one thing, Reardon was convinced, even against evidence to the contrary, that women were less criminally inclined than men – though definitely more devious – and it was hard to persuade him otherwise; for another, they could run rings around him if they chose. Especially when presenting a united front. United we stand, Ellen had said of the teachers here. Was that really so? Did they all know something about Isabelle Blanchard that they were keeping from him? He had a notion that at least one of them might.

SIX

Of those rooms Reardon had seen on his previous visits to Maxstead Court, what was now the art room was the only one virtually unchanged. Gone, for instance, was the gracious drawing room, and the small den once used as the business room by the Scroope family. But this place remained virtually unaltered. Then known as the garden room, it was now cleared of the horticultural disorder it had once housed, though it was no less cluttered now, being full of desks and easels and all the paraphernalia presumably needed to give lessons in art to the young. He glanced around, but didn't find much of their work was displayed or pinned up, though admittedly there wasn't a lot of wall space for that, most of it being taken up by the windows that let in the floods of light, making it an obvious place to use as a temporary art room.

Jocasta Keith was still engaged on the painting Ellen had described to him, or one similar, if the furious explosions of colour that looked as though they'd been hurled at the canvas were anything to go by. With exaggerated patience she put down the palette knife she was holding when he told her he'd like to ask her a few questions and perched on one of the desks, swinging an elegantly silk-clad leg. The overall she wore was paint stained, as were her hands, which he saw were not long-fingered and delicate, as the hands of artistic people were popularly imagined to be. Hers were square, rather blunt and capable looking. The nails, he noticed, were bitten to the quick.

'Ask away,' she said, waving him to another desk and offering her cigarette case.

'I don't smoke, thanks, but I don't mind if you do.' Reardon's last cigarette had been smoked an hour before the motorcycle accident in France which had given him his scar and earned him a medal and permanently scotched his taste for tobacco. She watched him over the flame of her lighter as she drew on the cigarette, a look which took him in top to toe.

'You're another new addition to the staff, I'm told, Miss Keith, like Mlle Blanchard.'

'Later than most of them. She and I started about the same time.'

'Where did you teach before?'

'I'm not a teacher, but Miss Hillyard is enlightened enough to realize you don't need diplomas to teach elementary art. If you're an artist yourself, you can show anyone the basics, the mechanics and techniques. They can be learnt, but after that it's up to yourself, what's in you.'

That sounded rather arbitrary to him, and he wasn't sure it could be right. What about all those art schools, and the professors who worked in them? But then what, if anything, did he know about art, apart from the fact that it wasn't renowned for bringing in much money? Miss Keith looked as though she might need quite a lot of that to keep her in the style to which she'd like to become accustomed. She hardly seemed the type to tolerate living in the proverbial garret.

His scepticism must have shown. 'It's all about self-expression, anyway. Getting rid of inhibitions,' she added.

She had a rather scornful way of looking at you if you didn't immediately cotton on. He was well aware what she meant, but he didn't argue. If what was on the easel was the expression of Miss Keith's rejected inhibitions, she must have amassed a whole lot she needed to dispense with.

'I didn't have any training myself,' she volunteered suddenly. 'I worked in a factory, prostituting my art if you like, designing – if you could call it that – china. I was good, and I could have gone to art school to learn more, but only how to paint more pretty tea sets.' Her expression said what she thought of that. 'This is only a stopgap. As soon as I have enough money I shall be off and get myself a studio. You won't see me for dust.' As if pulled by invisible strings, her glance was drawn back to the painting on the easel.

How much of her attitude was tongue-in-cheek, or bravado, he wouldn't know, but he hoped she had the sense to keep her intentions to herself. Miss Hillyard was not likely to welcome any hint that another member of her staff was poised to leave her in the lurch as soon as she could. If it should come to her ears, Miss Keith might find herself quickly dispensed with, whether she was ready to leave or not.

'Although, come to that,' she went on, almost to herself, as though a new and rather welcome thought had just struck her, her face suddenly becoming animated. 'I could, why not? There's nothing to stop me leaving now. I could easily get by – the salary here's not bad.' But just as suddenly, the excitement seemed to drain away and she shook her head. 'Not a brilliant idea, on second thoughts. Let me show you something.'

He followed her across the room, to where a sheet of paper was pinned to the wall. 'Stand back, so you can see it better,' she advised.

It was a pastel drawing of a horse and a boy in a field, nothing more. And yet so much more. A leaping chestnut horse with its forelegs raised, its mane streaming, a rope around its neck, a laughing boy, backing away and clad only in a shirt and trousers, holding a halter. It was simple, so much so that at first glance it might be dismissed, until you looked, and looked again, and saw the powerful, swiftly and confidently executed lines, which gave such a vivid impression of movement you could almost feel the horse leaping from the picture and sense the boy's joy. 'It looks good,' he said inadequately, ill-equipped to find the words to convey more. 'Yours?'

'Me? No, I couldn't do anything like that! It's by one of the girls. And that's why I'd better stay on – for a while, at least,' she added as an afterthought, making him wonder if that was the only reason. 'If I go, no one else will give her the encouragement she needs, and she's just beginning to find her feet. Before I came, they never realized what they had here, and her work went by the board. I'm not altogether sure they know *now*, apart from Miss Hillyard. She came in last week and saw this and I think it might have persuaded her I'm not talking completely through my hat.'

'Who is this treasure?'

'A girl called Antonia Freeman. She doesn't apply herself to anything else, so she tends to get overlooked. Or blamed for anything that goes wrong, poor child.' There was a softening in her voice, pity and perhaps understanding, as she spoke the girl's name. Might there be parallels here with Jocasta Keith's own life, a feeling they were both outsiders? Thinking about what she'd just said, Ellen's remarks about those practical jokes which had been played came back to him – she had mentioned a girl called Freeman, but he didn't recall her being thought of as the perpetrator. She'd been the one at the receiving end, hadn't she?

He could admire Miss Keith's passionate defence of her talented pupil, and he would like to know more about this Antonia, but they were rather getting away from the point of why he was here. 'Tell me, how did you find Mlle Blanchard?'

'I didn't have all that much to do with her.' She shrugged. 'They said she was a good French teacher, but so she should have been, being French.'

'*Was* she French?' he asked, not knowing why he had asked that. 'The name could be either.'

'Definitely, I'd say, typically so.'

'Typical in what way?'

'Like all the French, convinced of their own superiority and uncompromising about it – bloody-minded, if you like, as they say where I come from.' She paused and reached for another cigarette. Jocasta Keith might project violent colour into her paintings, but she obviously saw life in terms of stark black and white. Then she surprised him by adding, 'No, that's not quite fair, I suppose. I have to admit, she did know quite a bit about French art.'

He surmised all the same that Isabelle Blanchard's opinions had not been entirely in accordance with Miss Keith's own, and that she'd been rubbed up the wrong way by it. But she shrugged and went on, 'She thought a lot of herself, Isabelle, and she wasn't an easy person to talk to, but we both said what we thought and we'd found ourselves thrown together here in this situation, so I guess we did get along, in a funny sort of way. Actually, I suppose I did quite like her. She certainly didn't deserve what happened to her,' she finished abruptly.

What exactly had she meant by finding themselves together? It was interesting to think that the one person who had at first seemed totally uninterested in the Frenchwoman or what had happened to her now appeared might have known more about her than any of her other colleagues. He might have struck gold.

But in the end, nothing came of that. She had suddenly resolved not to give anything more away and he saw he was wasting his time trying to push her. Jocasta Keith wasn't by any means telling him everything she knew, but she had decided she'd said enough and wasn't going to go any further.

There was, however, more he had to ask before he left her. 'Do you have any idea why she left?'

'Oh, I think she got cold feet,' she answered, without giving it much thought.

'Cold feet?'

He'd taken her up too quickly, and for the first time she looked a little disconcerted. 'Just a figure of speech. I meant she'd realized she didn't fit in here. Like me, I suppose. All the other staff members were known to Miss Hillyard before they came here. They're very cliquey.' She shrugged and picked up her palette knife.

'Where did she go, or intend going, after she left here?'

'I haven't the faintest idea. And though I don't want to be rude, Inspector, I do have to get on with some work before my next class.'

She turned back to her easel and gazed critically at it. After a moment she put the palette knife down. 'Oh God, now I've lost it.' He assumed she meant inspiration, or something like that, for the painting. It looked quite mad to him, anyway, but he thought it would be tactless to comment. He had sensed something in her tone. Not annoyance. He rather thought it might be despair.

Several questions occurred to him as he walked away from the room. What had she meant about being able to leave Maxstead *now*? Because she had amassed enough money, or what? Clearly, she had regretted having spoken her thoughts aloud. She'd been momentarily fired with the possibility of quitting a job she obviously loathed, until it had occurred to her that for some reason it wasn't possible. Something was preventing her, and the excuse of staying on to provide support for a talented pupil didn't really hold all that much water, however much she might believe in the girl's need for it.

'So,' said Gilmore, catching up later with Reardon, who was still at Maxstead, 'it looks as though we have a missing woman now, as well as a murdered one. At least, let's hope Phoebe Catherall is just missing.'

'Whoa! We're not ready to go in that direction just yet.' Reardon had so far listened to Gilmour's account of his visit to Mrs Cooper with interest, though the information he'd gained complicated matters even further. 'All right, I take your point, but don't let it run away with you. Although I have to agree, it's damned funny – and I don't mean ha-ha – that Phoebe Catherall, untrained if we're to believe your Mrs Cooper, should be given the job of teaching French at a posh school.' Though in actual fact, didn't Miss Hillyard seem to be in the habit of taking on unqualified persons – at least one other, in the form of Miss Keith? 'Not to mention that the story about the hospital and the operation sounds like a load of codswallop to me. Cooked up so that Mlle Blanchard could take her place? Why, for Pete's sake? We need a lot more than that before we start making assumptions.' He drummed his fingers on the desk. 'And what about Miss Catherall's mysterious visitor?'

Gilmour shrugged. 'Mysterious only because it was unheard of for her to have visitors.'

'Which makes it a bit odd that it happened just at this time.'

'We have a photograph.'

'What?'

Gilmour grinned, 'Not of him, the caller. And not a proper photo, as such.' He dug out his wallet and produced a newspaper clipping, folded and beginning to turn yellow. 'Mrs Cooper cut it out of the *Birmingham Mail* and kept it. It's Miss Catherall.'

'What was her photo doing in the paper?'

'It was taken when they opened the rooms above the Springfield picture house for ballroom dancing lessons. Publicity, I suppose. That's her on the back row.'

It was a group photograph, posed in front of a white building with a modernistic domed frontage, the people pictured being those who were presumably concerned in the new enterprise, with the principal movers sitting on chairs in the front row, one woman clasping a large bunch of flowers. Most of them were grinning, eager to have their moment in the limelight, though the photograph was as dark, grainy and blurred as newspaper photographs usually were. Miss Catherall was the exception to the rest. She wasn't smiling.

'No oil painting, is she?' Gilmour remarked.

'She didn't have to be; she was only the piano player.' Reardon thought Gilmour was being uncharitable. You couldn't judge from a photo like this, though in no way could it be called flattering. On the back row because she was half a head taller than anyone in front, Phoebe Catherall seemed to be trying to efface herself. Her head was half-ducked, almost as if the large, horn-rimmed glasses she wore and the two heavy plaits curled low on her cheeks in 'earphone' style were weighing her down. Maybe she was shy. Or didn't want to have her photo taken. Either way, it wouldn't be much use as identification.

'I need to have a think about this.' Reardon stared out of the window at that east wing, grey and inimical and, now that the sun had moved, casting its shadow across the quadrangle. He almost shivered. After a while, meeting Gilmour's speculative look, he said, 'There's something not right here, Joe. And not only Isabelle Blanchard being killed. Something's not ringing true about this place. Dunno what it is, but I feel it in my water. Gives me the creeps.'

'What, the headless ghost wandering the corridors at the midnight hour?' Gilmour laughed, but the sentiments were unlike Reardon and, following his glance, he sobered, as if he too felt the shadow.

'I'd give a lot to know what's been going on here – something has, or I'll eat my hat. But something's warning me to tread softly. Very softly. On tiptoe, in fact.'

Gilmour thought about that. 'I get what you mean,' he said eventually. 'You're thinking anybody who can afford to send their kids to a school like this must be somebody. If you see what I mean.'

'That as well,' Reardon said, happy to go with that rather than his almost superstitious moment of unease. 'One false step and we could upset the applecart. The chief constable's daughter is a prefect.'

Gilmour rolled his eyes.

That wasn't the only thing, however. It was also a matter of not stirring up any more unnecessary trouble for Miss Hillyard.

He didn't think she was being straight with him on several matters, but she probably had reasons which were unconnected with his enquiry, and he couldn't entirely hold it against her. She was driven with a purpose you had to respect; she was trying to hold the school together, and what she'd done to turn the dismal old Maxstead Court he remembered into what it was today was something of a miracle.

'All the same, I reckon we need to go strictly by the book here – but that doesn't mean we shouldn't do a spot of digging. On everybody – what their background is, if any of them had anything at all against Mam'selle. And whatever we feel, we can't discount the head from that.'

'Dig the dirt on Miss Hillyard?' Gilmour looked distinctly alarmed. He was still in awe of teachers, who all wrote pretty much the same thing on his reports: *There is much potential in Joseph. Unfortunately that's where it stays.*

'I didn't say that. The mind boggles, I know, but we shan't let her know what we're doing. We can start by making some discreet enquiries about her, at any rate.'

'How do you suggest we do that?'

'I don't know.' Reardon cogitated, chewing his thumb. Then suddenly he grinned, 'But I can think of someone who might.'

DC Jim Gargrave was on his way to check the two taxi firms and the one bus company in Folbury. No abandoned bicycle or car had been found anywhere near Maxstead, and Sergeant Gilmour declared that common sense said that walking eleven miles on a dark night, especially if you were a woman, wasn't on, so unless the French teacher had flown there like Peter Pan, she had to have used either bus or taxi. Personally, Gargrave didn't believe either line of enquiry would be productive. He agreed with the DI, that she must have been taken there in a car and whoever had killed her had left after the deed was done, and this errand was a waste of time.

He'd been smart enough not to complain when the task of checking was allocated to him. He wasn't best pleased though. It was a boring job, but at least it was one step up from door-knocking – and he was ready to show willing and do anything to make his mark with the sergeant, and therefore Reardon, who'd given him his chance as a detective and on whom promotion, however far in the future, depended. He was a Yorkshire lad who had transferred from Bradford to marry a Folbury girl he'd met on holiday in Scarborough. When she'd changed her mind about getting spliced, Yorkshire bloody-mindedness was enough to make him stay on, devoting himself to furthering his career as a detective instead. Show her what she was missing – though by now he'd decided she wasn't up to much, anyway.

He was ambitious, and full of bright ideas which sometimes worked, eager to show he wasn't your usual plod, but this didn't altogether chime with his inclination to laziness, which might shipwreck his hopes if he didn't overcome it, and which to do him justice he sometimes tried to do. He went out of his way to please, not even objecting to his nickname, Gravy, accepting its inevitability. It had started in school, followed him here and would surely follow him into the . . . oh, God, there he went; you couldn't help it, with a name like his.

He cheered himself up with the thought that this job he was on shouldn't take him long, anyway. Midland Red's extensive fleet of buses didn't run out to Maxstead – that was left to the small local company which serviced both that village and the surrounding ones. And there were only two taxi firms in Folbury, the largest one catering mainly for weddings and funerals, the other which had started out as a one-man band, but now employed three or four drivers. The trouble was, bus drivers hardly ever noticed their passengers – and would taxi drivers be likely to remember a fare from as far back as around Easter-time, when the victim had last been seen? It was possible, Gargrave told himself, if the fare in question had been a well-dressed redhead and the destination Maxstead Court school.

He happened to have chosen a slack period, so his luck was in and he managed to speak to most of the drivers concerned at each taxi firm, both of which operated from garages near the railway station. But luck ran out when it turned out that no one at either place had ever had a fare resembling the woman he described. The drivers shook their heads. Maxstead Court was a familiar destination. It was a regular thing for parents who had arrived at Folbury by train to visit their children to take a taxi out there and arrange to be picked up later for the return journey. And of course they'd have remembered if any of the mothers they'd recently driven there had been either glamorous or red-haired.

He legged it half-heartedly over to Arms Green, in Folbury's industrial area, to the bus garage of Countrywide Buses (a gross misnomer, as their service was limited to the villages within fifteen miles or so of Folbury town centre). He had no expectations, so he wasn't disappointed. It was usual, on these rural bus routes, to oblige passengers' requests to alight at unscheduled stops near to their destination. The buses passed the gates of Maxstead, but few people asked to be put down there. And none had done so lately.

Even during the periods when she was not feeling depressed, my mother lived in the past. I now believe it was at the same time both a regret for what she'd so lightly abandoned and a solace, remembering the long-lost times when she had been happy, young and carefree. But when you've been at school all day, come home, and then delivered to the factory the buttons she'd made, and waited for them to be checked for any sloppy work; when you have a pile of homework that is really important to you and books you must read – well, it's hard to summon up too much interest in a distant place and a time which existed long before you were born. But if this escaping into the past helped to prevent the depression that descended on her from time to time, who was I to try and prevent it? She liked to talk as she made the cloth-covered shirt buttons, which then had to be stitched on to a card. She was very good with her needle and sometimes she got better work, silk buttons she had to cover with intricate fancy stitching. But that was harder, and often her fingers were raw.

Some of my teachers at school, one in particular, were pushing for me to stay on until I was sixteen, to matriculate and then perhaps go on to a teacher-training college. Did they not realize just how much of a fantasy this was, how cruel? If a fairy godmother had waved her wand to make such a thing remotely possible, I would have been delirious with joy. But fairy godmothers did not feature in the Hillyard family. And for another thing, Mother needed me to work. I knew the best I could hope for – her biggest aspiration for me – was for a future as a shop-girl in one of the big department stores in the West End.

And then came the miracle that one prays for, but never expects, that never happens in real life, by way of a letter.

And now, twenty-five years later, more letters.

Ever since that man first wrote to me with those increasing demands, despising my original offer, which was generous by any standards, I've been unable to get it out of my head. Letter after letter, and then, when he saw I would go no further, attempts to invade my personal space, my school. Maxstead. How dare he? How dare any of them?

SEVEN

ongreve Park is one of those little green London oases, small delights set amongst the great sprawl of the city when you come across them unexpectedly. Ellen, having taken the tube to Elephant and Castle, is further pleasantly surprised to find that the street where her friend Kate Ramsey lives isn't too far from this park, especially as it's absurdly called Green Street, when there is a distinct absence of greenery, not a tree in the pavement or a front garden in sight. After the quiet Shropshire countryside she used to love so much, and being basically an outdoor sort of person, Kate will appreciate living so near the park – even if it's scarcely big enough to qualify for the name. Most of the houses in the street, built of ubiquitous yellow, soot-streaked London brick, are large enough to have been converted into flats. This, too, is a compromise for Kate, but she is used to compromises. She had to leave her cottage when she changed her career path from teacher to her present job here in the city, but it's soon evident she has cheerfully accommodated the change.

Kate is the best type of friend – the sort you can meet after any amount of absence and take up with just where you left off. They had taught at the same school at the beginning of their careers as language teachers – German in Kate's case, which had turned out unfortunately for her during the war, since no one could countenance the enemy's language being taught. She now works for an organization dedicated to gaining equality for women in all walks of life.

Ellen has been looking forward to this weekend visit, planned some months ago. They embrace and soon catch up with their news and what has been happening to them in the twelve months since they last met. Kate is eager to hear about both Ellen's and Reardon's new jobs, the house in Folbury and her favourite canine friend, Tolly. Ellen is shown around the flat, which is actually dauntingly small, but is able to give genuine approval at how Kate has made the most of it.

'So, Edith Hillyard and all!' Kate says when they are sitting over what she calls a scratch lunch. She has never shown much interest in cooking, but it's never stopped her from eating well and the lunch is in fact quite a small feast. French bread and garlicky pâté, accompanied by interesting bits and pieces and unusual salads from a delicatessen round the corner, as well as eggs and tomatoes, and a bottle of good wine. 'Who would ever have predicted you'd be working for her?'

'It was good of you to put in a word for me. Your recommendation went down well.'

'What are friends for?' Kate spears a pimento-stuffed olive, watching as Ellen slowly picks at a hard-boiled egg which is refusing to be parted from its shell. 'Come on, Ellen, spit it out. Do I sense all is not well in the hallowed precincts of Maxstead Court?'

'Oh, it's fine.' Kate raises her eyebrows. 'It is, really; it's a nice school and Edith Hillyard is a . . . a good headmistress.' She had been going to say 'nice woman', but she isn't sure that would be right. 'Nice' is an anodyne word that implies neither one thing nor the other, and doesn't go anywhere to describing Miss Hillyard, certainly. She wonders if 'nice' is applicable to the school, either, at the moment. But she says, 'It's too early to make judgements, but as far as I can tell, she's doing a wonderful job. I know she's hoping to educate at least some of the girls to do something useful with their lives when they leave, rather than what most of them seem destined for.'

Kate smiles and raises her glass. 'I'll drink to that.'

She is one of the legion of widows left high and dry after the war. Being the sort of woman most men look for in a wife – not a beauty, but with bright eyes and a ready smile, energetic and, moreover, sensibly down to earth – she has not been short of offers of marriage, without ever having shown any inclination to take them up. She copes better than most with what life throws at her, and although it took her a long time to accept the fact that her husband wasn't ever coming home again, she isn't prepared to settle for second best, after losing the only man who could ever mean anything to her. She seems content with the work she does on women's behalf.

Ellen at last gets around to telling her about the horrible

event that has recently happened at Maxstead. As she had expected, Kate is suitably shocked – and obviously intrigued, though sanguine. 'Not a good start for the school, but at any rate the Edith Hillyards of this world are more than able to cope with that or any other sort of trouble. Goes without saying.'

'Yes, I'm sure she is.' The last bits of shell have at last succumbed and Ellen disposes of them and cuts the egg in half. 'How well did you know her, Kate?'

Kate reflects. 'She was a year or two above me at Agatha's, but being a small college, we all mixed pretty well. She was popular, and one of the high-flyers, but I hadn't all that much to do with her. To be honest, I couldn't say I ever really *knew* her.' She refills their glasses.

Ellen senses reservations. She thinks for a bit, then says, 'Kate, rescuing Maxstead Court and making it over to what it is now must have cost tons. Where would that kind of money have come from?'

'I've no idea. Edith never had money to throw around when I knew her. The only thing I do know is that her mother died, and the next thing I heard on the grapevine, she had bought Maxstead Court and was looking for staff. Years after we'd all left college, of course.'

'So her mother *was* rich. Or perhaps she inherited money from a wealthy family?'

Kate makes a wry face. 'I didn't have that impression, but either's possible, I suppose. Edith's never married, has she? So it couldn't have been a rich husband.'

'Then someone else must have put money into starting the school.'

'That seems a more likely answer, I agree – either way, she's doing something really necessary, so what's the difference? If it really matters, why don't you ask Eve Draper? They were always very thick.'

'Well, of course. I remember Eve Draper mentioning that.'

'She was at Agatha's, same year. And I think they were over in France together as well, driving ambulances.'

'That explains why she and Miss Hillyard are so friendly. She's deputy head, very efficient and energetic. You'd never guess she has a health problem – her heart. Not that she lets it stop her in any way. She didn't say she knew you when we spoke.'

Kate shrugged. 'We didn't move in the same set; she was above me and I only remember her because of Edith. I think they might have gone on to teach at the same school, too. Anyway, she'll be able to tell you more than I can.' She smiled. 'Meanwhile, pass your glass, I don't want to have to drink all this myself.'

The letter came when I was fourteen, from a solicitor who represented Thomas Pryde, a man I had never heard of.

It was a name from my mother's home town, in the Potteries. Thomas Pryde, owner of one of the largest of the hundreds of small, and some not so small manufactories that littered the landscape, which I had learnt, from listening to her ramblings about her past, were called 'pot banks'.

Pryde's was a family concern that had been handed down from father to son. It was Thomas who had made the name famous, though, due to the introduction of a range of bone-china tea services in simple, elegant white, decorated with three fine rings of gold around the rims, stamped with the Prydeware brand name on the base of every item made. It became hugely popular, and still is. No household that aspires to any sort of gentility is without it.

Mother had often mentioned this in her ramblings about her old home. What she had never said was that she had once worked at Pryde's. She had apparently been a skilled worker, expertly painting, hour after hour, day after day, without any degree of error, those three fine gold bands around the rims of teacups, plates and saucers, and so on, that made the Prydeware range.

According to Mr Gringold, the solicitor, Thomas Pryde in his old age had turned into something of a philanthropist. He had only married late in life and since it was now unlikely he would ever have children of his own, it pleased him to interest himself in helping any children he could find who seemed worthy. He had heard in some way – no doubt through my Aunt Louisa, Mother's sister, who attended the same chapel as he did, that I was now approaching the age to leave school, that I was clever and would benefit from further education, and I was to be one of the recipients of his good intentions.

My joy was not initially shared by my mother. At first, through an inborn unwillingness to accept charity, however well meant, she strongly objected to what was proposed in the lawyer's letter. Long, angry screeds arrived from my aunt. What was she thinking of? Thomas Pryde was a good man, his motives were of the highest. Underneath the hard-headed exterior he kept for business purposes, there beat a kind heart and a Christian goodwill which it would be wicked to turn down. Moreover, I was by no means the only recipient of his generosity, which took the edge off the idea that it was charity. In the end my mother succumbed, persuaded that refusal would have been un-Christian.

In fact, she roused herself so far as to write and thank Thomas herself, who instructed Mr Gringold to make money available to be used as deemed necessary and to include enough to provide for my mother while I was away at college, which pleased me greatly, though I was determined to pay it back as soon as I was earning.

Good fortune wasn't something I easily believed in, however. Something was sure to happen to prevent my dream actually coming true. I held on with bated breath, but nothing bad happened, and at last off I went to the Agatha Dean Teacher Training College to fulfil my dreams.

At the police station in Market Street, Reardon was pondering over the case file, impatient at any lack of progress. He found himself turning back, yet again, to the notes he and Gilmour had made at the crime scene. What had they gathered about Isabelle Blanchard's last movements? Depressingly little. Almost nothing, in fact. He was still trying to get a grasp on the sort of person she might have been. At the moment, he didn't have a clue what she had even looked like, never mind what sort of personality she had had. What he *had* learnt was not in fact building up to a particularly appealing picture of her which, paradoxically, was making him more sympathetic towards her. It was a melancholy thought that no one, so far, seemed to be shedding any tears for Mlle Blanchard.

It was a vile and ugly end to a life, but although the state of the body when he'd first seen it hadn't left much room to speculate on whether she'd been beautiful or ugly, an impression had been set up in his mind of a woman who had once been attractive in appearance. Small and slim, five foot three at the most, he guessed, with that mass of auburn hair which had made her immediately identifiable.

When she died she'd had on a light coat over her dress, but no hat, and what might once have been a smart but plainly cut dress in a material he'd been told was cloqué, in a colour he couldn't identify but was sure to have some sort of fancy name; greyish-brown, reminding him of the fur of a mole. The sort of dress Ellen might have described as understated. What the French called chic? Her underwear, too, had made him think: a matching slip and French knickers in delicate eau-de-nil silk crepe de Chine, trimmed with coffee-coloured lace.

The elegance of her clothes suggested she might even have been dressed for an evening out. Except for the shoes, which certainly gave pause for thought. They looked very odd indeed with the rest of the outfit – sturdy, even clumsy, brown leather brogues with a fringed flap. And more, striking the wrong note even to Reardon, to whom fashion was a closed book he never even tried to open, was a small diamanté brooch in the form of a spitting cat in profile, with a red glass eye, pinned to the shoulder of her dress. He turned it over. It looked tawdry in the bright daylight, as if it might have come from Woolworth's.

He picked up the torch that had come from her pocket. Thrust in so hard it had split the seam open a little. It wouldn't have been much good, since the battery was flat. But carrying a torch at all suggested it had been dark when she entered that building and met her death.

Who was she? How did she and Phoebe Catherall know each other? Moreover – another constant niggle – where was Phoebe now?

The telephone rang. Coming at that particular moment, as if tallying with what he'd just been mulling over, it was the doctor, Kay Dysart on the other end.

'We have the results of the PM,' she told him. 'Dr Rossiter

will be sending it in shortly, but I thought you would like to know now.'

She'd anticipated his impatience to know before the pathologist's written report came through, and although it didn't seem likely that anything would have emerged to contradict her original opinions, he thanked her for the forethought.

'You're welcome. I know you're always anxious for the results the day before yesterday.' She gave him a short summary of the report, which did indeed confirm her own first findings. Only what might have been expected – injuries consistent with falling from a high building, and severe enough to have caused death almost instantaneously. And rather more details than he wanted to know about the horrific damage resulting from landing face down on that treacherous rubble.

'There was nothing to indicate she'd been pushed? Bruises or anything?'

'We got to her too late for anything like that to show, I'm afraid.'

A silence fell between them. They were both accustomed to death, violent or otherwise. He couldn't know how doctors felt about that, but it was something he'd never got used to, and hoped he never would. You wouldn't want to, unless you were completely insensitive. The silence prolonged itself for so long he thought they'd been cut off. 'Hello?'

'There's something else,' she said. 'Your Mlle Blanchard was about three months pregnant when she died.'

He hadn't expected that. It gave him a nasty jolt, especially since the likelihood hadn't even occurred to him, when he told himself it should have done, given her age and her sudden departure from Maxstead. He'd been puzzling over reasons for her to have left, when a pretty obvious possibility had been there under his nose. A young woman, unmarried, finding herself pregnant in those circumstances, it would have rendered her situation there impossible. What else was she to do? Except leave, as fast as she could?

'She wouldn't be the first to take her own life in that sort of situation,' Dysart said, sounding tired.

Was it likely she was having second thoughts, coming round to the idea that suicide might have been possible, after all? That

Isabelle Blanchard had jumped from that door? On to that terrible pile of rubble? 'That's true, I suppose, and she won't be the last,' he said, 'but I'm finding it hard to accept that she jumped, given the facts.'

For, even if by some chance she had actually done so, someone must still have been with her. Someone who had reason not to want her secret to come out, who'd hidden her body and banked on her not being found for some time. The door had been fixed for the same reason, so that the body might not soon be found. Not everyone was aware of post-mortem procedures, or that an early foetus might still be detected after so long, and he didn't give the notion of suicide much credibility. 'If she had wanted to kill herself, Doctor, why come back to Maxstead to do it?'

'No ideas from me; you're the detective,' Dysart said, after a pause. She had sounded quite cheerful when they first began to speak, but now she was sad. Sad for another woman, a sister. Imagining herself in the same situation, maybe, empathizing. 'Find the one responsible for making her pregnant and I guess you've found her killer,' she said flatly. 'Killer in one way or another.'

He saw what she meant.

'One other thing,' she said before she terminated the call. 'Her underwear.'

He thought back to the report he'd just been reading. Green silk and lace-trimmed. 'What about it?'

'I don't know whether this might or might not be relevant, but it was hand-made.'

'She made it herself, you mean?'

'Hand-made in a professional way, if that makes sense. Exquisitely stitched. She could have sewn it herself, of course, but if not, there's a certain cachet in having your lingerie made and embroidered for you, personalized with your name or initials, which this was. Expensive, that goes without saying. I believe it isn't unknown for nuns to make money for their convents by doing that sort of sewing sometimes.'

Nuns? Now there was a thought.

He sat twiddling a pencil after the connection was broken, deep in thought. This new development opened up a whole new field of speculation; not only did they now have a believable explanation of why Isabelle Blanchard might have left the school so precipitately, but also a possible motive for her murder – if an association with anyone likely to be responsible for making her pregnant could be found. Here at Maxfield? Men were distinctly short on the ground in this environment. So far, only old Heaviside, who could hardly be counted, though stranger things happened. And Michael Deegan, who had said he'd known Mlle Blanchard only slightly.

He learnt from Miss Hillyard that Deegan was living in the house in Folbury which his late employer had owned, and summoned Gilmour to go with him. He decided not to telephone to make sure he would be at home when they called, but to take a chance on it. 'Let's surprise him.'

The house was situated in a short street just off Folbury's main shopping thoroughfare, a once busy but now quieter and less prestigious area than it had been, at a time when the bigwigs of the town had originally chosen to have houses built there for themselves. As the years had gone by and modern Folbury's businesses grew and expanded, as traffic increased and the town became noisier, the greener, quieter suburbs had come to have more appeal and the properties here had slid into a gentle, graceful decline. Most of them now looked as though they could do with a facelift. The house where Deegan was living, however, stood out from the others, its tiny front garden neat as a pin and its paintwork pristine, a demonstration to the world, if anyone was interested, of its late owner's evident competence as a builder and decorator.

As they mounted the steps and rang the bell, it struck Reardon as a slightly creepy notion that Deegan should occupy the dead man's house as well as hoping to take over his business. Besides, all Broderick's assets had been liquidated, hadn't they? So the house must have been sold along with everything else, and when Reardon had first seen him, Deegan had given him to understand that he was having trouble scraping up enough money to restart the business. How then had he been able to afford to buy the house? It was true that the recession meant that property was going absurdly cheap, but it didn't quite tie up with what Deegan had said, and his obvious need for money.

The man himself answered the door, and if the element of surprise was the object, they had succeeded. He was visibly taken aback at the sight of them, possibly disconcerted by his own dishevelled appearance – hair all over the place, a collar-less shirt with sleeves rolled up, flannel bags held up by braces. None of which upheld the image of the smart businessman he had been anxious to project when he and Reardon had first met; less smooth altogether, but at the same time slightly disarming.

He led the way into a bay-windowed front room, carpetless and unfurnished except for an empty bookcase and three chairs, apologizing as he waved them to two of them, armchairs which were patently past their best, and took the remaining seat, a straight, hard kitchen chair, for himself. He seemed embarrassed enough to believe an explanation was called for, and grinned ruefully as he gave it. 'Suits me to park myself here for the time being. I'm just renting the house from someone who bought it as a spec, until he can resell it when times improve. If I get the business on its feet again, as I hope, he's agreed to resell it to me. I plan to live here and use the place as business premises again, just as Frank did.'

Fair enough.

Reardon wasted no time in getting to the point of their visit, and began by telling him straight out what the post mortem had revealed. The effect was more than he'd bargained for. The voluble Deegan was rendered speechless. He turned ashen and dropped his head into his hands. Over his bent head, the eyes of Reardon and his sergeant met. There was little doubt that the shock was genuine, but he was decidedly more shocked at the pregnancy than he had been at the news of her murder.

As well he might be. He'd obviously been lying when he said his acquaintance with Isabelle Blanchard was slight. But even if he was only guilty of nothing more than making her pregnant, Deegan – Irish, and probably Catholic, lapsed or not – might well be facing a lifetime of remorse and repentance. He couldn't escape the fact that this was now a double murder – Isabelle and her unborn child.

At last he found his voice. When Reardon asked him if he had formed a relationship with the dead woman, he made no attempt to deny it. Was this because he was still so shocked to find out that she had been pregnant – or because he knew he'd been found out in a lie, and denial was useless? He had also been the last of the builders to leave the site at Maxstead and, despite his assurances about the safety of that door, he must realize that he was well in the frame for the crime, now that the truth of his connection with Isabelle had emerged. 'Yes, we had come to know each other,' he admitted.

'Why didn't you say so in the first place?'

Deegan shied away from that. 'I didn't think it mattered. We were never close.'

Gilmour shifted on his chair and gave him a hard look that said, *Close enough to get her pregnant.* His sergeant usually saw three sides to every question, especially where women were concerned. It could be bloody annoying, as Reardon found now when, treading where angels feared even to put a toe down, he pressed on, incredulously: 'She hadn't seen fit to tell you why she was leaving, then?'

'No,' Deegan said, bridling and flushing a dark red. 'I had no idea. But look here, Sergeant, I hope you're not implying that I . . . that I killed her.'

Reardon decided intervention was called for. Putting the man's back up wasn't going to get them anywhere. 'Where was she planning to go when she left, Mr Deegan?' He mumbled something Reardon didn't catch. 'Speak up.'

'I drove her to the station in Folbury. She was on her way to see that friend in Moseley who was in hospital, the one she'd replaced. I offered to drive her there, but she didn't want that. I left her waiting for the Birmingham train.'

'But you didn't see her get on it?' Gilmour asked. The fact that she'd *said* she was travelling to Birmingham didn't mean she had. There was no shortage of trains from Folbury to destinations all over the Midlands, and further possible connections. She could have gone anywhere.

'No, I didn't.'

There was a silence. 'Tell me what you know about Miss Blanchard,' Reardon said. 'You've obviously spent some time with her. Getting to know each other, talking about yourselves, as people do. She must have said where she came from, why she took up the position at Maxstead.'

He shook his head.

'And you weren't curious?'

'She used to say she wasn't interested in the past. It was only the present that mattered. I didn't press the point because I had the impression that she hadn't had a particularly happy childhood, though that was guesswork on my part. She wasn't easy to read, Isabelle. All I know is she'd lived in France all her life – until she came over to England – and she'd met that Phoebe woman there, when they were children. In fact, I think she stayed with her and her mother in Moseley until she came here to teach. That must have been where she planned to stay, after she'd visited the hospital.'

Gilmour soon disabused him. 'She never stayed at Miss Catherall's home, and she's not there now. Neither is Miss Catherall.'

'Well, it's likely she's still in hospital, isn't it?'

'I'm afraid that was a story cooked up between the two of them, so that Isabelle could come here. We don't know where Miss Catherall is.'

This was getting too much for Deegan. He looked bewildered. 'Why would they do that? And you're saying Phoebe Catherall's disappeared?' In a flash, calculation replaced confusion. 'Maybe she's gone for a good reason. You should be looking for her. Maybe *she* was the one who—'

Was he really trying to believe that? That Phoebe Catherall might have killed Isabelle Blanchard? An idea so far out it hadn't even crossed anyone else's mind? The way the enquiry was going, and if nothing better turned up, perhaps it would come down to that in the end, but they weren't there yet. 'Oh, I think you can do better than that, Mr Deegan. Like telling us more about Isabelle Blanchard, what sort of person she really was. Apart from being the sort who didn't wish to talk about herself.'

Colour was returning to his cheeks and, though he still looked devastated, he appeared to be recovering himself and giving out signs he was anxious to help. 'She was lovely, wasn't she?' he began. 'Lovely to look at, I mean.'

'We wouldn't know that,' Gilmour said.

'What? Oh God, no.'

Fortunately the sarcasm had slid off Deegan, who said

suddenly, 'Tell you what, I found a photograph of her the other day. Hang on and I'll fetch it.'

'Please do.'

He sloped off and left them in the bare, comfortless room and they heard him clattering along the ceramic-tiled passageway that led to the rear premises, as if glad of some action, or maybe escape.

'Amassing quite a rogue's gallery, one way or another, aren't we?' Gilmour remarked, no doubt thinking of the last photo they'd examined, that of Phoebe Catherall.

'Go easy on him, Joe. He's had a shock, and he's being co-operative.' Perhaps it was suiting him to be.

Deegan at that moment came back with a small snapshot in his hand. 'Frank – Mr Broderick – had a box Brownie for taking pictures of work he'd done – to show clients, you know. There was a roll of film in it when he died and I had it developed. He wouldn't have kept this one, though, because it was no good – useless for what he wanted it for anyway.' He handed it over and Reardon saw what he meant.

It was evidently spoilt in the sense for which it had been intended. A few inches square, it showed a view of the reconstructed wing at Maxstead. But the work it was meant to display was obscured by the woman who had evidently stepped into the picture just as it was being shot, and ruined it.

So this was Isabelle Blanchard. Looking at it carefully, Reardon decided her beauty was in the eye of the beholder, Deegan in this case. She was a good-looking woman, that was true, smiling as she held a black and white kitten close to her face, but attractive, or perhaps striking, rather than lovely, would have been his choice of adjective. There was something instantly, recognizably feline about her. He wondered if anyone else had noticed the triangular shape of her face, the almond-shaped eyes, and how much she and the kitten resembled one another.

'She loved cats. The kitchen moggy at Maxstead had kittens. This was the prettiest and she pleaded for it to be saved from being drowned with the rest of the litter. She called him Napoleon. Bonaparte was her hero.'

Reardon thought it best not to comment on that. Some

heroes these women teachers had! First Rupert of the Rhine, now Bonaparte. Was it something in the water at Maxstead?

'I hope they're looking after him, Napoleon, I mean,' Deegan said sadly. Fetching the photograph had temporarily diverted him from the main purpose of their visit, but now his dejection returned. 'It would have upset her if they're not.'

'She was wearing a little diamanté cat brooch when she was found,' Reardon said. 'Did you give it to her?'

'A what? No, I didn't. Maybe one of the girls did. They used to give her chocolates and things, sometimes.'

'Any girl in particular?'

'I've no idea.'

A gift from one of the girls? Possibly. It wasn't a piece of jewellery she was at all likely to have chosen herself, not in view of that expensive watch she'd been wearing. She might perhaps have worn it occasionally, to school, as kindness to the child who'd given it, but he wondered why she'd been wearing it on the night she died, when she was all dressed up. He also wondered if wearing her glad rags had been for a rendezvous with Deegan; though, if so, Maxstead would seem to have been a decidedly odd place to choose for it.

'Where did you spend your time together?' he asked, trying for the most delicate way of putting it. Deegan either didn't notice the implication, or chose not to, but he still looked discomfited.

'Here. I used to fetch her in my car, whenever she could get away.' He interpreted the silence and gave a short laugh. 'Not here in this room, of course. I'm living in the back.'

'Is it likely she left anything behind?'

'I don't think so.' He seemed uncertain and, after a long hesitation, he said there might possibly be one or two things. 'She might have, I suppose. You'd better come and look.'

They followed him along the passage, along the usual arrangement in houses of this type – two rooms, one behind the other, and the kitchen beyond – into a living room so spectacularly untidy and crammed with furniture it was hard to grasp at first glance how anyone could even find their way through it all, never mind a place to sit down. Possibly fairly clean, although a glimpse into the kitchen made Reardon glad they hadn't been offered tea. It was impossible to tell whether there was dust or

anything else under the welter of discarded clothing, old
newspapers, several used items of crockery and sundry other
miscellaneous objects. And Deegan obviously had a serious
addiction to Cadbury's Fruit and Nut, judging by the number of
wrappers tossed around. A dusty three-piece tapestry suite formed
a little island in the centre, chairs and sofa touching each other,
and a bed settee, still observing its function as a bed, and unmade,
was somewhere at the far end, its slept-in sheets scrunched up
in a tangled mess. Chaos didn't begin to describe it.

Did Deegan even see what it looked like? Not normally, that
was plain, but now, viewing it through someone else's eyes, he
looked around and spread his hands. 'Camping out,' he offered
feebly.

How was it possible it had got into this state in the short
time Deegan had occupied the house? Only by moving in and
dumping all his worldly possessions into this one room. In a
way that made sense – having everything together, he could
forget about taking care of the rest of the house. If this sort of
disorder extended to his business life, he was in trouble.

He did, however, appear to be one of those people who could
and did compartmentalize their lives, ruthless enough to be able
to shove aside what he thought was unimportant in order to
concentrate on what was. Amid all the confusion, there was an
open roll-front desk wedged into a corner, where papers were
neatly stacked, pens and pencils sprouted from a jar and files
were set in orderly fashion on its top.

Deegan was looking helplessly round at the shambles of the
rest of the room, understandably enough. Where even to begin
searching? 'Hold on, there's a box somewhere she asked me to
keep,' he said suddenly, clapping a hand to his forehead as he
remembered.

He swept papers off a small chest and groped about in the
top drawer, finally coming up with an old, flat chocolate box
with a picture on the lid of a simpering Gibson Girl with Cupid's
bow lips and quantities of hair. Across the corner a large red
ribbon bow which had been stuck on as a decoration still
adhered, now faded to a tattered pink. He handed it over and,
as Gilmour lifted the lid, a musky perfume arose. Inside was a
small collection of jewellery: a seed pearl necklet, a string of

corals, and a couple of rings with semi-precious stones, pretty but none of it looking very valuable. The source of the perfume was a small, attar-of-roses scent-card, meant for a handbag or a handkerchief drawer, priced at one penny, sold for the Queen Alexandra nursing charity. Resting on it was a well-thumbed miniature book of illustrated French fairy tales, the print so tiny it was scarcely decipherable.

These were personal mementoes, childish treasures of the deceased woman, pathetic in a way that brought her to life more than even the snapshot had been able to convey. As Reardon flicked through the tiny book he found, folded and tucked inside but protruding slightly, a scrap of paper that seemed to be have been torn from the last sheet of a letter, almost covered with spiky French handwriting. He scanned it quickly.

'What does it say?' asked Gilmour.

'It's presumably from her aunt, since she signs herself "Tante Mathilde". Basically, she's refusing to give Isabelle some information she seems to have written for. She warns her that she's playing a dangerous game, and tells her not to involve anyone else.' The tone of the letter was sharp and reproving. It looked as though it had once been screwed up and then smoothed out.

'And?'

'That's it. Not going to help much, is it?' Except that it was proof of a sort that Isabelle's purpose in coming to England had possibly not been entirely innocent.

He turned the paper over. On the back were a few scribbles, the tentative beginnings of what might have been a reply. But if it was, it wasn't one to the sender, since it was written in English and began, *Dear Nol.* Each attempt was scribbled out, as though it might have been a tricky letter to write, each beginning heavily scored through. *I have heard from . . . I have to tell you . . . I have had no luck.* And that was all.

'Do you know anything about this letter, Mr Deegan?' Reardon asked, showing it to him but keeping hold of it.

But Deegan, having peered at it, looked as mystified as they were.

'Ever heard her mention anyone called Nol?'

'Funny name. Nol? No, never. I'd remember if I'd heard that, wouldn't I.'

'Maybe it's a nickname,' Reardon said. 'Short for Oliver? Like Old Noll. That's how Oliver Cromwell was known, wasn't he?'

Gilmour had long since ceased to be surprised at what Reardon could come out with. 'Or even for Olivia,' he tried himself, not to be outdone.

'Well, I don't recall her ever mentioning anyone called Oliver, or Olivia, either,' Deegan said. He flopped down on the bed and sat looking miserable and defeated, as if the stuffing had been knocked out of him. Whatever else, the fact that Isabelle had been pregnant, and presumably with his child, had shattered him. Reardon hoped it was the only thing that he was feeling guilty about.

'Why did she leave this box with you?'

'Oh, she didn't trust the maids at Maxstead,' he said absently, wrapped in his own thoughts. 'She said they poked about in her things and she didn't want to lose these.'

'We'd like to keep this, Mr Deegan,' Reardon said, waving the letter.

'Take the lot, I've no use for any of it.' As he held the door open for them to leave, he said, 'I would have married her, you know.'

'I wonder if he would?' Easy to say, isn't? Gilmour remarked as they walked down the street.

'I don't know.' The truth was, Reardon didn't believe he had quite got the hang of Deegan. He was no fool, and he must realize he was a prime suspect. The pregnancy apart, he could be putting on quite an act. Reardon didn't really see him as a murderer, though he'd seen enough of them to know he'd met more unlikely ones. 'One thing that puzzles me,' he said. 'That letter, from this Tante Mathilde. It wasn't particularly friendly, you'd have thought she'd have chucked it away. What was the point in keeping it?'

He thought he would show it to Ellen. It had seemed perfectly clear, but his French wasn't such that he might not have missed some nuance that she might pick up to indicate why it had been kept.

EIGHT

Ellen has taken the first available train home and arrived in Folbury at an early hour. A visit to the capital where she had once lived and worked has been such a treat. She loves the bustle there, the crowds and the sense of life and things happening, but Folbury – or more correctly, anywhere where Reardon is – is now home, which means a great deal more. She has a lot to tell him and it's disappointing to find he has already left for work, though he has set the table for her breakfast and propped a note against the teapot. She has only spoken to him on the telephone, to tell him she had arranged to stay over another night with Kate. The note is apologetic. Duty says he's had to leave early to go over to Dudley and report to the new super before going on to Maxstead. Tolly has had his walk and is even now probably cadging a second breakfast with Horace Levett, their next door neighbour. He knows it's one of her days at Maxstead, so he'll look out for her there. With love and a few more remarks which bring a smile to her face.

She goes to see Horace, who lives in the nearest semi, to have a word before she leaves, and finds the little old man already at work, perched on a stool like a busy elf in a fairy tale, performing magic at the table under his window. Before his retirement he had owned a small jeweller's shop, with a sideline in watch repairing, and people still bring timepieces for him to mend, which he does with skill and for only a token payment, no matter how clapped-out the clocks might seem. He looks up from the glasses perched on the end of his nose and smiles the smile which transforms his ugly face into something memorable and heart-warming.

With a volley of frenzied barks, Tolly launches himself fervently at Ellen, forgiving her for abandoning him by trying to knock her down and wash her face with his tongue.

'All right, Tolly, I'm delighted to see you, but that's enough for now,' she says, giving him a hug and kissing the top of his head.

The old man has been lonely since his wife of over fifty years died and was delighted when neighbours with a dog which needed occasional dog-minding moved into the old house at the end of the street. They had taken to each other from the first, he and the dog. Tolly is happy in both houses, Horace's or his own, he can take it or leave it. He knows he's on to a good thing; he'll get his dinner either way and keeps his options open. His main priority is food, he's a thief of the first order where it's concerned, and neither is he averse to an extra walk, even though he's just had one.

He sits near the door where his lead hangs, staring fixedly at Ellen in silent reproach as she makes no move to take it down. 'Are you happy to have Tolly again today, Horace?' she asks, superfluously.

'Happy any day, you know that m'duck.' Horace has never lost his regional accent, or the habit of hospitality. 'Cuppa tea?'

'No thanks, I've just had breakfast. But I've brought you this.' She hands him a box of Florentines from Kate's favourite delicatessen, knowing what a sweet tooth he has. They chat for a while about her visit to the capital, while Tolly goes to sit on the staircase that leads from the living room, contemplating suicide as Ellen presently prepares to leave without him. She kisses the top of his head again and, as she starts up her car, sees he has leapt up on to the chair beside Horace's window and is watching sorrowfully as she leaves.

She drives over to Maxstead in an optimistic frame of mind and, as she steers into the parking spot by a rear entrance to which she's been allocated, she feels how good it is to be back in her own work environment. She hadn't admitted, even to herself, how much her real work is part of her, and it's only to Kate so far that she's confessed what the return to it has meant. Reardon himself knows without being told, without any need to have it pointed out.

The police car has already arrived, so Gilmour at least is here. If her husband has gone over to Dudley as he intended, he must have ridden over on his motorbike again. It's begun to worry her a little, that he's still riding it, but it might be more than her life's worth to even hint that maybe he's not as young as he was, that he won't see forty again. She leaves the Morris and makes her way into the school via the back entrance. Her previous stints here, taking separate Lower School classes, have gone down fairly well. She can't rate it better than that, because while her pupils have all given her a gratifying attention, though not without a certain curiosity, it's unusual to find girls of that age quite so obedient and industrious. She's a new broom, of course, and they haven't yet got the measure of her and how easy she might or might not be. On the other hand, considering what's happened to their previous French teacher, their quietness is understandable. Such a tragedy is highly unlikely to have entered their young lives before. What had happened to Isabelle Blanchard is sufficient to sober even the liveliest of girls and, if what Marian Golding had said was true, Isabelle Blanchard had been quite a favourite with them – contrary to what the staff had thought of her. Maybe that was because she'd had a more *laissez-faire* approach than the girls are used to from teachers, or maybe it was just because she was different – foreign, sophisticated, pretty clothes. *Scent.* It's by no means unusual for teachers like her to have this sort of effect on adolescent girls. 'Pashes' on teachers they admire and want to copy are a fact of life. Ellen fears they may find they have a poor substitute in her.

Her first lesson is with 5a. As she is walking towards their form room, she almost collides with Miss Draper, distracted and even more all over the place than usual, if possible, as she clutches Ellen's arm. 'Oh, Mrs Reardon, there you are, thank goodness! Is your husband with you?'

'No, but he'll be here soon, I expect. Is there something wrong, Miss Draper?' she asks, an obviously superfluous question.

Miss Draper inelegantly blows a damp strand of hair from her hot face and yanks it back behind her ear. 'One of the girls is missing!' she declares dramatically.

'Missing? Good Heavens! Which girl?'

Josie Pemberton, it seems, one of the senior girls Ellen hasn't yet met. Miss Hillyard has already questioned the girls she shares a room with, but so far all they've been able to say is that she hadn't been there when they woke that morning. They are in trouble, because for some reason best known to themselves they hadn't seen fit to mention that fact to anyone, and it was only at Assembly that Josie's non-appearance had been made apparent.

Miss Draper is almost in tears. 'We're all at sixes and sevens. I've set Daphne Cash and Miss Scholes to search the whole school, but there's been no sign of her. 'Let's just hope she hasn't had some sort of accident.' Her face registers horror at what she's just said, the fate of Mam'selle clearly uppermost in her mind.

'Is it possible she's run away?' Ellen asks uncertainly, to steer her on to another track. Maxstead Court is no Dotheboys Hall, but she can think of all sorts of reasons why a child would hate boarding school. Being separated from her parents and family, missing some sort of treat she might have been having with them, or even pining for her pet dog, anything. Such things can – and do – run deep with children. On the other hand, Josie is no longer a child, in that sense. She's nearly sixteen, and presumably long adjusted to the trials of life in a boarding school.

'Is there any chance she might be hiding? As a joke?' It's a feeble suggestion, but she can't prevent those other 'incidents' which haven't yet been fully explained to her from crossing her mind.

'Hiding? Why on earth should she? Oh, gosh, the attics!' Miss Draper's hand goes to her chest, as if to order her heart not to cause further trouble. 'No, no, she wouldn't, they're strictly forbidden to the girls – and why would she go up there anyway, when they're only used for storing trunks and so on?' She blanches, as frightening possibilities occur to her. There are doors from the attics with access to the roof, opening on to the leads, acres of rooftops with dangerous gullies between, and the narrow parapet which overlooks the Quad below – where Mam'selle's body had been found. The potential for accidents is endless.

'A dare?' Ellen suggests tentatively, then wishes she hadn't when Miss Draper looks even more horrified, though she doesn't dismiss the idea out of hand.

'Oh, Lord, perish the thought, but yes, you could be right! Josie has plenty of spirit. I believe she has an older brother at university, too, and you know what those graduates are with those rags of theirs, climbing to the top of monuments and leaving things and . . .' Her voice trails off. Someone will have to venture out on to the roof, it's clear. But who, among all these women, will have the pluck?

At that moment, Sergeant Gilmour appears in the hall and Miss Draper falls upon him as though Mafeking has been relieved.

'What's happening?' asked Reardon a few minutes later as Gilmour came into the cubbyhole/storeroom which everyone seemed to be calling the police room, though it was just a convenience, somewhere to park their papers, talk to people. At the present moment, the police presence was limited to himself and Gilmour, until the department's two DCs joined them to begin another, more thorough search of the derelict east wing, even though it was unlikely to produce much further in the way of results.

'A girl's gone missing,' Gilmour answered, his face as long as a wet weekend. It was also very red, and he was sweating. He had spent the last fifteen minutes on the roof, crawling all over it and trying not to look down, searching for a girl who definitely wasn't there.

'What?'

'And Miss Hillyard wants to see you in her study. Me as well,' he added, not happily. Miss Hillyard put the fear of God into him. Lowlifes twice his own size he could deal with, but clever women like her could reduce him to a pulp, though he'd be the last to own up to that.

Along with Miss Hillyard and a flustered-looking Miss Draper, they found Ellen herself also in the study, which didn't please Reardon. Not that it didn't lift his heart to see her after what seemed like an absence of weeks, rather than three days, but she had already been caught up more than either of them liked in the tragedy which had happened here, and he could see she was looking slightly ruffled at being drawn into this new development. He badly wanted to put his arms round her and say hello in a manner hardly appropriate at this moment. They exchanged a slight smile, in his case apologetic, acknowledging that it was maybe his fault she'd been roped in, and hers reassuring and saying that it wasn't. They settled themselves to listen as Miss Hillyard hurriedly launched into explanations.

After Josie's absence had been noticed in Assembly, which took place immediately after breakfast, enquiries revealed she had been missing for some time. The staff had immediately been instructed to carry on with lessons, and timetables were rapidly adjusted to allow Miss Cash and Miss Scholes to search the school.

'How old is she?' Reardon asked.

'Fifteen, nearly sixteen. A nice girl, bright, interested in sport, something of a tomboy.'

'Is it possible she has – er – run away?' he asked, posing the same question that had occurred to Ellen. It was a reasonable assumption, but Miss Hillyard did not take kindly to it.

'No, I do *not* think she has run away at all. I've spoken to her friends, the girls she shares a room with, and there's more to it than meets the eye. They know more about this than they have admitted, but at present they are choosing to say nothing.' Not for long, however, if she had anything to do with it, her expression said.

'Josie Pemberton is not the sort of girl to play tricks,' put in Miss Draper.

'I sincerely hope that's all it is, and not an escalation.'

'Escalation?' Reardon queried.

The headmistress exchanged significant looks with Miss Draper, then took a deep breath. 'I suppose you should know. I'm sorry to say, there has been a spate of rather foolish practical jokes being played here recently. There's a strong possibility, I fear, that this may be another, though hopefully one that has not gone too far.'

So this could be why he and Gilmour had been summoned here – and Ellen too, who, as far as he knew, hadn't yet been made party to the full extent of these schoolgirl japes. Everyone, she had said, seemed determined to play them down, if not to conceal them deliberately. Such things didn't happen in well-regulated schools. He could make a good guess at why the headmistress had now decided it was time to be to be frank about them, but Miss Hillyard was about to be disappointed, if he was right about that. Gilmour had already given help, it was the right thing to do, and Reardon was more than willing to do what more they could, unofficially, to assist, but unless she was still missing after the school had been thoroughly searched, the child's disappearance wasn't within the scope of the investigation here.

All the same, he listened carefully to what she had to say about the silly, childish tricks as she described them, such as balancing a dish of water on the top of a door left ajar, so that whoever pushed it further open got a small drenching. A toad had been placed between someone's sheets. The disappearing gym knickers, which Ellen had told him about. But then small sums of money, which was all the girls were allowed to keep, had also disappeared, as well as a quite valuable fountain pen, and later a Fortnum & Mason chocolate cake which had been sent to Selina Bright for her birthday.

'Forgive me, Miss Hillyard,' Reardon intervened. 'Money? That really does sound more than a practical joke.'

'I agree, but I do not believe we are harbouring a thief in our midst. For one thing, the gym things were later found stuffed behind a radiator in the locker room, and the money and all of the other stolen items – with the exception of the cake,' she added with a glimmer of wry humour, 'turned up in the end, so it had to be assumed they had all simply been lost or mislaid. I'm afraid it was the cake which caused suspicion to fall unfairly on one girl, with her fondness for sweet things.'

'Which girl was that?'

She sighed. 'Her name is Antonia Freeman.'

'But wasn't it *her* gym things . . .?' Ellen began.

Miss Hillyard said, 'That's true. And the missing fountain pen was hers, too.'

'Well, I don't believe it's unknown for that sort of thing to happen.' All eyes turned to Miss Draper, who went on diffidently, 'To divert suspicion from oneself, you know. Though one does wonder . . . would Antonia have the cleverness for that?'

'Eve!' said Miss Hillyard, gently reproving.

Miss Draper flushed brightly. 'Oh dear, I apologize. I

shouldn't have said that, poor girl. She's not unintelligent, of course, far from it, that wasn't what I meant.'

Reardon, who thought this was doubtless all very interesting, but should have been gone into more thoroughly by the staff before it reached this point, brought them back to what they were here for – Josie's disappearance. It seemed unlikely to him from what had just been said that this was just another joke. There would, as almost always in these cases, be a simple explanation, albeit one perhaps more serious, such as an accident. 'What exactly did Josie's roommates have to say?'

Miss Hillyard's lips tightened. 'As I said, they are being very silly and refusing to say anything more than that they found her bed empty when they woke – and that they thought she had gone out to the lake for some rowing practice.'

Lake? A quick glance passed between Reardon and Gilmour. They both remembered that lake, though to call it such might be a slight exaggeration. Not all that much bigger than a large pool, if Reardon remembered rightly. An idyllic spot, all the same, at the far end of the school grounds, abutting on to the forest beyond, not far from where a body had once lain beneath the snow. Very picturesque, fed by a gushing stream emerging from the woods and cascading down over boulders padded with velvety green moss into a deep, shady pool where fern fronds drooped to the water's edge. He also remembered with less pleasure and more alarm a large tree trunk, which had fallen across one end of the pool and offered a sort of bridge to the other side, slippery and undoubtedly dangerous. A ramshackle boathouse of sorts. Also a leaky little rowing boat, moored to the edge. He couldn't believe these women hadn't seriously taken all this into account.

But Miss Hillyard was continuing calmly, 'Our games mistress, Miss Cash, is keen to have the girls taught to swim, but I have not encouraged them to use the lake; in fact it's forbidden. I am not at all sure how safe it is. It's deep and there may be rocks underwater. I hope we may have an indoor swimming bath installed, sooner or later. Meanwhile, it's only Miss Cash herself who swims there.' Her tone spoke volumes. 'Although I *have* given her permission to teach rowing there to any girl who's interested.'

So the lame excuse Josie's two roommates had given for not being surprised to find her already up and out when they woke did have some validity, in so far as it went, if Josie had been one of those who liked to practise rowing on the lake, as it seemed she had.

All the same, Reardon hoped the leaky little tub he remembered had been replaced, or at least made seaworthy, or whatever the term was for waterproofing a boat – watertight, that was it. And even so.

'Oh, but that was the first place we looked,' Miss Draper said, before he had the chance to make the point. 'Miss Cash had been there, and we were satisfied Josie had not.'

Had Miss Cash been there all night, then, to know that? The pool was deep, as they had said. Reardon didn't know just how deep, and could only hope it wouldn't have to be dragged later. He had opened his mouth to say something they might not want to hear when there was a knock on the door.

Miss Hillyard frowned at the interruption, but called out a brisk, 'Come in.' A girl appeared in the doorway, making no move to enter. She looked ill at ease, especially when she saw the room was full of people. She stood there, blushing and tongue-tied, a solid-looking girl with dark eyebrows and long hair in two plaits.

'Well, Antonia, what is it?'

For a while she looked as though she might turn tail and run. But then she stammered out, colouring to the roots of her hair, 'I don't want to sneak, Miss Hillyard, but I think I know where Josie might be.'

NINE

V ic Wetherby levered himself upright from his armchair
and grabbed his walking stick. Steadying himself, he
took his first tentative step forward, followed by several
more confident ones round the room. He sighed with relief. It was
OK. The hospital could have the damned crutches back and no
regrets. He was going to be able to manage with just the stick
from now on, like he'd insisted he could to Gertie. In spite of this,
he didn't feel much more cheerful as he hobbled to the window
and stood there, smoking, despondently looking at the bolting
spring cabbages on his sun-baked vegetable patch. He began to
fidget again about getting back to his neglected garden. He drew
deeply on the cigarette and began to cough. For a moment or two
he held it between his fingers, watching it burn down, then suddenly
reached out for an ashtray and stubbed it out, half-smoked.

He was smoking too much and that was the truth. He'd given
up the fags years ago because of Mabel's asthma and even kept
off them after she died, because he *did* feel better without, just
as she'd always told him he would. And then he'd gone and
started again, after coming out of hospital. Living with his sister
and her husband was enough to drive anyone into bad habits.

He cut such ungrateful thoughts short. Gertie had turned up
trumps, when all was said and done. After he'd been discharged
from hospital, and was wondering how the hell he was going
to manage to look after himself, even to making a sarnie or a
cup of tea, hampered with them bloody crutches, she'd ordered
her husband to drive over here and take him back to their
bungalow in Kidderminster to stay with them until he could
move about better. She'd always been a bossy wench, Gertie,
and still treated him like her little brother, but she meant well.
After telling him off twenty times for not having the common
sense, at his age, to get someone else to look at the blocked
spouting, somebody who would have had more nous than to
reach out too far and fall off the ladder and fracture his thigh,

she'd shut up and got on with seeing to it that he had three square meals a day, his washing done and a comfortable bed. But instead of giving him an earful all the time about how daft he'd been, he was treated to a string of complaints about that Doreen, her half-soaked daughter-in-law. Spent every penny, that one, used too much lipstick, couldn't cook a decent meal, let alone keep her kids in order. Yak-yak-yak.

Vic had good evidence of that last – they were right enough, the little 'uns, but they'd rampaged all over the shop when they'd been brought to visit their grandparents, and the middle one, a right little 'erbert, had managed to get a hold of one of Vic's crutches, swung it round, and would have brained his little brother in the process, had Gertie not stopped him in time.

He sighed again and automatically reached for another cigarette, but stopped halfway and put a humbug into his mouth instead. Smoking again, what had got into him? But sucking sweets instead, plus sitting about doing nowt, was causing him to put on weight. Sooner he could get back to his garden the better, he'd told his mate, Ron Fairlie yesterday. Ron had brought a few beers with him and it had been a right tonic, catching up with all the workplace gossip, which he missed more than he liked to admit. He'd been due to retire at the end of the year, but this how-de-do had brought it forward. He wouldn't be into driving for a long time yet and, from what Ron had said, Ernie Woodman wasn't thinking of taking him back for such a short time as would be left, miserable old sod.

But it was only what Gertie had predicted. 'You should have made plans for your retirement, our Vic. You haven't, have you?' Vic hadn't. Except for more time in his garden. But he already grew so many veg he had to give most of them away, and he'd never seen the point of growing flowers. Leave them outside in the meadows and hedgerows, where they belonged.

He hadn't slept well last night, after Ron had left him. Facing that he'd have to do something about all that empty time ahead. And about that other thing he'd heard of from Ron. Which he'd better do now, or he might not do it at all. He wasn't good with pen and paper, but he hadn't much to say anyway. Just a few lines, and it was up to them after that.

*   *   *

'Don't rely too much on what Antonia says, Inspector,' Miss Hillyard said later, when she and Reardon were alone. She had asked him into her private sitting room, to avoid constant interruptions, she said. Unlike her study or the staff room, it was not only quiet and comfortable, but bordering on the luxurious. A thick carpet, graceful old furniture that was almost certainly antique, polished until you could see your face. Deep, squashy chairs and soft colours. An artistically arranged silver bowl of massed roses, filling the room with fragrance. Taken all in all, it threw a new light on Miss Hillyard. 'One doesn't always know what she's thinking and she may give you the wrong impression,' she continued. 'I'm afraid she is rather a difficult girl.'

'Are you saying she's a liar?'

'Of course not. But she's stubborn. She's been the main target of all this tomfoolery that's being going on and I'm convinced she knows who's responsible, but she won't say who it is.'

'Too intimidated, perhaps?'

'On the contrary. She isn't entirely without spirit. But these so-called pranks are annoying and must stop, and they will. I have my own suspicions about the culprits. Meanwhile, just beware of putting too much weight on what Antonia says.'

At the moment, she wasn't saying anything, though she had led them to where Josie had been found. And, short of using thumbscrews, he couldn't see how she could be made to say more. She had assumed a stubborn look which did not bode well for success and which told him she would be even less open to persuasion than Josie herself, who'd been too upset to make any sense. 'I'm not a tell-tale,' Antonia kept repeating stubbornly. 'I just guessed where'd she be.'

'Come along, Antonia, you can do better than that,' Miss Hillyard had said severely. A threat of punishment hung in the air.

She was shaking in her shoes but she still said no. 'I just did.'

They had left her to examine her conscience, Reardon thinking there must be better ways of getting her confidence so that she might give in and tell what she knew. Maybe Miss Keith, the art mistress, the one person who appeared to have any rapport with the girl, might be persuaded to get her to say more. And she must know more. She had taken them straight to where Josie had been fastened up, in one of the ground-floor rooms in . . . well, where else but that fateful east wing?

The terrified girl had been carried out, exhausted, dazed and disorientated at what had happened, and given into the care of Matron, a capable ex-nurse who took charge and who, after a brief check to make sure there was no physical damage, gave her a milky drink and put her straight to bed between clean sheets in a darkened room and ordered everyone else away. 'The last thing she needs is all this questioning just now. What she does need is to sleep the clock round, which she'll probably do. I'll let you know when she's awake.'

She was right, of course. There had already been too many anxious questions. Why had she gone there, in the middle of the night? the headmistress and Miss Draper had asked her. Oh, she couldn't remember, she must have been sleepwalking or something. Who had shut her in that room, with the door jammed so that she couldn't open it, however hard she tried? She didn't know, she hadn't seen. Could it, they suggested cautiously, even have been Antonia herself? Who had then led them to find her through guilt at what she had done? She shook her head vehemently and looked on the verge of tears, if not collapse, and Reardon was glad when Matron intervened and they had left off the questions and let the child go.

He was having to do a quick turn-round on his opinions. However reluctant he had been to get himself and his men involved in this latest development, wanting to believe it had nothing to do with the main enquiry, now that the girl had been found, and where, he was beginning to think there was every chance it might be. What was the attraction in that derelict, creepy old shambles of a building that drew young women to court danger and go exploring it in the dark? The question of whether Josie had been shut into that room by the same person who had killed Mam'selle couldn't be ignored, however horrific the implications of that were. If it was so, the indications were that the perpetrator was no outsider, but someone who lived at Maxstead Court, or had easy access to the premises. Not the first time that suspicion had cropped up, but it didn't make

Reardon any happier. He thought it was probably the reason why Josie was refusing to say anything, perhaps through a misplaced sense of loyalty, or not daring to incriminate anyone by breaking this non-sneaking code they seemed to have, the one thing that just wasn't done. Or she might actually be afraid.

Reardon sighed. He wasn't used to dealing with adolescent girls, but neither were any of his team. He didn't relish having to do it, but he'd have to give it a go. 'I'll need to talk to all of them – Josie, and those other girls, too, the ones she shares a room with, and Antonia. They must know something. I'd like to do it while it's still fresh in their minds that they're in trouble – if they are – and I don't want to leave it too long.'

'I'll arrange it, but can't it wait until tomorrow? Josie may feel differently after she's slept on it, and we've all had more than enough for today. They're not the only ones who need some time to consider.'

He saw the sense in this. At the moment, though, the girl who'd led them to Josie was the one who interested him the most and, after agreeing to do what she asked, he said, 'Tell me more about Antonia, Miss Hillyard.'

She didn't reply immediately. Playing for time, she reached out for a dark green glass paperweight, which stood on the walnut Pembroke table next to her chair, and stared into its depths as if scrying, using a crystal ball. 'She's a bit of a problem,' she said at last, looking up. 'The truth is, she hasn't made friends here and she's not much liked – mainly, I'm afraid, because she can be rather a bully.' For another moment or two she resumed her crystal gazing, then almost to herself she added, 'Or has she become a bully because she is disliked? Which comes first? I'm never quite sure.'

Reardon couldn't find an immediate response to that, but it seemed to be a rhetorical question that didn't require an answer anyway and she went on, 'Or even if it's due to her – well, let's face it, her plainness. That might well have induced feelings of inferiority which make it necessary to assert herself.'

She met his silence with a wry look, maybe chiding herself for thinking (quite wrongly as it happened) that he wasn't likely to be interested in such modern theories. He was thinking of Antonia, lumpy and unattractive, reputedly fond of cake – and surely born to be a victim of bullying rather than the victimizer. Those 'practical jokes' she had been suspected of carrying out, hadn't some of them been aimed at her, and wasn't that in itself a form of bullying?

'However, I am not prepared to put up with that sort of thing, whichever side it's on. I haven't been able to get to the bottom of it yet, but I will,' she asserted, the iron hand showing beneath the velvet glove. 'Meanwhile, I just don't know. She's fallen behind in her work lately, and it isn't through any lack of intelligence – quite the contrary, in fact. She's one of our scholarship girls.'

'Scholarship?' Reardon hadn't known girls were able to get to Maxstead Court via the scholarship route.

'We only have two, as yet, she and Catherine Leyland, though I hope to have more later. Clever girls can raise the standard for the others. I have great hopes of Catherine.' Her voice softened. 'She's all set for a university place and I'm sure she's going on to do great things.'

'Doesn't Miss Keith think the same thing about Antonia – artistically speaking?' He was remembering that compelling, imaginative drawing she had shown him.

'She has made it plain enough that she does,' Miss Hillyard replied, irritated, 'though Antonia's situation has troubled me too, for some time. I've seen her artwork, and no doubt she's very gifted, but I don't see that there's a great deal to be done about it.'

'I gathered Miss Keith believes she'd benefit from further training.'

'Yes. I dare say she's anxious for the girl to have what she missed. She hasn't had any formal training herself, and she's rather conscious of the fact. She came to us from industry.'

'In the Potteries, was it? Stoke-on-Trent?' She'd spoken of decorating cups and saucers.

'Somewhere like that. Yes, it was.'

'Presumably you have connections there, as well? That was how you knew her and asked her here to teach, I mean? You said you had invited most of your staff to join you here?'

'No, she answered an advertisement I put in *Teachers' World.*'

'My mistake. But she presumably knows places where Antonia could go?'

A spark of anger had lit her eyes. 'What Miss Keith *doesn't* know is how impossible that would be. Antonia will be leaving at the end of term. She's here on scholarship, as I said, which even so has been a great sacrifice for her widowed mother. Her husband, Antonia's father, was a successful solicitor, but he wasn't thrifty, and unfortunately he'd run through any money he had before he died suddenly, leaving her penniless. There are three younger children and the mother needs Antonia to find work and bring in some money, however much she might wish for her to continue with her education, or training.' She still held the paperweight and her fingers tightened round it. 'No one who hasn't been in that situation can realize what heartache such a decision can be for a parent, believe me.'

She spoke so vehemently he was prompted to wonder what had sparked it off, allowing him a revealing glimpse of Edith Hillyard he hadn't seen before; that few people would be allowed to see, he imagined. He had only seen her before as calm, fully in control, dedicated and perhaps ruthless in her ambitions. She'd struck him as a rather cold woman. But surely someone in her position must know of ways to help a girl in Antonia's situation?

He was in deep waters here, however, and for the moment he'd had enough of it, quite apart from the fact that all this was taking up time he could ill afford. 'I suggest they'll all soon think better about not speaking up, Josie and Antonia, as well as those other two friends of Josie.'

She sighed. 'That's another problem. I'm not altogether sure they *are* friends, in that sense. They share a room, but I've had my eye on them for some time, thinking they should perhaps be separated. It's not long to the end of term, however, when Avis Myerson will be leaving, and it will sort itself out then.'

He took a furtive glance at his watch. He should go, but he was intrigued, despite himself. 'Avis Myerson?'

Her expression hardened. 'A girl who needs watching, Inspector. A spoilt child of parents with too much money, who resents being here at all, and does all she can to encourage others to flout authority. I'm sorry to say I think she might be at the bottom of what's happened to Josie. At her last school she had some difficulties, I'm afraid, and was asked to leave

– and there's a big question mark hanging over whether she'll
be allowed to stay on here. I can't have disruption like this.'
She didn't say what had caused the girl to be expelled from
her previous school, and closed her lips as if she had already
said rather too much. With an air of winding up the subject,
she finally put the paperweight back and said, 'Maxstead is
only a stepping stone before she's old enough to be packed off
to finishing school in Switzerland; she's only here at all because
her parents don't really know how to cope with her until then.
I confess I shan't be sorry to see her go.'

'But you did take her on?' If her rich parents could afford
the Maxstead fees, who was Miss Hillyard to turn her away?
She was only human, after all.

'That's all part and parcel of being a teacher. I don't believe
anyone is beyond redemption, though I have to say,' she added,
'Miss Myerson tests my convictions sometimes.'

*I know I shall have to be more open with Inspector Reardon
sooner or later, and I will, but not yet. Even now, when it's
getting pretty near the bone, I can't plant suspicions in his
mind, implicating some who might, for all I know, be innocent.
Not until he has explored the full nastiness of what has been
going on and hopefully discovered it for himself. He's getting
there. He has just asked me about any connection I might have
with Stoke-on-Trent, which gave me a jolt, but I was able to
answer quite truthfully that I hadn't. Not personally, at any
rate. Mother came from a neighbouring town – yes, one of those
they call the Five Towns – but it wasn't Stoke.*

*What would she have thought of all this? She would undoubt-
edly have been proud to see me installed here, but I doubt
whether she would approve of how I'm dealing with the
situation (or* not *dealing* might be more appropriate).

*I think she must have been a sweet girl, my mother, before
my father's death and the sadness that took hold of her there-
after. Her photographs show her as a young woman with softly
waving brown hair and a dimpled smile. I don't remember her
like that. My father's death had left her without the wish to
smile very much at all.*

She was born Adelaide Beckwith, always called Addie, born

and brought up in that part of the country which is world famous for its ceramics, but nevertheless a place which is relatively unconsidered by most people in the British Isles, except for what it produces in the way of the crockery that graces their breakfast and tea tables, that provides kitchen- and sanitary-ware. The beautiful china that's also produced there is beyond most ordinary pockets. Addie worked in one of the factories during the week and sang contralto in the chapel choir at the weekend.

I've never visited the area myself, never having had the least desire to do so, but it seems almost as though it is mapped into my mind from the hours of listening to my mother's fond memories. It remains one of life's mysteries to me how anyone could feel as deeply as she did about what sounds like the last place on earth anyone could wish to remember; full of the grime of industry, and the threat of poverty for many hanging over it all, it seemed to me. And yet, it was all part of the reason why she did what she did and eventually left behind her family and everything that was dear to her.

The real truth was that she was swept off her feet by a young man called Jamie Hillyard. She liked to tell me she fell instantly in love, in the way women often do with someone bright, charming, footloose and different, I suppose. In this case a stranger to the town with his head in the clouds, who taught music and wrote popular songs which he hoped to sell. Unfortunately, he failed to take into account that there was little money in a working-class district for most of the parents, however proud, to indulge their children with falderals like music lessons. Or that the music publishers to whom he sent his songs would have little interest in buying them. All the same, Addie couldn't resist his charisma, and within a few weeks of their meeting they were married. She elected to continue working, because band workers like her could earn good money, and that kept them going until I was born. That was when she was forced to give up work to look after me. And when, I suppose, the trouble really started.

Nothing was coming in, and my father apparently never had the slightest idea about money except how to spend it, and the Micawberish attitude that things were bound to come better soon. If only the music publishers would see his songs for the little gems they were. If only the warm men, owners of the pot banks, could be persuaded that music was as intrinsic to their lives as making kitchen-ware and lavatory basins. If only money would drop from the skies like manna from Heaven.

Eventually, when the situation grew desperate, with hope triumphing once more over experience, Jamie decided he was bound to find both pupils and an outlet for his songs if he took us, Mother and me, with him to live in London. He was the only one who was surprised when no magic occurred there. Very soon the wandering minstrel was reduced to playing his fiddle and singing his songs in public houses for what he could get until, in the way things happened to Jamie, as I learnt many years later, he was accidentally drawn into a pub brawl in which he was entirely innocent and received a stab wound from which he never recovered.

I wonder if Addie ever admitted that the choices she made had committed her to years of hell? My poor dear mother. How different her life would have been if she had not married my father.

How different my life would have been had I not made certain choices.

By the time Reardon left Edith Hillyard's room, it was late afternoon. It had been a fraught day and he was tired, with work still to be done. After having agreed with her to leave questioning the girls until morning, he trudged back to the police room.

Once there, he found Gilmour despondently riffling through his notes. Normally as resilient as a rubber ball, he was looking as knackered as an old carthorse, more tired than Reardon felt himself to be. 'You look rough, Joe.'

Gilmour rubbed a hand across his face. 'Up half the night again, weren't we, me and Maisie?'

So, it wasn't the day's work that had got to his sergeant. He was talking about Ellie, their one year old, Ellen's goddaughter. Having passed through the teething stage so far without any trouble, little Ellie had recently taken it into her head that sleeping during the day and then waking up at three a.m., chirpy as a cricket and wanting to play, was what life was all about. Gilmour needed to catch up on some sleep, Maisie too, no doubt. Reardon took pity on him, told him to call it a day, and sent him home early.

Left alone, he settled down to try and get his notes and his thoughts in order. At one point, Miss Elliott looked in, eyebrows raised to find Gilmour already gone, but left without saying what she had come for, though no doubt it had been to check on why they hadn't found an explanation for Josie's imprisonment, or why they hadn't found the murderer yet. It wasn't an unusual reaction from those intimately concerned in an investigation like this. It never even entered their heads, understandably upset, and obsessed as they often were about their own tragic circumstances, that those working on their behalf might have a life beyond. Thinking of which reminded Reardon that he, too, had a home to go to, and a wife, as soon as he was finished with this lot.

The day had turned; the sun had passed from this side of the building, and this little storeroom, which never got much of it to begin with, had grown even darker. He rose to switch on the light, paused for a moment at the window. The slanting side view he had of the east wing made it look no less grim and inimical, and the shadows thrown across the littered space below didn't help. He'd already encountered Michael Deegan there earlier, pottering about with a clipboard, looking extremely pleased with himself, for reasons which became clear when Deegan told him that Miss Hillyard had given him the go-ahead to finish the work started by the late Mr Broderick. Even better, after a great deal of thought she had decided that the derelict wing was to be knocked down entirely at some time and new buildings erected as they became necessary. Reardon couldn't help but feel that the disappearance of the east wing would be nothing but a good thing, and in the interests of everybody, but he warned Deegan not to be in too much of a hurry over starting work there. 'We haven't finished here, yet.'

But Deegan had smiled sunnily and said not to worry, there was plenty to be done before they reached that stage. Miss Hillyard wanted the other half-finished work inside completed first. He was looking optimistic, and Reardon reflected how lucky it was for him that he could so easily put aside the murder. Maybe even the pregnancy, too. After the first shock of hearing about that, he was probably relieved that he would never now be required to face up to the consequences.

The already completed demolition of part of the wing now allowed a glimpse of open countryside to be seen, across fields which sloped up to a copse where starlings roosted year after year, just as generations of Scroopes had settled here in Maxstead Court. Reardon stood for a moment or two longer, his eyes on a great flock of the birds which were swooping home, wheeling and dipping in unison, to a compulsion only they knew. Awesome, beautiful against the deepening sky. He watched them, mesmerized for several minutes, then switched on the light and turned back to his desk.

Half an hour later, the door opened, and he raised his head with a frown that disappeared like a cloud before sunshine at the sight of his wife, bearing a tray. 'What are you still doing here, love?' he asked, jumping up to relieve her of it.

She smiled. 'I might ask the same about you.'

This weekend was the first time they'd been apart since they'd been married and he held out his arms to make up for that unsatisfactory greeting in Miss Hillyard's study. He kissed her, held her to him and rested his chin on her head. She only reached his shoulder, and he breathed in the clean scent of her shampoo. Apart from that brief conversation when she had telephoned him from Kate's, they had hardly spoken. 'I've missed you. Haven't even had time yet to ask you if you had a good weekend,' he said as she pulled gently away and waved him to sit down, though it must have turned out well, considering she had decided to stay on an extra day.

'I know, I've been waiting to see you, to tell you how I went on with Kate, but you've been up to the ears.'

'You could say that,' he answered, stretching, clasping his hands behind his head and leaning as far back as he could in the chair, which wasn't very far, considering it was one designed for the classroom rather than comfort.

'I got round the kitchen staff to make you a sandwich.' She whipped off the white cloth that covered the tray and set it in front of him. A man-sized sandwich, a pot of tea and one of

his favourite custard tarts. And two cups. 'Tuck in. I bet you
haven't eaten properly all day.'

He didn't need telling twice. He couldn't in fact remember
eating anything since a slice of toast for his breakfast, except
for the two ginger nuts that had come with a cup of tea.

'I didn't stay on with Kate simply because I was enjoying
myself,' she said with a smile, picking up on what he'd been
thinking, as usual. 'It was good to see her again, of course, but
it wasn't only that. Remember what I told you on the phone
about Miss Hillyard? That Kate thought she'd come into
money?'

He nodded, his mouth too full of sandwich to speak. It was
more than good. Brown bread and plenty of beef, not overdone,
and she'd remembered to tell them mustard, not horseradish.

'Well, I managed to get a bit more information, about her
time at the Agatha Dean.'

The bite he'd just taken went down without it being chewed
properly. 'Ellen. You didn't go scouting around there, surely!
You didn't ask to see the principal?'

He blamed himself. He'd told her, hadn't he, that he wasn't
averse to her keeping her eyes and ears open for a bit of gossip?
But that didn't mean she should be acting like some female
Sherlock Holmes and making enquiries which were the business
of the police. He always tried not to listen to her when she
joked that if she hadn't been a teacher, and if the Force should
ever be so enlightened as to take them, she could fancy herself
as a woman detective.

She smiled. 'Calm down and get on with your sandwich.
It was the former school secretary I saw. There was no need
for me to go to the college because she's retired now and she
lives quite near Kate and they still meet regularly. She has a
pension from Agatha's and a dear little house, so she lives
quite comfortably. We took her some éclairs she dotes on and
had coffee with her. She must be over eighty, but there's
nothing wrong with her memory and she still has her wits
about her. And guess what?'

'You're going to astonish me and tell me she remembered
Edith Hillyard.'

'Of course she did. Kate had told me she'd been there for

ever, remembered every girl that ever went through the college while she was there, and would be only too happy to have the chance to do some reminiscing, and she was. Her name's Chipperfield, but she was always known as Chippers to everyone.' Ignoring his rolled eyes, she went on, 'Kate was right, she was a thoroughly nice woman, a perfect dear, and I can see why they all loved her.'

'All right. So what did you learn?'

'She remembered Edith Hillyard extremely well, in fact; she'd always had a very soft spot for her. She remembered Eve Draper too, but only as Edith's friend. She was one who kept in the background, apparently. Before she retired, Chippers lived in at Agatha's, where she seems to have been a sort of mother confessor – apparently, everybody used to go to her with their troubles and she'd sort it all out over cocoa and biscuits. Even Edith, who'd always kept her home life to herself – until the day Chippers found her in tears.'

'Tears?' It was hard to imagine even a young Edith Hillyard in tears.

'Some family problem, to do with her mother, and money. Or rather, lack of it.'

'And?'

'And that's it, really. Except that wherever Miss Hillyard got her money, it couldn't have been from her family, could it? She and her mother were actually quite poor – and yet, Edith went on to college.'

'You said she was clever. Maybe she got a scholarship,' he said, scholarships being at the forefront of his mind at the moment.

'Maybe she did, at that, but it doesn't mean it wouldn't cost money. There would still be a lot to keep up with.'

As Miss Hillyard herself had reminded him a few hours ago, and now he understood why.

'Where did the money come from, then?'

She spread her hands. 'Well, her father had died when Edith was young and her mother came from a working-class family, somewhere near Stoke-on-Trent, I believe.'

'Don't tell me, let me guess. Her father's wealthy family had disowned him because he'd married beneath him, but relented when he died and sent money to support Edith through college. Then one of them miraculously left her a bundle in their will.'

'Chippers didn't think so,' she said severely. 'Hillyard *père* was a failed musician who came to London to make his fortune, which never happened. And she felt certain there was no family money in the background.'

They fell silent. Ellen drank her tea and Reardon polished off the custard tart.

'So it's all still a bit of a mystery, but does it really concern anyone else? Is it actually relevant?' she asked at last. 'To who killed that poor woman?'

'Why do you think I'm asking? Anything or anyone could be relevant, even Miss Hillyard.

'Oh, come on, Bert, you can't really suspect her. Why on earth would she do that, even if one could imagine such a thing happening?'

He had known equally unlikely suspects. And he had long since ceased to pin his faith on motive. True, when it came to murder, motive mostly came down to greed, anger or sex, but what could trigger it off, often something trifling and of no account to anyone but the murderer, remained a mystery. And yet, to think of Edith Hillyard pushing Isabelle Blanchard from a height, nailing up a door, covering her victim with that tarpaulin and leaving her to be found . . . no.

'No, I don't think that, Ellen. But there's something that needs clearing up. There was some skulduggery going on between Phoebe Catherall and Isabelle Blanchard about taking up a teaching place here – which, according to Miss Hillyard's account, she knew nothing about.'

'Why would she? She need not necessarily have known, surely?'

'Maybe not. But I'm mystified why she should employ so many unqualified teachers – Jocasta Keith, for one, and Phoebe Catherall for another, if what she gave her landlady to believe is correct. And the missing testimonials for Isabelle Blanchard seem to indicate she might not have been qualified either.'

'There's no reason why any of them should have been, you know. It's a private school. Anyway, uncertificated doesn't necessarily mean unqualified, or only officially. I've known excellent teachers who weren't. And they might come cheaper.'

'I suppose that could explain it.'

Ellen began gathering the cups and saucers tidily together. 'You haven't traced her yet then, this Miss Catherall?'

'She's disappeared into limbo. I've had Pickersgill out to Birmingham, talking to people at that picture place where she played the piano, but they knew nothing of her beyond working hours, and there's no one else we can contact. Mrs Cooper was right when she said she kept herself to herself, it seems. I suppose she'll turn up when we least expect it.'

He hoped that would not turn out to be as nastily prophetic as it sounded. Each time her name was mentioned brought another niggle of unease. 'Look, I'm ready to pack it in for tonight. Why don't we go home?'

As they left the room he said, 'Miss Hillyard's mother – did you say Stoke-on-Trent?'

TEN

'You look chuffed with yourself,' Reardon remarked as Gilmour came into his office at Market Street the following morning, waving a sheet of lined notepaper. 'As well I might. I bring glad tidings. We've had a breakthrough, from Woodman's, the taxi firm. You know Gravy didn't find anyone there who remembered taking a fare to Maxstead Court – but now, here's this bloke who's been off sick because he's had an accident and only just heard yesterday that we were making enquiries. Yes, I know, Gravy should have asked if they had any drivers off sick who might have remembered . . . but anyway, this chap hasn't got a telephone, and couldn't get out to post the letter, but he gave it to the milkman this morning and asked him to deliver it to us.'

'The milkman? Enterprise isn't yet dead, then.' It didn't take Reardon long to read the few lines of the letter. 'It doesn't say where he picked his fare up.'

'Doesn't say much at all, does it? He lives out at Little Sidding and I'm off to see him now. Unless you want me at Maxstead with you?'

'I think I can cope with talking to a few schoolgirls,' Reardon answered, with more certainty than he felt, given the negative results so far, and what he had heard of the Myerson girl. 'They may be a bit more amenable now they've had time for a think. Take Gravy with you, then, and I'll have Pickersgill with me. I'll see you both later.'

It had taken Josie a few minutes to recognize where she was when she woke that morning – alone in a bright, comfortable little room, nothing but the bedside locker and a chair, a washbasin and a small bookcase filled with books you'd like to read when you were feeling better. Of course, that was it: she was in the sick bay. She lay listening to a little clock on the wall that had a loud, self-important tick, then saw what time it was. She had slept most of one day, and then again through the night!

It all began to come back to her. All those horrible things. Then being brought here and put to bed, and Matron, who was usually so bossy, being really nice to her, tucking her up every time she wakened for a few minutes, and promising to give her a lovely, special breakfast on a tray today. And the policeman who had been there yesterday and who was coming back this morning and would want to know everything, which she simply couldn't tell him.

Oh Jiminy, no, she couldn't, she didn't even want to *think* about it, it was all too hideous, but even though she lay back against the pillows and closed her eyes, willing herself not to go over it all again, she knew she never would be able to forget what had happened. It rushed at her like a big savage dog and dragged her back into the darkness, and she was living the night before last all over again.

When they were sure all the rest of the school must be asleep, Josie had tried to let herself out of the pantry window. Their bedroom window only overlooked the rubbly old Quad, but it was high up and there was no drainpipe nearby, or any other way of climbing down. So the pantry window on the ground floor it had to be, but her shoe bag, stuffed as far as it would go into her pocket, made a big enough lump to prevent her from squeezing through. She yanked it free and threw it out on to the ground, but even then, getting through the window was a tight fit, though she was small for her age and agile. That was the reason she'd been picked to do this, she kept telling herself, though she knew really it was because Avis had decided she should be the one, in spite of her objections to the plan. At last she was able to wriggle herself free and dropped to the ground, grazing her knee painfully and tearing the leg of her pyjamas as she did so, meaning they would not only be filthy and probably have some blood on them from her scraped knee and she'd have to account for all that somehow to Matron, meaning a black mark. Picking her shoe bag up, she ran towards the east wing, stopping for a second to turn and wave to the others watching through their window upstairs that the coast was clear, forgetting she hadn't stuffed the bag back into her pocket and it was still in her hand. It waved like a white flag in the dark.

Her heart jerked, as much with fear as with running so fast. If anyone else had seen . . . Almost, she turned and ran back, but she could imagine the scorn she'd have to face, and forced herself to run round to the east wing's back door. She'd just known she would end up being the one to do this, in spite of saying she wouldn't. She didn't want the others to think her scared stiff.

Though she was. So scared she was sweating under her navy gabardine raincoat, which was the best disguise to cover her pyjamas she'd been able to think of. Her palms were slippery, her heart was banging. Was she going to have a heart attack and die, like Grandpa last year?

'You're in a funk, aren't you?' Nancy Waring had kept prodding spitefully, when she was getting ready, her little black eyes snapping behind her specs.

The answer was yes. More so than anyone could guess. But to say it aloud in front of the other Elites wasn't an option.

'You go, then,' she'd retorted, but Nancy had known she was on safe ground there. She was skinny, but she had big bones and was far too gawky to get through that small window.

Slipping out at night had been the only time to get into the east wing because the police were all over the place during the day. It still hadn't been easy, though she was lucky that she and the other two shared a room, so no one else needed to know.

Before, on their nocturnal expeditions, it had been easy, and they'd never been found out, but this was different. In the normal routines of the school it was the duty of the teacher who was responsible that day to see that all the doors were securely locked, so that no unauthorized person could enter the school, but all the same, the huge iron keys were always left in the locks, day and night. That was supposed to be in case of fire, and the necessity for a quick exit, so that although the school was protected from intruders, no one would ever be in danger of being imprisoned inside without the means of getting out. But someone had evidently been having second thoughts about safety procedures; since yesterday, when the

whole school had been abuzz with that awful news, all keys
had been removed.

When she thought of the terrible thing that had happened to
Mam'selle, especially where she had been found – and everything else – Josie's heart jumped into her mouth in terror, and
panic almost made her turn back. Miss Hillyard had informed
the whole school of what had happened and they had been
strictly warned not to talk about it, but of course everyone had
been whispering in corners ever since. Avis had said the police
went away every night, though she couldn't really have known
that was so. What she would do if they had left a policeman
on guard after all and he came round the corner and found her?
She crossed her fingers and took another step towards the oak
door with its heavy iron ring. A hand gripped her shoulder and
she uttered a choked, terrified yelp.

Petrified with fear, for a moment she literally could not move,
her insides turning to water, but somehow she found the strength
to break free and make a run for it. She had barely taken a
stride before she was grabbed by the belt of her gabardine and
yanked back. She managed somehow to twist round to face her
captor and, when she saw who it was, she couldn't believe it.
The last of her courage slipped away like water through a sieve.

And now it was all going to come out. She was going to
have to go over it all again, repeat what had happened, and they
would make her tell them why she had gone there at all. The
big policeman hadn't questioned her yesterday, just listened to
the others trying to make her talk. He was really quite nice, a
bit like her father, and quite handsome if you didn't look at the
scar on one side of his face. But he was the new French teacher's
husband, which wasn't so nice. Teachers had a way of making
you confess, and policemen must surely be worse.

Vic Wetherby's house was one in a row of four identical cottages
built on the roadside just before you arrived in Little Sidding,
with the village itself still half a mile away. They might once
have been tied cottages, originally built for the workers at the
farm whose roofs could just be seen at some distance. But
though identical, each cottage had its paintwork, normally a
standard, serviceable dark brown for this sort of house, done

in a different colour, a sure sign that the farmer had been forced
to sell them off to different owners. It was highly unlikely
that the original occupiers, farm workers, would have had the
money to buy them, even as sitting tenants. But whoever owned
them or rented them now, Gilmour liked the non-conforming
colour schemes. It gave him some hope that all individuality
was not yet dead.

They had to wait some time for an answer to their knock,
the reason being apparent when it was eventually opened
by the man they'd come to see. He was balding, middle-aged
to elderly, with a pink face, at present screwed up with effort,
a bit corpulent, and could only walk slowly, and with the aid
of a stick. The result of an accident, he told them, that had kept
him off work for several weeks.

'Twenty-fourth of April, few days after Easter when I picked
her up,' he said promptly, after showing them into his front
room and letting himself down into his armchair with a thump
and a sigh of relief. 'I can tell you the exact date, 'cause it were
the last job I did. Fell off the bloody ladder next day. Off me
head, I must've been, climbing ladders, according to our
Gertie, and I dare say she might not be wrong, but it's hard to
admit you're not as spry as you was at one time. Been off sick
since then; things didn't go as easy as they should have, and
I've lost me job an' all.'

'That's hard lines,' Gilmour sympathized.

'Well, that's how it is. Ernie Woodman isn't a charity, not
likely. What do you want to know?'

'Let's make certain we're talking about the same woman you
mentioned in your letter, for a start – for which thanks, by the
way. What did she look like?'

'Very smart, though she didn't have no hat on and it was
blowing like the clappers. That's how I remembered her, particular – you can't hardly miss hair that colour, can you? Nothing
personal,' he added, looking at Gilmour, but Gilmour was used
to it. 'She wanted to go out to that school over to Maxstead.
Very nice and polite she was, but she just sat quiet in the back.
I tried to make conversation with her, but she didn't want to
talk. Some do and some don't. And she gave me a good tip
when I dropped her.'

'What time was this?'

'Eightish when I picked her up, if I remember right. They could have told you that at Woodman's. She'd booked earlier on.'

'They didn't remember her. They might have done if we could have given them more to go on. Seems quite a few trips out to the school were made around that time, though.'

Wetherby nodded. 'Easter holidays, see. There's a lot of to-ing and fro-ing between the station and Maxstead round about then, parents taking the kids home and bringing them back. No reason to remember anybody in particular. It was only when my mate Ron said you was looking for somebody with red hair I remembered her meself – and with it still being the school holidays, and that time of night an' all.' He reached towards the packet of Woodbine's on a table, hesitated, but decided against them. 'One thing I did think was funny. She asked to be dropped at the school gates, told me not to bother getting out. Them big heavy gates, see, they leave 'em open when they're expecting deliveries, or guests, otherwise you got to do it yourself, or if you're on foot, there's a side gate. Used to be a gatekeeper lived in the lodge, but all that's long gone. She didn't want me to take her right up to the house, although it were a wild night and it's a long drive. But if that was what she wanted.' He shrugged. 'That's where I left her, by the gates.'

'You know why we're asking about her, Mr Wetherby?'

'I do, poor wench. She's been murdered, Ron told me. I hear it's been in the *Herald,* but I've only just got back home and haven't had time to catch up with the papers yet.' He waved to a stack of newspapers piled at one end of the sofa.

It had of course got into the papers by now. The editor of the local, the *Herald,* had gone to town on the news and Folbury was humming. It had also received a mention in one or two of the nationals, but it wasn't big enough for them to make headlines. Gilmour wondered how long it could stay that way. 'And you picked her up from where, Mr Wetherby?'

He named Melia Street, in a run-down area of Folbury both policemen recognized. 'Funny thing, though,' he went on. 'I was told to pick her up round the corner, in the lane round the back of the house, not at the front door. So I can't give you the house number. I doubt you'll need it though.' He laughed, but didn't explain.

Making the constant trek between Maxstead and Folbury was tedious, but the enquiry couldn't be wholly conducted from Folbury, and Maxstead was where it was centred. It gave Reardon excuses to use his motorbike whenever he could, though he was beginning to use it less and less since he and Ellen had bought the car. It was understood between them that she was to have the Morris when she needed it, though. He was thought eccentric (and not only by Ellen), and so he was, when it came to his BSA. He didn't much mind. He liked to imagine it kept him in touch with his younger self, even if he didn't roar along like an Isle of Man TT competitor, but kept it (mostly) at a speed more in keeping with advancing years, as Gilmour kindly put it. Today, since Gilmour had the police car to visit that taxi-driver, was a good chance to use the bike. He took an elated Pickersgill along with him, riding pillion.

He had a lot of time for this latest recruit. Dave Pickersgill had once, when he'd still been one of the dreaded Inspector Waterhouse's uniformed constables, nearly come a cropper over a young woman reporter at the *Herald*. Now, Reardon having rescued him from Waterhouse, and as a newly fledged detective, he was watching his step, but learning fast.

At Maxstead, they made their way in the direction of the sick bay. Josie was still under Matron's care, until her possessions could be moved to a new bedroom, which Miss Hillyard had now sensibly ordered, so as to split up the trio of Josie, Avis Myerson and Nancy Waring. He couldn't question the wisdom of this; if what she believed about them all being concerned in the escapade was correct, separating them would remove any temptation to concoct some sort of subterfuge to explain what had happened to Josie.

They had almost reached their destination when they encountered Matron, who waved them back, saying Josie was up and about and waiting for them in the music room. 'She didn't want to stay in the sick bay. But I'd like a word first, please.'

Matron, who wore a wedding ring and was otherwise Mrs Benson, though the name was never used, had struck Reardon as a basically warm and kindly woman, but like all nurses she was inclined to be blunt, and she didn't mince her words in this instance. Josie had had a nasty experience, she went on to say, but she shouldn't be pampered too much. She had youth on her side and she'd soon recover. 'It'll be good for her to talk to you and get it off her chest, but don't let her forget what she's done. It won't help her in the long run. Some of these girls think they can get away with anything.'

Having delivered the homily, she set off to find Miss Scholes, who had asked to sit in while they talked to Josie.

Reardon understood what she was saying, but he was prepared to go easy on the girl. It was by no means certain yet that what had happened to her was relevant to their enquiry, but she *had* been found in the east wing and he was prepared to act as though it was. He'd been afraid that Miss Hillyard was going to insist on being present herself, thus scuppering his chances of getting anything useful from the girl, who he thought would be more than likely to shut up completely in the presence of any of the mistresses. But when Miss Scholes, who was Josie's form mistress as well as her music teacher, had offered to be there, Miss Hillyard had seemed relieved.

'That's good. Miss Scholes gets the best out of her,' she assured Reardon, 'mainly because Josie likes piano and does her practising, I suspect. She's only average at her other subjects, though she does at least try – basically she's sensible and she's such a nice, lively girl to have in class. Everyone likes Josie.'

Sensible? If so, then how had she come to be involved in what had at first appeared to be nothing more than a silly escapade, but which had led to such trouble? She hadn't been in any state when he'd seen her, just after she had been delivered from her night's ordeal, for him to tell what sort of girl she was.

The music room was situated at the end of a corridor, its door slightly ajar. As they approached, the opening notes of 'Für Elise' being played over and over could be heard, but when they walked in, the music stopped, discordantly. Josie was at the piano in the far corner, her hands resting on the keys – small hands which looked barely able to span an octave. She swung round on the piano stool to face them, already looking slightly defensive.

Apart from the piano, which was an upright, the room was simply furnished with several music stands, three rows of chairs, and a few shelves where sheet music and songbooks were kept. More shelves held music cases of various kinds and several recorders. A blackboard on an easel stood facing the chairs, with a few bars of music chalked on it. Altogether, it was a bare-looking and functional room, but at least it wasn't intimidating for Josie, a far better choice than the dark little place the police had to work from, in view of its proximity to that grim building where she had been imprisoned.

She was still wary of them, and the tremulous smile she summoned now was shy, but she seemed to have a natural appeal about her; a smallish girl with a still childish figure and thick, wavy dark hair, a lively face. The colour had returned to her cheeks since yesterday, he was relieved to see. As Matron had said, she was young and, he thought, would normally be of a happy-go-lucky nature, though that wasn't apparent today. After the small smile her features settled back into misery.

Pickersgill began to pull chairs together as Miss Scholes arrived in a flutter of apologies, though she'd been only just behind them. The DC beckoned Josie from the piano stool to join them and Reardon gave him points for that. The four of them in an informal group was a far better alternative than sitting as inquisitors facing Josie.

Miss Scholes, however, touched her gently on the shoulder, gave her an encouraging smile as if to say she was there, but only if needed, and then placed herself at the far end of the first row of chairs, as though trying to make herself invisible. She was a faded blonde with a faraway look in her eyes and a soft voice that was scarcely above a whisper, an indecisive woman who blushed easily and left her sentences unfinished. Despite the warm day, she was wearing a long droopy cardigan over a brown dress, and a diamond ring on her engagement finger from the fiancé who would never return.

Josie perched on the edge of her chair, her head drooping as if waiting execution.

'So what have you decided to tell us about why you went into the east wing at night, Josie?' Reardon asked, going along with a fiction no one could believe in for one moment – her convenient loss of memory. She hadn't been knocked down, hit on the head or concussed, though she'd certainly been manhandled, and there were bruises to prove it. The unwillingness to admit to anything at all was far more likely due to a refusal, or perhaps a fear, of saying too much. Altogether, she'd spent a wretched night that couldn't have been wished on anyone, much less a young girl like her, and that hadn't come about through anything but a deliberate act on someone's part. Reardon now thought he had a good idea of *what* might have happened, and possibly *why*, but he hadn't yet worked out the *who* part of it. 'Don't be alarmed, Josie,' he reassured her. 'I promise you won't be in any trouble over anything you have to tell us.'

The music room overlooked the tennis court, and Josie was avoiding looking at him or Pickersgill by staring out of the window, watching the two girls on the tennis court, following the ball with her eyes. It was stuffy in the room, although the windows had been thrown open to what promised to be yet another hot day, and the thunk of ball on racquet, the exasperated shouts from one girl as the other continually muffed a shot came clearly into the silence.

It wasn't going to be easy to get her to talk and he wondered what, or who, she was afraid of. At the same time he thought she looked as though she was normally a girl with plenty of spirit and might conceivably have been provoked into accepting a challenge, so he took a chance on that. 'They say the east wing is haunted, don't they? Did you go there for a dare?'

She looked wary for a moment, but then she answered rather too quickly, grasping at an excuse that probably hadn't occurred to her before, 'I might have done.'

'But it wasn't a ghost who shut you up in that room, Josie.'

She caught her breath, but said nothing. Like Antonia, she evidently had a streak of stubbornness. All the same, she'd been reminded of the person who had shut her up, and she lost colour. 'I don't know if anyone did shut me in. Maybe the door was just stuck,' she said, rather desperately now.

Miss Hillyard had said she was a truthful girl and most likely she was, in normal circumstances. But she would have to learn to lie better than that if she wanted to be believed. 'You know that won't do, Josie,' he told her gently. 'There was a lump of old wood wedged under that door to stop you opening it.' She looked down at her hands, taking pinches of the skirt of her print dress and pleating it into folds. 'How did Antonia know where you'd be?'

'I don't know. I – I suppose she just guessed.'

'That's possible, I suppose. But not just out of the blue. What could have led her to guess?'

She shrugged slightly. 'How should I know?'

If she went on like this she would exhaust his patience, however much he was disposed to like her. 'That wing has been placed out of bounds because it's dangerous, you know that, don't you?'

'Not if you know where to go.'

'So you've been in there before?' He'd tripped her up and she bit her lip. 'Look, Josie, we know you have. We've found things in there.' He paused. 'Cigarette packets, candles. Empty bottles.'

He didn't say that this had in fact not yet been mentioned to Miss Hillyard, but the way her face blanched, he guessed that was probably the terrifying prospect that had occurred to her.

The door of the room where she'd been forced to spend the night hadn't been locked (any keys to these doors had almost certainly been lost years ago), nor had it stuck accidentally. It had been jammed tightly shut with the aid of that bit of wood driven in at floor level. It was one of the few rooms with windows, and even its shutters were still intact, and they had been closed, making the room totally dark. When they found her, her voice almost gone with shouting for help, Josie had wedged herself into a corner and fallen, utterly spent, into an exhausted sleep that was more like torpor, from which she was only faintly roused when the door was at last opened, as if she had lost hope of ever being rescued. As well the poor child might, Reardon reflected, after spending all night in that bare, foul-smelling black hole.

In the initial, somewhat cursory search of the rabbit warren that was the east wing, after the discovery of Isabelle Blanchard's body, most of the rooms and hidden places had been revealed as empty of anything except rodent droppings and the rotting corpses or skeletons of birds which had fallen down chimneys.

Those bottles, the cigarette ends and other rubbish found in one room had been discounted, put down to the builders, who'd most likely taken their lunch in there sometimes, out of the rain. But in the search for Josie, it had been given more attention.

Not much stretch of the imagination was needed to surmise pretty well what had been going on. The empty bottles into which candles had been stuck were sherry bottles, hardly builders' tipple, and the cigarettes were black Russian Sobranie with gold tips. The remains of a would-be sophisticated version of a midnight dormitory feast, only spoilt by the quantity of decidedly unsophisticated sweet wrappers and biscuit packets scattered around. Josie had been wearing her pyjamas underneath her raincoat when she was rescued, and she had been crouched on the floor in an exhausted doze, resting her head on her shoe bag. A very inadequate pillow, it must have been, but handy as a receptacle for the rubbish which had clearly been thought incriminating enough for her to venture out at night to remove. But that didn't provide any answers as to why she'd been shut up in there, and why she was refusing to say who the person was who had done it, when clearly she did know.

She still wasn't looking at either of them. She'd pivoted round on the piano stool again, half facing them, but still keeping her eyes fixed steadfastly on the game going on in the court.

'I think you're shielding someone, Josie,' Reardon said at last.

She swung round from the window. She seemed to draw herself inwards, head down, and Miss Scholes made a hesitant, protective move towards her. 'I've told you! I can't remember, I can't!' she whispered.

'That's not quite true, is it?'

He was quite unprepared for the terror in her eyes as she at last raised her head and looked towards him. She was being driven into a corner, but since he wasn't accustomed to bullying little girls – and that was all she was, a frightened little girl, though frightened of what? – it was enough to make him feel he'd gone far enough.

'All right, Josie, we'll leave it for now. But think about this. It doesn't look as though whoever put you in that room and left you alone all night had any good intentions towards you, so why are you protecting them? If it could happen to you, it could happen to someone else.'

She turned away and gave a choked little sound. For a moment, he thought he had her, but she kept her head averted, ashamed of her tears, and repeated stubbornly, 'I didn't see who it was.'

He stood up. 'We have to go now, but we're going to be around here for a while, so if you change your mind . . .'

'I won't,' she said. 'I can't, I really can't.'

He met the teacher's look over Josie's shoulder, a look that said: 'Leave this to me. Trust me.' And somehow he knew he could do that, though Miss Scholes was not someone you immediately felt would be capable of giving support. From what he had heard about her past, she was a woman unable to put her sadness aside and step into the future, a shy woman who still cried for her lost lover. And yet, it appeared she cared enough for the girls in her charge to put her diffidence aside and come forward and help them.

'Thank you, Josie, Miss Scholes, we'll leave you now. Take care.'

The look Josie gave him was astonished, relieved, apprehensive, all three. Unable to believe she was going to be left alone.

'Phew! And there's still those other girls to see,' Pickersgill said, as they passed the now empty tennis court. 'If they're all as stubborn as she is . . .'

It wasn't something Reardon faced with any prospect of pleasure. Ellen had reminded him of the possibility of angry parents descending on Maxstead like an avalanche. The last half-hour with Josie and the prospect of more girls to see didn't make him feel any better.

They had hardly walked more than a few yards when he felt a touch on his arm and turned to see Miss Scholes, who had followed them. She said hesitantly, 'If you can spare a moment I . . . I'd like to thank you for having so much patience with Josie.'

'I'm not sure about that. I was afraid it might give out, I

have to confess,' he said drily. 'I think it's you who should be
thanked for being with her. I could see she appreciated it.'

'Oh, goodness, that was nothing! I wanted to be with her
because well, Josie's not foolish, and I'm sure she will . . . Just
give her time. She's very upset just now.'

He forbore to say that time was something they didn't have
to spare. 'I'm sorry to have upset her. I didn't enjoy pressing
her like that, Miss Scholes.'

'No, no, of course not, I know that.' She still stood there,
uncertainly.

'Was there something else you wanted?'

'What? Oh, yes.' She drew her droopy cardigan tighter round
her thin shoulders. 'It's nothing, really, but that night I went
outside for a minute or so – I don't sleep very well, you see,
and I wanted some fresh air. Such a hot night . . .' She finished
in a rush, 'I might have seen . . . I *think* I saw someone moving
from the direction of the east wing.'

'You did? Who was it, Miss Scholes?'

'No one I recognized.'

'A man or a woman?'

'I couldn't see that. It might have been a man, but it was
dark and I, I wasn't sure at first whether I'd just imagined it,
whether it wasn't just another shadow. In fact, I'm not sure
even now, but in view of what's happened—'

'Where did you say this was?'

'Oh, in the garden at the side of the house that runs from
the Quad.'

'Which direction was this person going?'

'You know, I really couldn't tell. I only saw it for a moment.
Merely a fleeting impression of movement that stopped. That's
why I haven't mentioned it before, but now . . .'

'Could it have been Heaviside?' The old gardener was the
only man who could legitimately have been wandering around
the school grounds. But in the dark?

'Heaviside? Oh, no! Goodness, no! Oh, look, I've told you,
I don't even know if it was a *person* at all.' Her initial confidence was rapidly dissipating. She was regretting the impulse
that had driven her to follow them. 'I'm sorry, I shouldn't have

spoken. I'm sure now I was mistaken, that it was just a shadow I saw. I must get back to Josie.'

Clearly, he wasn't going to get much further by pressing her, rather the reverse. 'All right, Miss Scholes, but thank you for letting us know.'

He watched her as she scurried back in the direction of the music room. What she'd seen, or not seen, was vague but unsettling, because there just might be something in it. But you had to admire the woman. She might have regretted the impulse which had made her speak, but she had been sure enough at first about what she'd seen to give her the nerve to come forward with it.

ELEVEN

After talking to Vic Wetherby, Gilmore and Gargrave had gone straight from Little Sidding to the street he had mentioned. Situated on the edge of Arms Green, Folbury's least salubrious neighbourhood, it was in a desolate area, much of which was scheduled for clearance and rebuilding by the council. It was the nearest to a slum area that Folbury came. Corner shops, home workshops and sheds, a betting shop with grimy windows. A fish and chip shop, midday fumes still lingering. Children too young for the brick-built elementary school further along playing in the dirty streets which, if they hadn't been scheduled for demolition, ought to be. Gilmour thought of the gardens and playing fields surrounding Maxstead Court School, and the green fields and country lanes where Vic Wetherby lived.

Some clearance had reached as far as most of Melia Street, but the rebuilding hadn't happened yet – nor did there seem to be any likelihood, in view of the present economic slump, that it would happen in the foreseeable future. The only buildings left in this unlovely spot comprised what had once been a Methodist chapel with 'Ebenezer' incised in stone above its lintel, standing alone and desolate with a derelict warehouse further along – and the tail end of what had once been a longer terrace of small homes. Wetherby's cryptic remark about a house number not being important was explained. There were only three left, the sole indication that life might still exist in these few hundred square yards. They were not pretty, nor was their appeal enhanced by the pop-bottling factory stretching out somewhere behind, its conglomeration of low buildings crouching threateningly, and its chimneys contributing more layers of dirt to the already grimy red brick of the houses.

The arrival of the two detectives coincided with the departure of a taxi, of all unexpected things to see here, just drawing away from the first house of the three. Like the others, its paintwork was shabby, though the doorstep was defiantly donkey-stoned in white and the lace curtains at the one downstairs window were dazzling behind shining panes. The passengers in the departing taxi were an elderly couple. Gilmour watched it drive off and shrugged philosophically. One house down, two to go.

Gravy knocked on the door of the neighbouring property. Here, there was no scrubbed doorstep, the curtains were drawn, and it was no surprise when the knock elicited no response. If you were a copper, you developed a feeling for an empty house, or that's what Gilmour told himself, and this one said there was no one at home. He jerked his head towards the last of the three houses and Gargrave stepped over to try there. This time, the knock was answered.

Nothing like nosy neighbours when it came to getting information. If you were in luck on this sort of job, you might get someone who took enough notice of the comings and goings of the folk next door to remember what they'd been doing. The woman who opened this door, however, was a late middle-aged, respectable type, who looked as though she minded her own business. Plump, cheerful, and no doubt with a brood of grandchildren. 'It's Mr Newman you're wanting, then?' she said. 'I heard you knocking next door.'

Gilmour said yes, seeing no reason to tell her they had no idea of the occupant's name, or even whether that was the house they wanted.

'Well, you're out of luck then. He's not in.'

'Any idea when he might be back?'

'I don't know. I haven't seen him about for quite a bit as it happens.'

'You mean he's gone away, Mrs . . .?'

'Ainsworth, Miss.' So much for easy assumptions. 'No, I didn't say that.' She looked uncertainly at them, wanting to know who they were and why they were enquiring about her neighbour, not liking to ask.

'We're police officers.' Gilmour gave their names and showed his warrant card. 'It's actually the lady we want to see,' he added, making a stab towards what he hoped might be the truth. But she shook her head.

'There's no lady there. He lives on his own, when he's here, that is. That's what I meant, he's not just out of the house, he might be away, as you said. He does go off, sometimes for a day or two, or a week. Looking for copy, I expect.' The word came out self-consciously, as if she wasn't quite sure it was the right one.

'Copy?'

'He's an author, isn't he? At least, that's what I think. I haven't had a lot of conversation with him. He's writing a book or something, I reckon.' She hesitated, then perhaps remembering they were police and wanting to have her curiosity satisfied, she said, 'Look here, step inside a minute, won't you; we can't talk on the doorstep.'

The front door opened directly off the street and into the living room, which was dominated by a large table in the centre. A treadle-operated Singer sewing machine stood next to it, and most of the chairs were occupied by swathes of fabric and pieces of sewing in various stages of completion. 'Excuse the mess. Now that Father's been taken and his pension's stopped, I have to take sewing in to make ends meet, you know how it is. A bit of dressmaking when I can get it, alterations and that for Baxendale's,' she said, naming the town's best ladies' dress shop, which had lately expanded into a small department store and now called itself an emporium.

She swept her work aside, making room for them to sit.

'What makes you think your neighbour's a writer, Miss Ainsworth?'

'Well, I just assumed, you know. On account of the typewriter. You can hear a pin drop, these walls are that thin. The Dawsons on his other side are both so hard of hearing it doesn't bother them, bless 'em. They're just off on holiday, to their daughter's. But I don't mind, not really. Mr Newman's very quiet otherwise, and very polite when I see him, which isn't often, I have to say. And I dare say he has enough of me at times. You can't use a machine like this old thing here without making a right racket. I don't see much of him at all, but I have to say, he's very gentlemanly when we do meet.'

'Lived here long, has he?'

She shrugged. 'I couldn't say, exactly. Three or four months?'

She was the sort who'd never admit to being seen as nosy, just 'interested' in her mysterious neighbour, but she had evidently decided she wasn't going to give anything more away until she'd got something in exchange. 'What's he been up to, then?'

'Nothing, as far as we know. You say he's often away?'

'Well, he doesn't seem to go out much, and when he does it's in his car. Keeps it behind the house. There's just room between the back yard and Shefford's fence.'

'What sort of car is it?'

'Eeh, don't ask me! One's the same as another, as far as I can tell. It's black is all I know.'

But she was on surer ground when it came to the man himself. Tall, dark and handsome was how she described him. *Very* handsome, like a film star when he smiled.

'What about his wife?'

'He doesn't have a wife – or if he does, she doesn't live here. I told you, there's no woman living there.' She looked curiously at them. 'What's all this about?'

Gilmour said, 'Just routine enquiries.' Ever the answer in response to such questions.

He was disappointed. There was nothing to say Isabelle Blanchard – or any other woman – had been living at 43, Melia Street. But despite Miss Ainsworth's certainty, there was nothing to say she hadn't. There would have been no need for anyone to have known, if that was what she had wanted. She could easily have kept herself out of sight, which would account for that request to be picked up round the back of the houses. And if Newman had left before she did, taking his car, that would account for her need of a taxi.

They would have to leave it at that for now, but Gilmour handed Miss Ainsworth his details before they went. 'If anything else occurs to you, Miss Ainsworth, or as soon as Mr Newman returns, will you let us know?'

If he returns, he added, but not out loud.

TWELVE

O riginally built for a gamekeeper, when such a person had been employed on the Scroope estate, Heaviside's home was a small cottage in a sheltered, sunlit clearing in the woods that abutted on to Maxstead Court. With the afternoon sun glinting on its red brick and scalloped eaves, it looked charming, a Hansel and Gretel gingerbread house with red-and-white checked gingham curtains fluttering at the open windows. It stood on what was still part of the school land, and Miss Hillyard had seemingly extended her good work here, even to having the roof retiled against the plague of grey squirrels which had once been a great problem in the main house. A neatly tended plot of vegetables at the front sat inside a white picket fence, and a few chickens scratched about in a run at the far side.

Pickersgill had been doing some scouting around, asking about Heaviside, and was itching to pass on what he'd found. As Reardon seemed absorbed in his own thoughts, he managed to contain himself. They were nearly there and were emerging from under the heavy shade of thickly planted trees, when Reardon turned to him and asked him what was up.

'I've been talking to one of the women who works in the school kitchen, sir.' He was good at that, winkling information from those below stairs who often knew more about those they worked for than the same people knew themselves.

'And what did she have to say?'

'She lives in Maxstead village; she's known Heaviside all her life and swears he's harmless. A right old miser, though, she says he is. Do anything for a bob or two, it seems.'

Even to providing cigarettes and alcohol for rebellious teenage girls who regarded breaking school rules as a caper? He could see Reardon thinking that, though it didn't seem much to have offered, now he'd said it, but Reardon nodded acknowledgement. 'Useful to bear in mind, Dave.'

The old man answered Pickersgill's loud rat-tat on the open door and, after an initial hesitation, stood aside to let them enter.

Inside, the cottage was as neat, clean and tidy as the deck of a small ship, and something savoury bubbled in an iron pan on the old-fashioned range. As far as Reardon was aware, shooting and fishing rights had been sold along with the estate, but very likely Heaviside didn't feel that prevented him taking a rabbit for the pot. He'd been peeling potatoes and the knife was still in his hand as he waved to them to sit down. Pickersgill took his six-foot frame inconspicuously aside, choosing a chair as near the open door as possible. Reardon took his point. Today had turned out hotter than ever and the sun, plus the glowing fire, made the small room hot as Hades, despite the slight breeze coming through the door and window, but there was no help for that: the only means of cooking was on the range.

Other than that, the whole place spoke of modest comfort. A line of winking, polished horse brasses hung on nails from the mantelshelf above the range, and the windowsill was home to a row of geraniums in pots. The windows shone and the gingham curtains were crisp and fresh. You had to admire Heaviside. He might be an old curmudgeon in his seventies and live alone, but after working at a tough job all day, he still found the energy when he came home at night to keep the snug little place spick and span. He put aside now the potatoes he'd been peeling, ready to add to the pot for his supper, and seated himself in a Windsor-backed chair by the fire. He didn't seem to notice the heat.

'You've been working down at the school today, Mr Heaviside,' Reardon began. 'I suppose you've heard of the latest happening?'

'That little wench getting herself shut in? Ar. No telling what they get up to, is there? Times I've told 'em to keep away from that there old bit.'

'It's more a case of what somebody else has been up to. That's why we're asking everyone to account for their movements last night. Can you tell us where you were?'

'Me?' He eyed them both sardonically as he struck a match and lit one of his cigarettes. 'Well, I weren't at the school. I walked across to the Scroope, like I do every night.'

'That would be the Scroope Arms in Maxstead village?' He nodded. 'So you would pass the school?'

'Nah. No call for me to go anywhere near the Big House,' he answered, which was what the school evidently still was to him. 'Use the path up behind here, short cut, I do, save me legs.'

'So you didn't see Josie?'

'I don't know no Josie. I don't have nothing to do with them down there.'

'She's the girl we're talking about,' Reardon explained patiently. 'The one who was shut in all night.'

'So they tell me. But I still don't *know* her.'

'So it wasn't you that shut her in, then? To teach her a lesson, not to go wandering around there at night?' he asked, keeping in mind those bottles and cigarette ends they'd found, though not in the room where Josie had been imprisoned, but in another small room at the back of the building. A room which also still had its shutters intact, where the lights from the candles stuck in the bottles would not be seen from the house.

There had been something dubious right from the start about the old man's concerns with that old half-ruin. He'd been too anxious, after Isabelle Blanchard's body had been discovered, to steer them away from closed doors and had taken them directly to that other door on the next floor which had been nailed up. He'd known what they were going to find there, moreover. Reardon repeated his question.

Heaviside coughed and spat into the fire. 'Not up to me to learn her, is it? What have they got teachers for? Any road, I've already told you, I weren't anywhere near there.'

Reardon said, 'We found things in one of the rooms. Bottles, cigarettes. Were you paid to get them for those girls?'

He gave a short bark of laughter. His cigarette had burned down. He lit another one from its stub. It was little surprise that the savoury smell of the stew on the fire and the open door and window weren't enough to mask the stale reek of tobacco which hung heavily in this close little room, despite its cleanliness. 'No, I weren't.'

Reardon was inclined to believe him. It had been worth a try, though it hadn't actually ever been a realistic possibility.

Heaviside smoked Woodbine's himself, and where would he have found Balkan Sobranie to buy? In the village shop? Not even in Folbury, if Reardon was any judge. But if Heaviside hadn't provided the goods, who had? It hadn't been the girls themselves. Smuggling forbidden delights like Russian cigarettes and sherry into a well-regulated school such as Maxstead, like someone passing a knife to a prisoner in an old spy story, wasn't an option that could be considered. Discipline at Maxstead Court was not severe by any means, but rules were made to be kept and just punishments meted out. The girls would be allowed only a limited amount of pocket money, strictly supervised. Having a midnight feast which included smoking and drinking alcohol in forbidden, out-of-bounds and possibly dangerous territory was a shocking breach of school rules that Miss Hillyard would not be willing to overlook under any circumstances. It was hardly surprising that Josie had refused to talk. The girls concerned would be in serious trouble when she learnt of it, possibly facing expulsion.

'Look here,' Heaviside said suddenly. 'I never got them girls nothing. I knowed summat were going on but it were none of my business.'

'That building, and what they're calling the Quad, with all that equipment hanging around. It was out of bounds to the girls because it was dangerous; you knew they were using it and you never thought of reporting it? Why not?'

'Weren't my business,' he repeated stubbornly.

'Somebody paying you to keep quiet about it, were they?'

'You got no call to think that.' But Reardon did. Especially after what Pickersgill had told him about the old man's keenness for money.

'We've been told you're not averse to earning a bit on the side. Spot of poaching, the odd pheasant, venison?'

The taciturn old codger suddenly became eloquent. 'Look here,' he said again. 'I've a son. Out in Australia, and I've a mind to go out to him. Haven't seen him for years, nor my grandkids. Saving up. He can't afford the money for me passage, he's struggling himself what with four kids and making his way – they don't all make their fortunes when they go out there, you know. But if I can get the half of it, he'll see me all right

with the other half. The wife would have wanted me to go.'
His glance flickered to the old-fashioned mahogany chiffonier
that stood by the far wall, and the photograph which took pride
of place there – a faded sepia likeness of a young woman with
a baby on her knee, and a young Heaviside standing with his
hand on her shoulder.

This unexpected side to the grim old man brought silence
for a moment or two: Heaviside as a once happily married man,
with a wife and son. Now a grandfather whose family lived
halfway across the world, all of whom he was longing to see
again. It presented a different and more appealing picture to
the one they'd so far seen of him.

He'd had enough of them. He stood up and walked to the
sink, where he picked up the knife again, a potato in his other
hand, and began peeling it. 'Well, I'm sorry the little wench
had such a fright,' he said gruffly, not looking at either of them.
'She all right?'

'She is now,' said Pickersgill

'Well, then, no harm's done.'

But Reardon wasn't ready to leave it just yet. 'One more
question. Was it you who re-nailed that door up?'

Heaviside took his eyes from the potato long enough to throw
a derisive look. 'Me? I'd have made a better job of it if I had.'

But he knew that it had been reopened, after Deegan had
made it fast, and knew all about it being nailed shut again after
Isabelle Blanchard had gone through it to her death. So he'd
been poking around – why? It wasn't part of his duties to look
after the derelict wing; he was employed as the gardener. He'd
admitted he knew something was going on – had he suspected
something other than illicit midnight feasts? Reardon would have
given a lot to know how much he knew, or suspected, but
Heaviside had decided he'd said too much already. Getting blood
from a stone would be easier than getting him to say any more.

'Well,' Pickersgill said, as they made their way back to the
school, 'the old skinflint might not have got the stuff for them,
but he knew about it. Paid to keep his mouth shut, wasn't he,
sir? Never mind what he said.'

'So it would seem.' The old man's last outburst had been an
admission of sorts. Trying to scrape enough for his passage to

Australia explained why he'd acted as he had to get the money, but didn't excuse it, never mind that Heaviside himself obviously felt quite justified in what he'd done.

He'd been paid not to report what had been going on, all right. But why had someone felt it necessary to do that? The old man had known what the girls were doing was irresponsible, and Reardon thought he regretted now having taken money from someone who evidently didn't think the same way. A person who felt it was more dangerous to expose the situation than to allow it to continue, and Reardon had begun to doubt whether he was going to get any light thrown on the subject from the girls he was now due to see, before prep began.

He had been irritated with himself for consenting to be drawn into what had initially seemed to be a purely school matter. In the middle of a murder enquiry, the promise he'd made to Miss Hillyard had afterwards seemed rash, something they could have done without. All the same, when evidence was short on the ground, something which didn't seem to have any connections could turn out to be the key that fitted the lock. Now, after the last half-hour with Heaviside, links between Isabelle Blanchard's murder and what had happened to Josie Pemberton didn't seem all that unfeasible.

Too much was happening in that ill-fated east wing. To misquote, one fatal incident may have been a misfortune, two incidents looked like deliberate malice.

The long day was destined to go on longer. He still had to talk to two more reluctant schoolgirls, when he should have been on his way home to supper, a glass of whisky and a quiet evening with Ellen, a chance to see things in perspective. He found them waiting for him in the small anteroom adjacent to Miss Hillyard's study. Side by side on the small sofa, facing a small coffee table, a chair for him on the opposite side. Miss Hillyard left him alone with them.

The moment he set eyes on Avis Myerson, Reardon identified with the headmistress's assessment. Trouble. More trouble. Sixteen years old and trying desperately to act twenty-six. Straining at the leash, ready to be off like a greyhound out of the trap when she was released from the childish restraints of school. Clever in her own way, he suspected when he first heard her speak, but choosing not to show it. She wasn't overawed by his police presence, had in fact given him a look from under her eyelashes she evidently thought was provocative. He wasn't having any of that and ignored it, but how sad. A young girl, so eager to throw off the best years of her youth and step into the world he was only too aware she was more than likely to be inhabiting soon. A world of wild young men in fast cars, equally fast young women, seeking nothing but the shallow pleasures of the moment – spending a fortune on clothes, night-clubbing, smoking, the next fashionable cocktail. And no doubt cocaine, currently the recreational stimulant of choice.

Nancy Waring was a different matter. A colourless, awkward girl with a mean mouth and spiteful dark eyes behind horn-rimmed glasses. The sort girls like Avis deliberately chose as a foil for their own good looks and personality, and sometimes as a mouthpiece, getting them to fire the bullets they themselves had already manufactured. The sort you could never be sure of because she would say whatever she thought was necessary.

Together, they presented an entirely different proposition to Josie, although they were still children in his eyes, however hard they tried not to be. But he began by addressing them as 'Miss Myserson, Miss Waring', to show them he was going to treat them as young women and would expect a grown-up response, without recourse to childish behaviour.

They didn't, of course, know exactly how much he already knew about their activities. So he told them as much as was expedient at the moment: what had been found in that room of the east wing, and that he knew they had been using it. He deliberately left out the word forbidden. Judgement and everything else that would follow was for Miss Hillyard. The only thing he now wanted from them was to know who had helped them in such a mad escapade, and why. 'Josie went there to remove the sherry bottles and the cigarettes,' he said.

'I suppose she told you that,' Avis said scornfully.

'No, she didn't.' He smiled faintly. 'I'm a detective, you know. It didn't take long to work out.'

The attempt at humour was lost on both. He tried another

tack. 'I suppose you realize you're going to have to face the music?'

Avis shrugged. 'Expelled, I shouldn't be surprised.'

She didn't seem to care. In fact, he wouldn't be surprised if she didn't actually welcome the possibility. It couldn't have been a new thought to her.

It was new to Nancy, though. Her face screwed into a ferocious scowl, the result, he guessed, of trying not to show she was upset. 'Daddy will simply *kill* me! She can't expel us, she just can't!' The prospect of Miss Hillyard's wrath seemed to scare her more than her father's. Hadn't it occurred to her before now? She wasn't a particularly bright-seeming girl but he wouldn't have put her down as stupid.

'Don't be such a muggins, Nancy,' Avis said, not looking at her.

Nancy bridled. 'It was only a joke, what we did.'

'Well, it was odds-on you'd be caught, wasn't it?' Reardon observed mildly.

'I don't see why. There was no reason why anyone should have known about it,' Avis retorted. 'They wouldn't have, if Josie hadn't got herself locked up.' Her eyes held a spark of excitement. She was enjoying this. She could see where it was leading, but it wasn't upsetting her in any way. She didn't look or sound either guilty or scared at what was now sure to come. Yet the don't-care attitude was overdone. Under it, he saw a still rather uncertain young girl.

'Ah yes, poor Josie. She spent a terrible night. Who do you think would do that to her?' He addressed both of them.

Nancy gave Avis a shifty glance.

'Well,' he went on, when neither replied, 'how did you get hold of that stuff? Who got it for you?'

He didn't expect an answer, but for a moment he thought Nancy would say. He waited. But even as she opened her mouth to speak, Avis quelled her with a look, then to Reardon she said, butter not melting in her mouth, 'We can't tell you that. We don't want to get anyone into trouble.'

If she was trying to imply it was one of the staff, that wouldn't hold any more water than the idea that Heaviside had been their supplier. Almost certainly it would not be any of those village

women employed to work at cleaning duties under the strict
eye of Mrs Jenkins, the housekeeper. But it did give rise to the
possibility, however remote, that it could, in fact, have been
one of the teaching staff. Not as unlikely an idea as it might
seem at first. Miss Keith, for instance, he didn't believe would
be averse to breaking rules; might even turn a blind eye in fact,
though he couldn't actually see her going as far as encouraging
such flagrant behaviour. Still, he'd received the impression she
was perceptive, and she might suspect who would have been
prepared to do so, and he resolved to speak to her, if only for
his own satisfaction.

'It was Heaviside who got that stuff for you, wasn't it?' he
tried, convinced now that it wasn't, but simply to get a reaction.

Neither girl replied. Nancy was attempting the same noncha-
lance as Avis, and not entirely succeeding, He kept his eyes on
her, but she'd grown dumb.

'It was only a few cigarettes – and *sherry*!' Avis said at last.
'Not even a Hanky Panky or anything,' she added, showing as
much bravado as she dared.

Hanky Panky. Gin, sweet vermouth and something bitter, a
name that shouldn't have been in any schoolgirl's vocabulary.
'You sound very familiar with fashionable cocktails, Miss
Myerson. I hope you're not thinking of trying that one out, too.'

'I already have. My father doesn't object. He lets me smoke
as well, when I'm at home.' She couldn't be aware how much
like a defiant child she looked and sounded.

Reardon sighed inwardly. The softly-softly approach wasn't
working. 'Why did you let Josie go alone to get rid of the
evidence?' he asked sternly. 'In fact, why did you need to clear
it up at all? No one would have thought anything of an empty
bottle or two.'

His two lads who'd done the first search should have thought
of it, considering the sort of bottles they were, of course, but
that aspect of it didn't concern these girls.

'Catherine said that, but that was potty. It had to be cleared
up before anybody saw it.' Nancy was shifting uneasily on her
chair.

'Catherine?'

'Catherine Leyland. She's such a goody-goody. Things had

been left in a real mess. We had to leave in such a hurry, because little Josie felt sick!'

Did that mean they were *drunk*? Well, he didn't subscribe to the theory that just because they were nicely brought-up girls they wouldn't have succumbed to those sort of temptations. But what Nancy said was interesting. Josie seemed to have been the weak link, all the way round. And what about the other girl? 'Catherine?' he asked again, and looked from one to the other. 'How many more were there?'

'In the Elites? Well, only three actually, that night. Catherine wouldn't come with us. She *said* she had some reading to do,' said Nancy with disgust.

The Elites. So that was what they called themselves. He almost laughed.

'What about Antonia Freeman? Was she one of the – one of your group?'

'Heavens, no,' Avis said. She didn't like the way this was leading. Not going so far as to yawn, she began to examine her nails minutely, seemingly switched off, boredom seeping through every pore.

'Then how did Antonia know where Josie was? She said she guessed, but if she did, she was spot on, luckily for Josie. You two knew where she was, but you didn't tell,' he said severely. 'That was a bit hard on poor Josie, wasn't it?'

'We didn't know she hadn't come back until we woke up,' said Nancy at last, when Avis declined to answer.

'And you still didn't think to say anything?'

'Everyone was looking for her. It wouldn't have been long until she was found.' Avis went on examining her nails.

'Who got you that stuff?' Reardon asked suddenly, sharply. This larking around with him, wasting his time, had gone on long enough. 'Come on, let's have the truth. We'll find out sooner or later, but it'll come better from you.' He could look pretty intimidating when he chose, which was now.

And suddenly Nancy was giving in. She opened her mouth to speak. Avis sat up and threw her a look that said, *Don't you dare!* but it was too late.

'It was Mr Deegan,' Nancy said.

*   *   *

There was still one more girl to see yet. He hesitated, thinking that what he'd just learnt meant Antonia, as well as Catherine, was off the hook. Then he sighed. Despite the clock relentlessly eating into the evening he'd been looking forward to, he might as well get it over with. He found her alone in the art room, staring moodily at a drawing pad, surrounded by screwed-up balls of paper. She'd drawn something or other on the pad, but threw the pencil down with something like relief when he came in. The relief became palpable when she heard what he had to say. 'They're a stupid crowd, those *Elites*,' she said, scornfully stressing the word. 'Except for Josie. She's all right, really. I didn't want to get her into trouble.'

'They're the ones who upset you with those silly tricks.'

'Tried to,' she returned with some spirit. 'They wanted to make me look a fool, but it didn't work. I just ignored them. So they tried to make it look as though I was a thief, or she did.'

'Avis?' he surmised.

'Yes. She hates me.'

'Why?'

She blushed. 'I wouldn't join their silly set and – well, I did a picture of her she didn't like.'

He grinned, and suddenly she laughed as well.

She was a big girl, at the unprepossessing stage of puberty. She was never going to emerge from the chrysalis as a stunningly beautiful butterfly, but she had nice, steady eyes and a smile (when she thought to use it) that said, when she had gained confidence in herself, she had the potential for being a warm, talented and attractive woman. That confidence must already be growing, if she was able to regard the practical jokes played on her with such coolness, and it was rather admirable, considering her age.

She picked up her pencil again as he left, and bent her head over the drawing pad.

The day still wasn't over, however. Reardon sighed as he encountered Gilmour, who had just arrived at Maxstead, eager to catch Reardon before he left for home, and tell him everything that had transpired from his visit to Wetherby and subsequently to

Melia Street. But Reardon asked him to hold explanations until they'd seen Deegan. Together they sought him out and found him in the as yet incomplete room destined to be the science lab. He was bent over an open file of papers lying on the windowsill, a pencil in one hand and a large, leather-bound builders' tape measure in the other. When they came in he turned, looking pleased with himself, and told them he was taking stock of what was to be done, as Miss Hillyard had given him the go-ahead for the unfinished interior work to begin, as soon as he could get things together, as he put it. When he heard what Reardon had to say, he lost his smile.

'It was only the once,' he said, looking defiantly from one to the other.

'Once?'

'Well, yes, for the sherry, that is.'

'Two bottles. Isn't that two too many for children? And God knows how many packets of cigarettes.'

'Children? They're no children! Leastways, she isn't, that Myerson girl.'

'She's only sixteen – and she's the oldest of them,' Gilmour said. 'You could get into serious trouble for that, and for what else was going on with those girls—'

Before he could finish, Deegan interrupted him furiously. 'What do you think I am? I'm not interested in little girls. My God, you coppers!'

He had leapt in too soon with protestations. 'That wasn't what I meant,' Gilmour said stiffly, and much as Deegan rubbed him up the wrong way, Reardon knew he hadn't.

'She's a spoilt little madam,' Deegan said, calming down.

'And you took advantage of it, encouraging them to break the rules. And sixteen or not, Avis Myerson's not averse to a spot of blackmail, is she?'

'Blackmail?' He tried to look entirely innocent, and failed. His hand clenched on the tape measure, he'd been fidgeting with. 'No, she just asked me to get her that stuff.'

'And you obliged, for no particular reason? Come on, man, you can't expect us to believe that.' He still said nothing. Reardon sighed. 'She knew about you and Mlle Blanchard.'

Deegan kept pulling on the brass ring of the tape measure,

irritatingly drawing it out a foot, then letting it go with a snap. He saw the looks he was getting and stopped. 'If she did, what was wrong with that?'

'Dangerous knowledge. Since you were meeting Mlle Blanchard in one of the empty rooms in the east wing.'

Reardon had had difficulties from the first in being convinced about Deegan and Isabelle Blanchard meeting on a regular basis in that tip of a room in the house he called home. After all, Isabelle's frequent absences from the school couldn't fail to have been noticed, whereas the east wing was at least convenient, if scarcely a love-nest, until the girls had started taking an interest.

'That little bitch,' Deegan said, suddenly and viciously, and Reardon didn't think he was referring to Isabelle. 'I don't know how she does it, but she knows everything; snoops around, or gets other people to do it for her. You wouldn't believe how much these girls know, where they get to. They don't have enough supervision, that's what it is.'

'Oh, I expect they'd always find ways of avoiding it. But Avis Myerson wasn't the only one who knew what you'd been up to. How much did you bribe Heaviside to keep him quiet?'

His face turned the colour of clay.

'Did you push that girl, Josie, into that room and leave her there all night?'

'Jeez, I wouldn't do a thing like that!'

'Tell us where you were that night and we might be inclined to believe you,' Gilmour said.

'I was at home.'

'Alone, I suppose?'

'Yes, like I always am. I had my head down, trying to sort out the paperwork for all this, if you must have chapter and verse. I need a bank loan and God knows if I shall be able to get one. It's keeping me awake.' He nodded towards the file on the window ledge, rubbing his thumb on the leather tape-measure case again, as if wishing it were Aladdin's lamp to summon a genie who would miraculously grant him the money he needed.

'And were you at home on the night of Thursday the twenty-fourth of April?'

He looked puzzled, then aghast as the significance of the date hit him – the night Isabelle had been murdered. His face reddened. 'April? I haven't a clue what I was doing then. Do you remember exactly what you were doing six weeks ago, either of you?'

'We've got him,' Gilmour said.

'You think so?'

'He gets Isabelle Blanchard pregnant, then kills her because a pregnant woman he felt obliged to marry was the last thing he needs at this time, when he's so obsessed with getting his business going. The Myerson girl got wind of what was going on and blackmailed him into getting that stuff for them.'

'He said he would have married Isabelle.'

'Well, he would say that, wouldn't he?'

'I can't see him killing her, just to be rid of the obligation.'

'There's plenty who would.'

'And Josie?'

'He pushes her into that room, to show them not to muck about with him.'

'He wouldn't have left evidence lying around – that sherry and so on he'd got for them. He'd have cleared it away himself.'

'If he'd known it was there. I shouldn't imagine these girls are accustomed to tidying up after themselves, but he wouldn't think of that. He's not exactly tidy-minded himself. And he has no alibi.'

Reardon sighed, that single malt he was looking forward to receding ever further into the distance. 'What's this about the taxi driver, then?'

'Miss Hillyard isn't going to accept that as an explanation,' said Ellen, over supper, at last. 'I mean, midnight feasts! That's lower-school stuff. Those three are past that stage.'

'It was more than lemonade and chocolate biscuits, Ellen. Miss Hillyard doesn't need to know about that, though.'

'Why not?'

'It may not be necessary. She would probably expel them, wouldn't she?'

'Almost certainly. But perhaps they deserve it.' She helped him to more shepherd's pie, and passed him the HP. After a moment, she went on, 'I'm not sure you're right, but I suppose you have your reasons. And in that case Miss Draper mustn't be told, either. She keeps nothing from the head.'

Reardon watched his wife through the steam rising from his plate. She was finding her feet at the school, getting to know her colleagues as individuals: Miss Scholes was gentle, but a very good teacher, Miss Elliott was less of a dragon than she appeared, though she terrified the girls. Miss Cash and her oblivion to anything but games for the girls was a good egg, really. It seemed to be Miss Draper, however, the girls' favourite teacher, with whom Ellen had established a real rapport. They were already on Christian-name terms, and he didn't doubt what she'd just said was correct.

He knew that if it should ever get to the ears of parents that pupils had access to cigarettes, never mind alcohol, the fat would be in the fire. And that Miss Hillyard certainly wouldn't be content until she knew what had happened to Josie. At the moment, however, the full truth would only complicate matters.

'When I spoke to those girls, they mentioned Catherine Leyland,' he said, pushing his plate away and waving off pudding. The shepherd's pie had been good – for Ellen. She wasn't a brilliant cook and he didn't want to push his luck with the rice pudding, although it had the burnt skin on it that he liked. It could be warmed up for tomorrow, or there was always Tolly, the canine dustbin, to dispose of it. 'She's in with that group, but I'm not sure how far.'

She raised her eyebrows. 'Catherine? Are you sure?'

'That's what they said.'

'Well, if you say so. But I wouldn't have thought it. She's not the sort to get up to silly antics like that. She seems to be a very steady girl. Very clever, way ahead of her peers.'

And one of that clique, those so-called Elites, as he'd just been told. He remembered seeing her, just after Josie had been found. He'd been walking along a quiet corridor when he'd noticed a girl in earnest conversation with Miss Draper at the end of it. She might even have been crying, and Miss Draper had given her a hug, smoothed her hair back and sent her on her way with a gentle kiss on her forehead. 'The child's a little upset about Josie,' she'd told Reardon, knowing he'd seen. He'd wondered if such tender care was standard procedure in all boarding schools, or if it was just Miss Draper's kind nature.

Yesterday, I watched that flashy, vulgarly yellow limousine purr away up the drive, and felt nothing but thankfulness to see the end of Avis Myerson, finally able to admit that it had been a bad decision on my part, right from the first, to take that troublesome girl. Mistakenly, I fancied that the quietly regulated routine of Maxstead, mixing with girls like Josie Pemberton and Catherine Leyland, in a healthy, wholesome atmosphere, would bring out the best of her qualities. Whereas . . . well, I can only hope it wasn't Maxstead which had precisely the opposite effect, and pray that her influence here will not be lasting.

She is cleverer than I gave her credit for. Sly, rather. After the inspector spoke to her and Nancy Waring, she managed to steal a march on me, sobbed down the telephone to her silly mother about how unhappy she has been here, and of course her mother responded like one of Pavlov's dogs, rushing here immediately to snatch away her blameless daughter before I could punish her for doing nothing. And, incidentally, leaving the other girls concerned to take the rap.

Nancy Waring, I still have to deal with, and Josie too. Catherine, of course, is a little more of a problem. I would not have expected her to have truck with such childish nonsense as secret societies, and I have yet to find out how Antonia Freeman was mixed up in all of this. It seems they were all involved in what happened to Josie, one way or another, as well as in that spate of inexcusable mischief and bullying which has so disrupted the school. Since I am convinced that too originated with Avis Myerson, the problem is halfway solved. And yet . . .

Inspector Reardon is not telling me everything he has discovered. I don't entirely blame him. I had reasons for not wanting to question the girls myself and he obliged me by doing so, though I don't for one minute think it was entirely altruistic. He knows I am not a fool and that I am well aware he's keeping much of what he's found out to himself. So be it, the facts will out, sooner or later. At the present, it suits me to turn a blind eye. What exactly went on there, in the east wing, I refuse to contemplate, but then I think of the dangers involved, and what happened to Isabelle Blanchard here . . .

It stands there, that building, always there, like a silent reproach. The sooner it is razed to the ground, the better, and I can forget. Perhaps. I haven't yet come across a way of preventing the subconscious, the mind, and perhaps the heart, from going their own way.

PART TWO

THIRTEEN

'Everything comes to he who waits. We're in luck, at last.' Gilmour was still feeling chuffed after his visit to Wetherby, and the subsequent foray to Melia Street.

Luck? Maybe, thought Reardon. And maybe the harder you worked on something, the luckier you got. If Gargrave hadn't given up too easily on his visits to the taxi firm, this information would have been available sooner. His ambition hadn't yet taught him that the lowlier, more boring jobs were a necessary adjunct to becoming a high-flyer. Young Pickersgill knew this. He was steadier, not so showy, but in the end would go further.

Anyway, by luck or otherwise, they now possessed the precise date Isabelle Blanchard had returned to Maxstead, plus the reasonable assumption on why she had made her summary departure from there. But the question of why she had felt it necessary to go back at all after leaving was still giving Reardon a headache. He couldn't see any rational reason for her return. Since she had taken the taxi from the insalubrious area around Melia Street to get there, it seemed to suggest that was where she'd been staying, up to the time of her death. Unless Deegan was lying, which of course he might well be, he had left her at the station, believing she was taking a train to Birmingham, but he hadn't stayed long enough to see her board that or any other train. And although Miss Ainsworth had sworn there was no woman living next door to her, that wasn't necessarily so, either. If Isabelle, and this man Newman, had wanted her whereabouts to remain hidden, keeping out of sight wouldn't have been any great problem. Only going out at night. Remaining indoors. Slipping out via the back entrance. Until she had been picked up by Vic Wetherby's taxi on that fateful night.

Who was Newman? If he did have some connection with Isabelle Blanchard, it followed he might also have been the mystery man who had called on Phoebe Catherall. And maybe he was the man Edith Hillyard had been fighting with on the steps of her school, the one who had passed Ellen in a fury? For a moment, Reardon's pulse quickened, but only for a moment. Just as one swallow did not a summer make, neither did the dubious appearance of two, or even three unknown men – if you counted 'Nol' in the murder picture – make a certainty. Even if they had been the same man. And speculation was useless, unless at least one of them could be traced; one who might, possibly, be this Nol to whom Isabelle had been writing?

'There's a woman out front, Sergeant Longton, a Miss Doris Ainsworth,' Pickersgill announced, popping his head round the door of the back room and interrupting the desk sergeant's elevenses. 'She's asking for Sergeant Gilmour. I've told her he's not here, but she says he gave her his card and it's something he'll want to know. He saw her yesterday.'

'Yes, I know. All right, I'll see her.'

Longton finished his tea in a leisurely swallow, took his feet off the desk, heaved his not inconsiderable bulk upright, brushed the last crumbs of a bacon sandwich from his tunic, and went out front with an air of martyrdom to do his duty.

He found Miss Ainsworth sitting on a bench in the front office with a large parcel on the chair next to her, looking put out not to have found Gilmour there. She'd made time to come in on her way to deliver some sewing to Baxendale's Emporium, just around the corner in Market Street, and she was in a hurry, she said. 'He *did* say I was to come in if there was anything more I could tell him.'

Longton gave her his ponderous look and told her he was quite au fait with the situation, that DS Gilmour had given him a full account of what had transpired at their meeting yesterday, so that he would know what it was all about if Miss Ainsworth came in when he wasn't there. Longton would make a note of everything she had to say and pass it on as soon as he came in.

'Oh, I see.' Somewhat mollified, she came to the point. 'Well, I don't know if this matters, but the rent man came round yesterday, and we got talking about my neighbour, you know, the one Sergeant Gilmour was enquiring about.'

Longton knew all about that, too, having been roped in to

set in motion local enquiries about this Newman, according to
the details Sergeant Gilmour had given him. Nothing at all had
emerged at present, but there was no need for anybody, least
of all him, Longton knew, to break into a sweat trying to find
him. If there was anything known about Newman, he was
confident it would soon emerge. Nothing remained hidden for
long in Folbury, especially when it involved a stranger, reputedly handsome, and owning a car, what was more. Cars weren't
yet so common in the town that they would pass unnoticed
(though the accidents Longton recorded testified to the increasing
hazards of crossing the ever busier roads) and anyone who was
well off enough to own one would have been marked down by
someone or other, sure as eggs. 'Mr Newman, that's the name,
right?'

'Yes, only it turns out his name's not Newman – leastways
it is, but it's his Christian name.' She sounded affronted. Longton
remained impassive. 'But you know,' she went on, justifying
her mistake, 'he did introduce himself as Newman – and when
I said, "Pleased to meet you, Mr Newman," he smiled, but he
didn't correct me.' She looked even more put out, obviously
feeling she'd been made to look a fool.

'Understandable mistake. I've never heard Newman as a first
name,' Longton said, making it sound as though, since he hadn't,
it wasn't possible.

'I have to admit he did seem to like a joke, but he shouldn't
have let me go on thinking that, should he?' The neighbour
she'd invested with glamour had definitely gone down in her
estimation.

Longton agreed that he shouldn't, but he'd been under no
obligation, had he, to tell her?

'I suppose not.' She didn't look as though she agreed.

'What is his last name, then?'

'The rent man said it was Liptrott, Newman Liptrott.'

Longton licked his pencil and wrote it down. After a moment,
she said, 'He's in trouble, isn't he?'

'We don't know that yet.'

'Well, I'm sorry if he is. I still think he's all right, even
though he did have me on.'

'This landlord of yours, who is he, then?'

'Oh well, it's Shefford's, isn't it,' she said, naming the pop-bottling factory that abutted on to the backs of the Melia Street houses, and then, forgetting her hurry, went on to air what was obviously a long-standing grievance. 'They own all three houses, the ones that are left, that is, bought the whole street years ago, and they want us out, you know, to knock 'em down like they've pulled down the rest of the street, but they can't just turn us out because they want to expand, or so they say, can they? We have rights – old Mr Dawson, my other neighbour, has made enquiries. They won't do any repairs or anything and they think that'll make us throw in the sponge, but it won't. We're staying put.'

'Quite right,' said Longton. He offered nothing further and silence ensued.

'Well, that's it, then,' she said at last. 'I've said what I came for.' She picked up her parcel from the chair.

Longton was overweight and didn't care for bestirring himself, but he was good-natured. He thanked her for coming in and asked if he couldn't get somebody to help her with her parcel; he could spare one of his constables for a few minutes and Baxendale's was only round the corner, after all. She told him she could manage, though she looked pleased at the offer.

'What's the name of the man who collects the rents, by the way?'

'Oh, it's Shefford himself that comes round, so he can keep an eye on what's going on. It's not a lot of trouble for him to do that, with only three houses left,' she said bitterly as she departed.

'Newman Liptrott, you couldn't make it up,' Gilmour said when he came in to Reardon's office with Miss Ainsworth's information.

'Well, it has a certain ring to it, you have to admit.'

'You could say that, but I'm wondering. What if he has a middle name? Oliver say, or Oscar, or anything else beginning with an O.'

'So he calls himself Nol?'

Gilmour grinned. 'Who wouldn't, saddled with a name like that? And Nol could still be Olivia, couldn't it?'

'Even if it is, it doesn't get us much further.' Reardon thought a bit. 'A word at Shefford's wouldn't come amiss, if he's been living in one of their houses.'

'Right,' said Gilmour, and went to find Gravy. 'Job for you,' he told him when he saw him. On second thoughts, remembering the boy wonder's not altogether successful questioning at Woodman's taxis, he said, 'I'll go myself, and you can come with me.'

Shefford's bottling factory wasn't a big outfit. It employed about fifty people, and in its entirety comprised only a collection of low, shed-like buildings that had seen better days, and a red brick-built edifice resembling a public convenience that was the office.

Gilmour sniffed the sickly, fruity sort of smell that pervaded everywhere and pulled a face. There were two lorries in the cobbled yard, one being unloaded of the carbon dioxide cylinders that gave the pop its fizz, the other being stacked with crates of bottles intended for delivery: dark-brown bottles of dandelion and burdock, lemonade that was unlikely ever to have made even nodding acquaintance with a lemon, sarsaparilla. And what was in that was anybody's guess.

The man superintending the loading wore a brown smock and held a clipboard in his hand, and was too occupied to pay them much attention. He ticked off another crate as it was loaded, not bothering to raise his eyes when Gilmour asked for Mr Shefford, just jerking his head towards the brick building. They left him to it and walked across. The door opened on to a brown tiled vestibule, taking the municipal look even further. Here they waited patiently after obeying the pencilled instructions drawing-pinned to a wooden flap in the wall that ordered tersely, 'Knock and wait.'

Shefford had presumably heard the knock, and he made them wait, as per instructions. Eventually he stuck his head through the flap and bade them enter the door next to it. A very short, stocky man, with a red face, small sharp eyes, a comb-over hairstyle and a trick of bouncing from one small foot to the other, like a boxer. It made him look as though he was stretching up to make himself look taller, and perhaps that was why it had become a habit. After introducing himself and shaking hands, he offered them chairs, while he perched on a high stool that was drawn up to a sloping desk, swivelling it round so that he had the advantage of looking down on them.

'We're a growing concern here,' he responded self-importantly, when Gilmour introduced the subject of the houses on Melia Street. He spoke with a strange accent, his vowels strangulated, a shot at gentility. 'And we'd like to rebuild and develop, but to do that we'd have to pull down what's left of that row, you understand.'

Presumably this was the royal 'we', since Shefford Soft Drinks was this Reginald Shefford himself, son of the father who had started the factory, and who was now sole owner. But develop? A more likely scenario was the prospect of a profitable sale on a vacant parcel of land for the council houses waiting to be built when times improved.

'Which we shall, sooner or later,' Shefford went on confidently. 'They're slums, falling down and of no use to anybody.'

Except to the poor sods who live in them, thought Gilmour. And if Shefford considered them slums, which Gilmour didn't, whose fault was it that they were in disrepair and falling down? He hadn't liked Mr Shefford at first sight and he wasn't improving with acquaintance.

'We've offered the tenants other accommodation,' Shefford added self-righteously, 'but they're being damned stubborn and won't accept.'

Gilmour had a good idea what sort of accommodation that would be and saw every reason why they wouldn't accept. He put such thoughts aside and addressed the real reason for being there. He asked him about Liptrott and was pleased to see Shefford's face darken as he asked, 'If they're going to be pulled down, what was the point of letting the empty one?'

'Only short-term renting, it was. Furnished accommodation. No point in leaving it unoccupied after the old cove who lived there died. I put an advert in the *Herald* and Liptrott answered straight away. And now he's buggered off owing me a month's rent!' Reminded, his face became even redder as he contemplated the crime. As though it was a king's ransom the absent tenant owed, when it was probably not more than a few pounds, at most, regardless of whether Shefford classed it as furnished accommodation or not. 'Just let me know when you find him! What's he been up to, then?' His accent was slipping, becoming broader by the minute.

'Nothing that we know of,' Gilmour said truthfully. 'It's a friend of his we're trying to connect with. But since we can't get hold of him and there seems to be no indication when he'll be back—'

'Back? You'll be lucky! He'll not be coming back this side of the millennium. Take it from me, he's done a moonlight. I went in there yesterday and had a good look round, to check the inventory. You can't trust folks. But I have to say he'd taken nowt but his own stuff with him.' He seemed disappointed to have to admit that.

Inventory? It was all Gilmour could do not to laugh. 'Didn't you ask for credentials when you took him on as a tenant?' he asked instead, being deliberately provocative, and got the look from Shefford the man obviously thought such a stupid question deserved. He would have rented the house to Vlad the Impaler if he had been alive and well and living in Folbury – providing he had the wherewithal to pay the rent.

'And besides,' Shefford went on, adding up the grievances, 'I wanted my keys back. But the bastard's gone off with them.'

'Did you know he had a woman living with him?'

'What? No, I didn't!' For a moment that had caught him off balance, but he was quick to cover up. 'Well, I suppose it was his own business if he did. No skin off my nose.'

'We'd like to take a look around the house, if that's all right with you,' Gilmour told him. And even if it wasn't, his tone implied.

Shefford said testily, 'I can't go round there just now. I'm too busy. And there's nothing to see.'

'You don't need to come with us.' Gilmour looked bland.

Shefford paused, on the point of refusing, then gave in, remembering they were the police, after all. 'All right,' he said grudgingly, 'as it happens I do have a spare key. But I want it back, I've already lost the others, haven't I, and I don't want to lose any more.' Reluctantly, he rummaged in a drawer and handed it over.

*   *   *

Jocasta Keith slapped paint viciously on to the canvas and stood back, biting her lip, scowling ferociously at what she'd just accomplished – or not. Drat the thing! It was no good, she was all over the place lately, her concentration nil, and it showed. And now that the light was going it was too late to start again. The few free periods she had during the day, and the short time after lessons were finished, were the only times she had to get on with what she considered her real work.

She cleaned her brushes furiously. It shouldn't have happened like this. None of it should have happened at all, in fact. Nobody had ever intended that, had they? But he had been persuasive, knowing instinctively which nerve to press, in a way that made it impossible to refuse. Or it had seemed so, then.

It still shouldn't have happened. It was all due to what they called coincidence anyway. Coincidence, or Fate? She didn't believe in either, or only in the Fate that dealt you a rotten deal in life – which might have been exactly why they'd bumped into each other in a London street, of all places, at a dark time for her, another black spot in what was beginning to look like an increasingly bleak future. Or, more precisely, she had bumped into him, not looking where she was going, to be honest, colliding with him because it was pouring with rain and she had her umbrella up and her mind elsewhere. Torn between going back to the café she'd just passed for a reckless splurge on sausage, mash and onion gravy, plus pudding, for one-and-eleven all in, or settling for beans on toast again in her bedsit. Her stomach was rumbling. Her waistband had felt even slacker that morning. With the grand total of seven shillings left in her purse, no prospect of any more to come and still less of anyone buying any of her work, either, not even any of the odd potboilers she was reduced to doing to keep body and soul together.

She had been an easy target.

'Joan!'

Even in her bemused state she'd turned round at that blast from the past, one she needed as little as yet another rent demand from her landlord. When she'd finally found the will and had shaken the dust off, she'd never wanted even to think about her home town, much less meet anyone who'd been part of it. But there he was and, knowing him, he would not be got rid of easily, and she herself did not want him to go, to tell the truth. Not when he was offering to buy her lunch and asking where the nearest place was.

'I'm not Joan any more. It's Jocasta now,' she'd told him while they waited for apple pie with custard, already feeling better and more confident after the sausage and mash.

He had been amused. 'Jocasta? I like it. Jocasta Keith, famous artist.'

The annoying blush she always found it hard to contain rose from her neck. 'There's no call to be sarcastic.'

'No sarcasm intended. You were always good.' He smiled, reached out and pressed her hand, and, despite herself, she'd smiled.

And that was how it had started. Soothed by a full belly, seduced by images of more meals whenever she needed them. New silk stockings. That pair of lizard-skin shoes she'd briefly coveted. But more than anything else, the prospect of time in which to devote herself to what really mattered, what she burned to do. She had done what he asked, and in the end she hadn't had any regrets. Not really. Coming here had meant that at least there was no need to worry about where her next meal was coming from, even if it was of the school dinner variety. Money in her purse and decent clothes. She could even afford to go up to London from time to time to have her hair cut and waved properly. It meant the open door to freedom. Time to focus on her real work, with no imperative to try and sell rubbishy crowd-pleasers in order to live, the joy of being free to tell the philistines to take a running jump if she wanted to. And the price? Truth to tell, when she thought about that she'd had qualms, right from the beginning, but they'd been easily suppressed. Especially when she thought of what she'd left behind, and just how near the brink of the abyss she had been when he'd found her, gripped with the black despair that took hold of her sometimes, always when she least expected it, like it was doing now. What her father used to call the black dog, threatening to savage her with its fangs bared.

Her father, a worker in the Potteries. When she mentioned where she came from, most people seemed to regard it as distant as the North Pole, if they'd ever heard of the region at all.

Nobody seemed to know exactly where it was, a sort of hole in the middle of England; so she usually compromised by saying 'the Midlands'.

Sometimes she thought briefly that she ought to have stayed there. But she had fumed at not only being unable to use her real talents, but also at not making money. Not real money, anyway. She wasn't going to satisfy either need by devoting her life to painting chinaware. By local standards she'd been earning good money, but the foot-treadle she used to operate her work-table came to feel more and more like a treadmill. Even when she graduated from that to hand-painting designs, she was bored and frustrated beyond belief.

For a time it hadn't been so bad, living in London, trying to establish herself and lose all traces of her provincial past. She wanted to make money, yes, and plenty of it, because she knew herself and that she wasn't cut out for a life of scrimping and scraping. Success had to mean artistic fulfilment, but must also mean more. The arty, floaty, precious world typical of the Bloomsbury set she had once so admired from afar had not made itself available to her, and living the so-called romantic life in a garret she had found was distinctly overrated. Her ambition was boundless, but not enough to make that bearable.

And in the end, in a contradictory sort of way, that ambition was what had made up her mind. It was a self-defeating decision, had she but known it then, and she had taken the plunge and left.

FOURTEEN

A nasty smell greeted them when Gilmour unlocked the door at 43 Melia Street. The hairs on his arms stood on end as he stepped inside, Gravy following, hoping to God it just betokened an old, damp house and not another corpse.

But it wasn't that sort of smell. It was the sour odour of unaired rooms, past fry-ups, air that was used up. Yet, despite that, and whether Liptrott had left in a hurry or not, an initial quick glance around suggested he might have done a half-hearted tidy-up before he went. The place wasn't cluttered, the carpets looked more or less swept and there was only a thin layer of dust and grime on the surfaces.

This house was a repeat of the one next door – the familiar layout of front room, a kitchen/living room at the back and two bedrooms. There was no bathroom and the privy was outside in the yard. Gilmour started a systematic search with the parlour at the front. Unlike Miss Ainsworth's, which at least served as her workroom, this room had probably remained unused for years. Shefford's assertion that the house was furnished didn't agree with his own estimation, but maybe it was, if that was how you regarded one with no more than a few sticks of tired old furniture, and without a single book, picture or ornament of any kind to make it welcome and homely. Not even a cushion graced the old-fashioned horsehair-stuffed, tabby-cat-patterned plush sofa and chairs. Shefford wouldn't have needed any inventory to check with one glance that all his furnishings were still intact.

The drawers in the one chest were empty, except for a little trail of detritus that had accumulated in corners, been missed or left behind. An exploration down the sides of the dusty plush chairs unearthed a little cache of small denomination coins, a pencil stub and a betting slip dated three years earlier, but all in all, this room at least turned out to be nothing more than the bare bones, scraped clean, of what had been the life of the old man who had previously lived there.

The state of the kitchen-living room, however – always a give-away – seemed to say Liptrott hadn't been a complete slob. The sink in the corner was clean and a tea towel hung neatly over a wire stretched across the cold kitchen range. Was it Gilmour's imagination that it was ever so slightly damp? He decided it was. Here, too, the cupboards had been cleared, except for a few tins, a packet of tea and some sugar that he'd seemingly not thought worth taking.

It was becoming depressingly obvious that Liptrott might indeed have done a runner, as Shefford had said, and most likely for good. But there were still the rooms upstairs to look over, accessed by a narrow staircase steep enough to make the north face of the Eiger look like a nursery slope. Gilmour wasn't hopeful of finding anything there, though, and he was right. The brass bed in the front room had been stripped to its flocked mattress and striped ticking pillows, and in the only other piece of furniture, a chest of drawers, was nothing but a cheap Californian Poppy scent bottle, its contents evaporated, and a dried-up lipstick of an improbable orange colour. Unlikely property, either of them, for a fastidious and fashionable woman who wore custom-made underclothes. If Isabelle Blanchard had ever been here, she had left no more traces of herself than Newman Liptrott had.

Yet the nasty premonition persisted, and when they came to the firmly closed door of the other small bedroom – it could be no more than a box-room as it was partly over the stairs – the feeling intensified. Houses like these didn't aspire to have locks on their inside doors, the other bedroom didn't have one, and neither did this. But nothing came of it when Gilmour tried the knob and, even when he leaned on it, the door refused to budge. He put his eye to the keyhole. He could see nothing. He rattled the knob and shouted. There was no response.

The door itself looked flimsy enough. 'Go on then, Gravy.'

The hefty DC gave it a summing up, grinned, then stepped back the few paces the tiny landing allowed, charged forward and put his shoulder to the door. It gave way with a tremendous crash as the chest of drawers which had been pushed against it was overturned, and Gravy was catapulted into the room under the terrified gaze of a woman sitting on the edge of the bed.

The downstairs parlour seemed too full, what with three large policemen – Gilmour, Gargrave and now Reardon – as well as the weeping woman now hunched up in a chair. When she stood, she was almost as tall as any of the men in the room.

It must be hard for a woman to be so woefully plain, Reardon couldn't help thinking. On the other hand, she wasn't helping herself with the heavy, horn-rimmed glasses, centre-parted hair and earphone plaits, none of which enhanced a long, thin face. Wearing, what was more, frumpy clothes that even he could see were years out of fashion, as was that hairstyle, one most modern young women wouldn't be seen dead with. Yet when she took her glasses off to wipe away the tears – which she had to do every minute or so – her eyes were large and slate grey and, he thought, intelligent.

At present she was hunched on one of the hard-stuffed plush chairs, a sodden hankie clutched in her fist. She looked as though she might never stop crying.

'Are you – you're not going to arrest me, are you?' she asked tremulously.

'I don't think so, Miss Catherall. Not yet, not unless what you have to tell me says you've done something wrong.' Something about this woman bade him speak gently, as if to a child.

'I haven't! I swear I've done nothing wrong.' Her voice rose, panic-stricken. The slow tears continued to trickle down from behind her glasses.

'Who did you think it was downstairs, that made you barricade yourself in that bedroom?'

'I thought it was . . . There was a man here, yesterday. I – I thought he'd come back.'

At first he imagined she must mean Liptrott, then he remembered that Shefford had been there the previous day, or that was what he'd told Gilmour. In which case, he must have known Miss Catherall was there, but had chosen to say nothing about her, most probably having ordered her to leave, terrifying her

so much in the process he had confidently expected she would
be gone when he'd handed the front door key over to the police?

'Take it easy,' Reardon told the sobbing woman gently. 'You
don't have to rush this. In fact, you don't have to tell me anything
at all just yet,' he decided, resigning himself to the fact that a
witness in this incoherent state wasn't likely to be much use.
'It'll keep. We'll find somewhere else for you to stay tonight
and you'll feel more up to it tomorrow.'

'No, no, I won't!' she cried urgently. 'Not until I've told you.
But I . . .' She looked nervously from one to the other of her
audience and Reardon sensed it was the presence of so many
of them that was bewildering, if not actually intimidating, her.
How deeply she was implicated in all this, he didn't yet have
any idea, though he suspected it might be less than she herself
imagined, given her overreaction to the possibility of being
arrested. He somehow didn't see her playing a major part. She
appeared altogether too timid, and though guilt at something
or other hung over her like a pall, he was prepared to go easy
on her. Not, however, to the extent of letting her get away with
anything.

'All right.' He inclined his head to Gilmour, who took the
point. Happy to leave Reardon to it, he at once made a move
to the door, nudging Gargrave along with him.

When he heard the outer door close behind them Reardon
said, 'Well now, maybe a good place to start, Miss Catherall,
would be by explaining to me how you came to be living here,
and how you know Newman Liptrott?'

'Nol, you mean?' Her face closed. So the improbable nickname did belong to Liptrott. 'It's a long story.'

'And I want to hear the whole of it, but there's no rush. Take
your time; I'm not anxious to leave before I've heard what you
have to say.'

They sat facing, on those unforgiving chairs, one each side
of a cheerless grate filled with yellowing, almost crumbling
newspaper, pitted with spots of soot the rain had brought down.
She was sitting with her shoulders hunched, arms across her
chest and her feet splayed, pigeon-toed, an awkward, graceless
and curiously immature pose.

'I don't know him,' she said after several minutes. 'Not what you'd call *know*. In fact, the first time I ever saw him was a few months ago, when he came to see me at . . . where I was living at the time.'

'In Moseley, with Mrs Cooper.'

Her eyes widened, but she didn't ask how he knew that. 'I suppose she's told you all about me?'

All Mrs Cooper had known, which hadn't been enough, he thought. He said, 'She's been very worried about you, not hearing anything, you know.'

'I'm sorry about that. She's nice, her husband too, but I had no choice. Oh, it's all such a mess, I don't know where to begin.' Her eyes filled with tears again.

He wondered if she knew just how much of a mess. 'How about starting from how you came to be living there, in Moseley?' he tried again, patiently.

'I came to see England. I'm half French. My mother was French, but my father was English, and the stories he told me about this country made me want to see it. I'd lived in France all my life, and he always said I must visit here one day – that I should be missing out if I didn't, but somehow he never wanted to come back himself. He was trained as a historian and he was writing a book about Napoleon, you see, so his work was centred there. But after he died and I was left alone, I plucked up courage and came.'

She made it sound as though crossing the Channel on her own, and taking a train to Birmingham, was akin to undertaking a lone expedition to the Antarctic.

'Why pick Birmingham?' *One has no great hopes of Birmingham.* Perhaps Jane Austen's Emma might have had a point. The Second City, that great hub of industry in the smoky Midlands, was not the obvious place of choice for visiting tourists.

'Oh, Father was born in Edgbaston, though he never left France after he married my mother, and was quite content to stay in France, even before she became an invalid and died, when I was young. But I'd always wanted to see where he'd come from and, when I did come eventually, I just stayed. I like England. Or I did until, until . . .' She couldn't go on.

Until she had heard about Isabelle Blanchard's death? When

they first began to speak, he had told her why they were here and that it was in connection with her murder, but of course she had known. It had been no news to her.

'How did you get yourself mixed up in all this, with Liptrott?' he asked again, in an effort to get her back on track and prevent more tears.

'It was Isabelle,' she managed at last. 'I was all set to start teaching at Maxstead, so happy about it after all the time I'd spent working at that awful picture house – and then, and then . . . Oh, maybe if I hadn't done as she wanted, it would be me who was dead! I wish it was,' she finished with something like a wail. And more tears.

Well, they were real enough, but who were they for, Isabelle or herself? He would have put her in her mid-thirties, yet here she was, a grown woman sounding more juvenile than the adolescent schoolgirls he'd recently been talking to. Or was the display of ingenuousness, as well as the emotion, overdone? He wasn't sure. His initial impression of her was fading fast and he was beginning to think Phoebe Catherall maybe wasn't the sharpest pin in the pincushion. He could see, despite what he'd said, that it was going to take more time than he wanted to spend in getting to the nub of the question if he allowed her to tell the story in her own way.

'So tell me how you came to get that teaching position at Maxstead.'

'Well, Edith knew I was bilingual because of my father and mother. So when she told me about Maxstead and needing someone to teach French, I asked if I could have the job. I'm not a qualified teacher, but she was delighted, and told me I didn't need qualifications.'

Hold it. This was now going too fast. 'You knew Edith Hillyard *before* you began to teach at her school?

'Oh, yes, we've known each other for years. We met in France during the war, when she and her friend Eve were ambulance drivers, working from the British military hospital near Boulogne, where I lived. I never could imagine how she, how anyone could bring themselves to do that. Some of those poor men had the most horrific wounds and she had to help lift them into her ambulance, you cannot believe . . .'

She stopped, realizing where he'd most probably received the blemish on his face, blushed with embarrassment, but to her credit didn't look away.

He'd leant to live with it, as others had had to do with the disfigurements and disabilities that were the legacies of the war. One sleeve pinned across a chest, a crutch making up for a lost leg. Injuries to the body, and to the mind, that didn't show.

'You know how it was, then. The chaos, especially at night.'

'Yes.' He still relived it in his dreams. 'Yes, I know.'

'Well,' she went on after a moment, 'I was employed as a translator in the communications section. They needed people to do that, when we French and the English were working together. To translate documents, write letters and so on, which I could do, of course. It was my war effort, you see, small though it was. We all did what we could against the Germans, didn't we?' She paused, but he didn't think he was going to have to prompt her to carry on. Phoebe Catherall seemed to have a lot she was anxious to get off her chest.

'There was one night when the weather and everything else was simply frightful. The guns seemed to have been going on for hours. Nobody knew what was happening. Everything was all over the place. Somehow, one of the badly wounded men taken into Edith's ambulance was a Frenchman; how or why he'd come to be fighting alongside the British Tommies, no one ever found out. He asked for water, in his own language, and Edith had answered him with what little French she knew. Once they had got him into bed, he begged her to write to his mother. She couldn't refuse the request of a dying man, but she didn't think she knew enough of the language to find the right words herself, so she went in search of a translator, and found me. That was how we first met, and after that we met off duty, and soon became good friends. When the war was over and she had gone back to England and her teaching, we kept in touch, though not all that regularly.' She paused again and scrubbed at her damp face. 'Then my father died and left me some money; although it wasn't much, I decided I would do as he'd always told me I should, and cross the Channel to see something of the country of his birth. I hoped that perhaps Edith and I could meet again. It was a year or two before I finally decided to come over here.'

'And Isabelle? Did you meet her the same way?'

'Heavens, no, we grew up together. She lived with us and we were as near to sisters as it's possible without being related, although she was several years younger than me. I fact, she became my stepsister later. She was – she was everything to me – I'd known her since she was a year old.' Again the tears welled. It took several moments before she could go on. 'Isabelle's mother was a widow, but she had been a nurse, and when my mother became ill, she came to stay with us, and afterwards, after Maman died, she agreed to stay on as house-keeper. On condition she could bring her little girl, too.'

He took a moment to get this together while she sat twisting her sodden handkerchief, trying to find a dry spot. 'Let's get this straight. You were very happy at getting that job at Maxstead with your old friend, Miss Hillyard, yet you agreed to that rigmarole with Isabelle about you needing to go into hospital, so that she could take your place?' She didn't deny it. 'That was a long shot, surely? How did you know Miss Hillyard would agree to take her on, for one thing?'

'Well, she knew that Belle was as fluent as I am in both languages, didn't she?'

Edith Hillyard had known not only Phoebe, but Isabelle, too. She had lied, at least by implication, by deliberately omitting to tell him that she, the murdered teacher and the one who had replaced her, had in fact all known each other. And pretty well, it seemed.

'Actually, Belle was better qualified than me for Maxstead, because of her teaching English in France for years,' Miss Catherall admitted.

'Yes, at the Lycée Honoré de Balzac in Metz,' he said, while his thoughts raced as he attempted to pull what she had just told him together.

'*Metz?*'

'That was where she had been teaching, according to Miss Hillyard.'

She looked confused. 'You must have got that wrong. She only gave private lessons, when she could get them, and that only in the last few years. She wasn't trained, but she turned out to be a good teacher.' Reardon thought that any teacher who was popular with her pupils, as Isabelle Blanchard seemed to have been, would have a head start, so that was probably true. 'But to my certain knowledge, she never lived in Metz. It was Paris where she lived after she left home.'

So Isabelle, too, had not told the truth to Edith Hillyard. Or maybe it had been the headmistress who had made up the lie about Metz, the references and God knew what else. Lies and more lies, coiling together like a nest of snakes. For reasons that were as yet obscure, Miss Hillyard had omitted to say she knew the two women previously. He found no difficulty in believing she might be capable of blatant untruths. But why? Simply to add verisimilitude, as someone or other had it, to an otherwise unconvincing narrative? That didn't seem very likely.

Phoebe Catherall was weeping again. He thought she might now be taking refuge in tears to drum up sympathy and stop his questioning. Being married to a woman he was very happy to know had no such tendencies didn't incline Reardon to go along with that, and his tone hardened. 'All right. You met Miss Hillyard through working at that hospital. Did Isabelle work there too?'

'Oh, no, she was too young for that! I suppose they first met when Edith visited me at home,' she said vaguely, 'for a meal, you know – as I said, we'd become friends, Edith and I. We didn't have much food to share at home but it was better than at the hospital.' She gave a very French shudder at the memory. And then she said timidly, 'Can we go, now? I'm very tired.'

'Yes, I can see you are, and we'll leave in a minute.'

It was a big tangle that was going to take some sorting out, but he doubted if telling Phoebe Catherall to start from the beginning would produce a more lucid explanation. There were huge gaps in her story, such as whether she had been here in Melia Street ever since she had left the house in Moseley, and what her connection with the evasive Liptrott really was. And that was only the beginning. But she did look tired and he was sure she wasn't going to be persuaded to say more. She had the look of a stubborn child who knew she would be punished if she confessed. 'But just tell me one thing before we leave. Why was it so important to Isabelle to take that job at Maxstead?'

'She wouldn't say. She just said she had to.'

He raised an eyebrow. Now *she* was lying, or at best being evasive, and whichever, it was beginning to irritate him. He found this unquestioning obedience to Isabelle hard to believe, to say the least. Here was a woman who had landed herself a worthwhile job, which would provide her with status and income and take her away from a lifestyle she had obviously hated, and yet she had been willing to surrender it to Isabelle Blanchard for some unspecified reason. He found it incredible that any woman could let herself be used in the way Phoebe seemed to have been used. Did she actually enjoy playing the martyr?

He was afraid that might be true. Why else would she have been content to earn a pittance by playing the piano in a picture house? God knows, jobs were difficult enough to find, but even in slump-bound Britain she could surely have found something more suitable to the other talents she possessed. Miss Hillyard, for one, had been willing to employ her for her language skills, unqualified as she was, and surely that wasn't solely out of friendship? He was beginning to suspect Miss Catherall was someone who drifted along where the wind took her or, more to the point, where her 'friends' – who may have included Liptrott, despite what she'd just said about hardly knowing him – dictated she should go. Not to mention that Isabelle, adored friend, not-quite-sister, had clearly had some overriding influence over her.

He made one last try. 'You let Isabelle Blanchard take your job without asking why?'

'You didn't know Isabelle,' she said sadly.

And that, he was sure, was the best he was going to get at this stage.

'She's lying, of course, or at any rate sparing us the whole truth,' Gilmour said when all this was relayed to him and the rest, back at Market Street.

'Well, we haven't finished with her yet. We'll see what we can get from her when she's pulled herself together a bit more.'

'Meanwhile, what are we going to do with her?'

Phoebe Catherall had been near hysterical at the thought of having to stay on at Melia Street, as well she might, and Reardon had suggested the Shire Hotel, which had had almost the same effect. It was Folbury's one and only hotel, and perhaps she was thinking of the cost, though she had said she had enough money to tide her over. In the absence of any other ideas at what to do with her, he had brought her back to Market Street, hoping for suggestions. For the moment she was sitting in his office with a cup of tea and her belongings in a suitcase at her feet while they decided on somewhere for her to go. The possibilities for accommodation in Folbury, other than the Shire, were few.

'We can always take her back to Moseley, to Mrs Cooper,' Gilmour offered. 'She'd be glad to have her, I'm sure.'

'I need to talk to her again. She hasn't told us everything, not by a long chalk.'

Longton had been listening in and now stirred himself and coughed. 'She could come and stay with us,' he said stolidly.

Heads were turned in amazement. Gargrave smirked. 'You smitten, Sarge?'

'Don't be dafter than you can help, Gravy.' Longton was unfazed. He was middle aged, carried too much weight for his age, and didn't have flighty tendencies.

But Gilmour suddenly understood. 'I thought your mother had stopped taking in lodgers, George.'

'She has, she said she was too old for it now, after the last one left. But there's a room, a bed. I reckon she'd be happy to oblige in the circumstances.'

FIFTEEN

'You can't bother the young lady when she's poorly,' Mrs Longton said next morning. 'She's been sick this morning.'

Gilmour's eyebrows lifted.

'Now, now young man! Definitely not, what are you thinking? She was sick last night as well, though my meat and tatie pie and plum duff never upset anybody before, Mr Reardon. I'll tell you what it is. I reckon she hasn't been eating properly for weeks and maybe it was too rich.'

Too heavy rather, by the sound of it. If this was the usual fare his mother provided, no wonder Longton was bursting out of his uniform. 'Maybe one of us could just speak to her for a minute, Mrs Longton?' To Gilmour, Reardon said, 'I'll see her myself,' thinking that two policemen appearing in her bedroom might be too much altogether for Phoebe Catherall's tender susceptibilities.

'You can try. But not for more than a minute, I wouldn't. The kettle's on. Make the tea when it boils, there's a good lad,' she instructed Gilmour. 'We'll have a cup when we come back down.' She was not intending to leave Reardon to his own devices.

She hadn't been exaggerating. Phoebe Catherall was looking poorly. She turned to face the wall and pulled the blankets up further around her shoulders when Mrs Longton opened the door. Mrs Longton stood on guard in the doorway as Reardon approached the bed. Her temporary lodger's indisposition had brought out the protectiveness in her.

'You'll have to give me time,' Phoebe muttered, her voice muffled by the bedclothes. 'I've been through so much, and I don't feel well.'

'I'm sorry, but I need to ask you a few more questions, then I'll leave you alone until you feel better.' Silence, but Reardon didn't intend to be so easily put off. He began with the first question that occurred to him. If he could get her started, she might respond to more. 'We found a letter from her aunt, Mathilde, among Isabelle's possessions.'

After several moments' silence, Phoebe pulled the blankets down and turned her face towards him. 'Her aunt *who?*' She stared at him and then, surprisingly, laughed. '*My* Tante Mathilde, don't you mean? Mathilde Blanchard is Isabelle's mother. I've called her aunt ever since she and Isabelle came to live with us, after Maman died. And even after she married Father, two years later.'

'She was writing to *you?*'

'If she signed herself Tante, she must have been.'

'It appeared to be a warning not to go ahead with something.'

'I don't remember any such letter.' She spoke almost sulkily. Clearly she remembered very well whatever it was she didn't want him to know about. But he must not let the fact that he found this woman so annoying sway him, and no one could really have the heart to force her to talk further, the way she looked. White as the sheets on the bed, dark circles under her eyes, although, even so, minus her heavy glasses and her hair undone, she was better looking than she had been the day before. And more vulnerable, he thought guiltily. All the same, he'd had just about enough of women, young and old, who took refuge in untruths, and turned to go.

'Do you know where Newman Liptrott is?' he asked, as a parting shot.

'I've told you, I have no idea. Just leave me alone,' she said again. 'I'm ill.'

He had a strong impulse to shake her. 'Very well. But you're going to have to tell us what you know, Miss Catherall, sooner or later.'

She turned her face back to the wall. Mrs Longton was clucking behind him. He had no alternative but to leave.

Downstairs the kettle had boiled and Gilmour had made the tea as Mrs Longton had instructed, had helped himself to a cup and was tucking into a flapjack from the plate she'd left out, but Reardon was too frustrated with the woman he'd left behind to waste time on drinking tea.

*   *   *

Phoebe knew the inspector was right. The day of reckoning had come and the facts would have to be made known. The truth was she was rather intimidated by Reardon. The face – that honourably scarred face – he'd showed her, although he probably wasn't aware of it, could turn rather frightening, not because of the disfigurement, which wasn't really all that terrible, but because she thought he might be a rather uncompromising man, when faced with lies. And more lies were what she would have to tell.

She couldn't tell the whole truth, feeling him watching her and weighing every word, judging her. She was always uneasy when she felt people didn't have a good opinion of her.

But as she thought of that letter he'd mentioned, a brilliant idea came to her and she immediately began to feel better. The pain in her stomach had miraculously gone. She got out of bed and scrabbled in her suitcase for her writing case, a pencil and enough writing paper amongst all the old letters from Tante Mathilde she had kept. This was going to be a long epistle.

She had no need to go through them all to know that particular letter the inspector had mentioned wouldn't be there amongst all the others. She remembered it well, of course. She had written to Mathilde asking her for more details about what had happened so long ago in France, and Mathilde had been upset and had written back to tell her not to meddle in something that was over and done with. She had showed the letter to Isabelle and she in turn had shoved it in her bag, absent-mindedly or not, after reading it, and Phoebe hadn't asked for it back because it really wasn't anything of importance. And when had Isabelle ever needed a reason to take anything? Whatever Phoebe had, Isabelle had always wanted it, even if she had no use for it. She had always been greedy, for possessions, for status, not caring too much how either was obtained. She had left home and gone to live in Paris as soon as she was old enough for her mother, Phoebe's beloved Tante Mathilde, to allow her to leave and make her own living. Phoebe never really knew for certain how it was she managed to buy such beautiful clothes and some rather good jewellery, just from the money she earned giving English lessons. But Tante Mathilde's lips had tightened on the occasions when she visited, and Phoebe had put two and two together.

There had been nothing incriminating in that particular letter, as far as Phoebe could remember, but then, she didn't store facts away for future use like Isabelle had always done, watching with her veiled cat's eyes that missed nothing, waiting for an opportunity to use it. No reason why she should have kept it, except that it belonged to someone else. Especially if that someone was Phoebe.

Nor did Isabelle ever forget. She had been fifteen, and Phoebe twenty-two when it happened but, fifteen years later, she still remembered.

Phoebe picked up her pencil.

Before I became a headmistress, it never occurred to me that responsibility can keep you awake at night. I used to take seven or eight restful hours' sleep for granted; now I'm grateful for much less. Last night I scarcely slept at all. It was so hot, and while I have been sitting here, I've watched the dark night sky gradually lighten from black to the colour of charcoal, then into pewter, and finally into pearl grey. Now it's turning the tender blue, touched with rosy pink, that hopefully heralds rain later.

I was a fool ever to have had dealings with that woman. But there is no point in dwelling on that now. The bell will be sounding for breakfast in half an hour, the blessed routine of the school day will be commencing. I stand up and I'm leaving my seat by the window when I see a figure running towards the school from the direction of the woods. Eve, Eve Draper. Running!

Stuff was in the habit of piling up on the desk if you were away for more than a day or two, and for Reardon today in his office at Queen's Road it was no exception. Having shuffled through the snowstorm of papers, he could see that most of it, as he'd expected, was backlog from the previous week that he'd being shoving to one side, with Isabelle Blanchard's murder needing to take priority. It was routine stuff, but couldn't be shuffled off indefinitely. He decided to get down to shifting some of it before he had to go out to Maxstead once again. He was halfway down the pile when he saw the envelope.

Longton came in with a cup of tea and placed the thick white mug on the desk. It would be strong, as Reardon liked it, but there would be too much sugar in it. Longton was incapable of understanding that not everyone liked their tea as he did. 'I take it you brought this in, George?' Reardon asked him, holding up the envelope.

'Miss Catherall asked me to give it you.'

'And you put it on my desk.'

'Yes.' He sounded surprised at the accusing note.

Where someone else had dumped more papers on top of it. Just as well Reardon had had a stab of conscience about them. It could have lain there for another week, gaining more layers each day. 'All right, thanks. But next time you're asked to give me something,' he said, giving the constable a look, 'hand it to me personally, right?'

'Yes, sir.' Looking pained, as only Longton could, he left the office.

The handwriting on the envelope was immediately recognizable. Small, spiky, upright, an unfamiliar style that wasn't easy to read. The same as on that letter he'd asked Phoebe Catherall about. Tante Mathilde's handwriting.

But it wasn't the unknown Tante Mathilde who was writing to him. The letter was from Phoebe herself, the handwriting only similar because it was French in style.

She was writing this, she explained, because she feared she would be too emotional when faced with him to be as clear as she ought to be. He raised an eyebrow. He had been *très sympathique* when they spoke, she went on, and hoped he would forgive her, but it was easier to put difficult words on to paper than to speak personally.

This was, of course, her way of avoiding direct confrontation. She was prepared to communicate, but she was setting her own boundaries. At least it was one better than keeping her face turned to the wall.

'I will be honest with you because I feel I may have given the wrong impression of my relationship with Isabelle and I would not like you to think that I didn't love her very dearly.

'I think I must start by telling you how I met Edith once more after so many years, as what transpired then only happened because I was, I have to confess, at a very low point, very dissatisfied with my life. England had drawn me here but I had not found what I had expected. I had hoped it might somehow change my life, but after I had been here some time, I could still see no bright future for myself. Yet what was there for me back in France? A spinster, untrained for anything except to play the piano, though not with anything much more than average competence? And then came the meeting with Edith that I thought would change my life. As it has done, though hardly in the way I expected, or wanted.

'I had already written to my dear Tante Mathilde and to Isabelle to tell them I was coming home. I had never told either of them that I had hoped my visit to England would be permanent, and Mathilde had been writing continually to ask me when I would be returning. So of course she was delighted at the prospect of having me home at last. But now I had to write and tell them both that my plans had changed. I was sure they would be pleased that Edith and I had made contact again and that she had given me a position in her school.

'Mathilde is not well now and had so looked forward to us being together again, and she was sad and disappointed that it was not going to happen. I was sad too, I hated to disappoint her, but I promised I would visit, as soon as the school holidays permitted.

'Isabelle's response to my news, however, astonished me. She came straight over to England to see me herself, though not to persuade me to change my mind, as I had first thought. She confessed herself delighted that I now had the position with Edith, and she was very happy to hear of her good fortune at becoming headmistress of her own school. I had planned various things she and I could do together before I started work at the beginning of the new term. When she arrived, we met briefly, but after that she wanted to be off on her own pursuits, whatever they might be. Secretive as ever.

'I think you may have guessed now that I was perhaps a little jealous of Isabelle, just a little. I am sorry for it now, that I shall never be able to make up for it. It wasn't only her clothes and her glamorous Parisian lifestyle. It was more that, although I was my father's only child, she had always been his favourite,

ever since Mathilde brought her to live with us when she was
only a year old. In comparison with her I was plain and rather
dull, nor could I share his only interest, his lifelong preoccupa-
tion with writing that life of Napoleon, his hero. Whereas
Isabelle did, or pretended to. She even named her cat Napoleon
to please him, although when she found out the Little Corporal
had been mortally afraid of cats (a weakness he always tried
to hide), she laughed and said she was sure he would be *beau-
coup amusé* by the idea of having one named after him, wherever
he was now. My father's pet name for her was Minou.

'She had been very enthusiastic about the three of us meeting
again – Edith, herself and me. When she arrived, I arranged to
meet her in the hotel where she was staying. I felt she might
despise the modest lodgings where I'd ended up if I asked her
to visit me there, although they were quiet and decent and
neither I nor my landlady, Mrs Cooper, had anything to be
ashamed of. But it was the sort of place which would have
caused Isabelle to raise her elegant eyebrows. She would see
that I had made a poor job of looking out for myself, as she
used to put it, and she always despised anyone who couldn't
do that. I think now that she saw the truth as soon as we met,
although she didn't say so. Over a very English tea of scones
and jam, she wanted to know all about Edith's good fortune,
and was eager to meet her, but she said there were things she
had to do first. She didn't say what they were and I didn't ask.
As I said, Isabelle had a passion for keeping things to herself.

'It wasn't until later, after we had made that arrangement to
change places, that I found out what she had been doing, but
by then it was too late. The letter had already gone to Edith
about my "illness" and my suggestion that Isabelle should replace
me before that man Liptrott chose to visit me at Mrs Cooper's
house. He said he had come to make sure I went through with
the scheme, that I wouldn't suddenly get cold feet and feel
obliged to give the game away. He tried to threaten me with
what would happen if I did. Vague threats but nonetheless
alarming. He is rather a stupid man, Newman Liptrott, although
he doesn't think himself so, and I was surprised Isabelle trusted
him. I could only believe that her hopes at what would transpire
from including him in this exploit overwhelmed her common

sense. And it turned out he was half right. Had I known what they were planning, I would never have agreed.

'I was already bitterly regretting having told Isabelle about the money with which Edith had been able to start her school. She had wanted to know all the details, and now I know where she had gone, and that she had found out where the money had come from, and why, and that she had ferreted around until she was led to Liptrott, who was already making Edith's life a misery with his demands for what he considered his share of the money.

'I didn't know what was happening then, but I was already feeling I had got myself into a frightening situation and I couldn't see my way out of it. I went home, back to Mathilde, leaving Isabelle to take up the position at Maxstead. She promised to keep me informed, but when she didn't write, I wrote to her at an address she had given me in Folbury. No replies came and that worried me, so I came back three days ago and went straight there, to Melia Street, to see what was happening. And that was when I heard the terrible news. I couldn't go back to Mathilde again until I knew the truth of how and why Isabelle had died. Liptrott said he would help me, and meanwhile I could stay there. And then he disappeared. I was there on my own until you found me.'

SIXTEEN

Reardon's motorbike stuttered to a stop behind the school. He parked, dismounted and removed his goggles, divested himself of his leathers, his heavy coat and helmet and made his way towards the school door and Miss Hillyard's study, taking his time. He'd become familiar with school routines and knew that this was the time, after breakfast and before lessons began, when the bell rang for the girls to assemble in the school hall for morning prayers, hymns and the day's notices, and he was surprised to see they were still hanging around in disorganized groups outside. They seemed cheerfully normal and looked happy enough, however, and made the disagreeable effect Maxstead was increasingly having on him seem ridiculous, as did the unwelcome, recurring thought that he was beginning not to like the idea of Ellen working here very much. Wasn't it something of a hothouse, a closed community of possibly neurotic women, with secrets and passions under the surface, resentments, jealousies, that couldn't be particularly healthy? He tried to laugh it off now. He was the one who was being neurotic. Ellen was showing more enthusiasm for her day's work than she'd shown towards anything for a very long time.

Inside, he passed the hall which had been created by knocking together two of the large reception rooms of the old house, and saw the double doors were open wide, and the hall empty. He wondered what had happened to Assembly.

Miss Hillyard didn't respond to his knock. The door was ajar and her study empty. Curiouser and curiouser. He left the building and went outside again. The morning was still fresh, before the sun gained strength for what promised to be yet another hot day. This weather couldn't last. He was passing the music room, near the tennis courts, when he became aware of some sort of noisy commotion coming from the direction of the lake and the woods behind it. The hairs on the back of his neck stood up. He'd come to know by now that this sort of to-do at Maxstead was all too likely to signal disaster. He sprinted across.

This time the fuss was centred on the lake, where a knot of hysterical women – seeming at first to be made up of every teacher in the school, including his wife, whose day it was here – milled around, but the crowd parted like the waters of the Red Sea to let him through to where Matron and Miss Hillyard were kneeling by the body.

He was forcibly reminded of another young female he had seen fished from a lake several years ago. Except that this one, contrary to first impressions, wasn't dead. Jocasta Keith was still of this world. Miss Cash was there too, also very much alive, also fully clothed and equally soaked to the skin.

The rest of the staff were flapping around her, clucking like a group of mother hens. She had, it appeared, arrived for her daily swim just in time to save Miss Keith from drowning. He let them carry on with their fussing, keeping his ears open, and after a while managed to get some idea of what had happened. Daphne Cash, it seemed, had seen what was happening when she arrived at the lake and – with commendable good sense – had immediately used her games whistle before plunging into the water. It had been heard by one of the daily maids using the short cut through the woods from the village to get to her work here, and she had lost no time in running for assistance. Miss Draper had been the first to arrive on the scene, and it was she who had then hurried back to the school to ring for an ambulance.

'You all right, love?' Reardon found time to ask Ellen.

'Yes, of course; it's Miss Draper I'm worried about.'

Together, they walked across to where she was sitting, a little apart from the knot of people at the water's edge. She had returned to the scene at the lake once more after making her telephone call, and was now uncomfortably perched on one of the large mossy rocks, some way from the pool, her breathing laboured, her head down. She looked up as they approached. She looked dreadful. 'Shouldn't have run like that . . . had my pill though . . . my stupid ticker, you know . . . be all right soon.'

Reardon and Ellen exchanged glances. What had she been thinking of, rushing around when she had a bad heart? It was only by good luck she hadn't added to the emergency. But even as they stood there, it seemed that her medication was indeed working: her lips were looking less bluish; her colour was coming back to normal.

He left Ellen to stay and keep an eye on her and went back to the others. Suddenly, amid all the talk of stretchers and ambulances and who was to fetch the canvas wheelchair that was kept in the sick bay for emergencies, Miss Keith was sitting up, protesting that she could walk, thank you very much, and what was all the fuss about? She wasn't going into any hospital.

'Of course you are, goodness knows what you've swallowed,' Matron retorted, in a dark reference to the possible proximity of the lake to soakaways for septic tanks, a disagreeable necessity of life in country villages far from town amenities, and which Maxstead Court was sure to have.

'Oh, rats to that!' came from Miss Cash. 'The water's quite safe.'

Matron bridled, while Jocasta repeated through chattering teeth, 'I didn't swallow any water and I don't need an ambulance. I'm not about to die.' It didn't appear that she was and, though she was shaking and her voice croaked, it seemed to be more from shock than anything, and it didn't prevent her from glaring at Miss Cash and managing to say once again, '*I just fell in*. I can swim and I wasn't in any danger at all.'

'That's as maybe, but it's hospital for you all the same, Miss Keith,' Matron replied implacably. She ignored the games mistress, stung by her previous remark. If Miss Cash wanted to take the daily risk of swimming there, that was her funeral – and probably would be, her look said.

Miss Hillyard intervened. 'The ambulance people will decide what's necessary when they arrive with the doctor. They should be here soon.'

Jocasta Keith said crossly, 'What a ridiculous fuss over a fall!'

Fallen, had she? Then why was she shoeless, and what was that pair of fashionable, high-heeled, lizard-skin shoes, totally unsuitable for walking in the woods, doing neatly placed together at the side of the pool?

She tried to struggle to her feet, but halfway there she swayed, and no one was in time to catch her before she fell forward in a faint, which seemed to settle any arguments about hospital, no matter that she came round almost immediately.

In the end, they managed to get the two women over to the school. Miss Keith was installed in the wheelchair and this time made no protest, while Daphne Cash stalked across on her own two feet, plimsolls squelching. Presently the ambulance arrived and Reardon was pleased to see the doctor accompanying it was Kay Dysart, who told him she had been doing emergency duties at the cottage hospital when it was called out. After a brief examination, Miss Keith was summarily lifted into the ambulance on her instructions. 'She needs to be checked over, no arguments,' she said firmly.

'What about Miss Cash?' Reardon asked.

'She refuses to go, and I dare say it'll take more than that to hurt her, especially as she swims there every day. It's not contaminated water I'm afraid of. Miss Keith fainted because she probably bumped her head when she went in. She has a sizeable bump and she ought to be looked over.' She appeared to be about to say more, but then changed her mind and hurried into the ambulance after her patient.

Matron had decided to ignore the games mistress's previous declaration that she was all right, and between them she and Miss Hillyard almost frogmarched her into the sick bay. A few minutes later, Reardon followed.

Matron's province comprised a few rooms with three single beds in each, and others where girls could be isolated if any infectious disease was suspected, plus a bigger room, where she had cupboards in which she kept first-aid kits and medicines. It also held a doctor's couch, a stand-on weighing machine, and a strong smell of disinfectant.

Here Reardon found Daphne Cash. He had grown accustomed to seeing her bouncing around the place in that well-filled gymslip, but now, divested of her wet clothes and bundled into warm blankets, she presented a very different picture.

She allegedly swam in the little lake every day, and he would have expected her to have towelled herself off briskly by now and be regarding her fully clothed swim and the rescue of her colleague as all in a day's work. But here she was, huddled in a basket chair, with a hot-water bottle at her feet. Inside the blankets, the pneumatic Miss Cash looked oddly deflated, with no apologies for the word. She was drying off, but she was pale, and she had her hands clasped around a cup of steaming tea which had evidently replaced the cold one standing untouched on the table beside her, but she wasn't drinking from that, either.

'Drink your tea, dear,' Matron urged. 'I've put plenty of sugar in it.'

'I don't take sugar.'

'A hot drink will help you feel warmer, all the same. Drink up, there's a good girl.'

'I'm not cold.'

'Shocked, though,' said Matron unarguably as she left them. Miss Cash took a sip of the tea.

Reardon said, 'It's been a nasty experience, but if you can bring yourself to tell me what happened.'

'I didn't see her at first. I went towards the boathouse to change and I saw her. I don't know what made me look.'

'So you jumped straight in.'

'You don't stop to change into your swimsuit before you try to save someone!' she retorted, some of her pep coming back. 'Jocasta Keith was fully dressed and, in spite of what she says, she must have been in danger.' Her indignation was evident, but he was amazed to see she didn't seem far off tears. She'd been badly shaken by the episode, more than he would have expected of her. Shaken, or maybe humiliated at having been thought to have made such a mistake.

'You're a brave woman, Miss Cash.' And he meant it. Not many women would have done what she'd done. He might even forgive her the gymslip.

'There was someone else there before me,' she said suddenly. 'I didn't see anyone but I heard someone crashing through the woods, running away. I don't think she fell in at all, I think she was – well, I think she was pushed.'

'*Pushed?* Are you sure about that, Miss Cash?'

'I'm not given to much imagination, Inspector,' she said tartly, as if that were an asset, daring him to contradict. 'I know what I heard. It was someone running away.'

She was not at her best, but the dip hadn't deprived her of her wits. 'I believe you,' he said. 'You've no idea who it might have been?'

'I didn't see, I simply heard.' She was coming back to herself by the minute. She even took several gulps of her tea, now cool enough to drink, pulling a face at its sweetness.

'It's an extraordinary claim to make, all the same. Why should anyone want to push Miss Keith into the water?'

She gave him a look. 'Why should anyone want to do any of the things that have been happening at Maxstead?'

He'd been right, she was sharper than she was given credit for. She was adamant about Jocasta Keith having been pushed into the water, and if she was correct about that, it was the third attack here, and might have been the second murder had it not been for her. It was getting harder to escape the fact that the incidents weren't connected. Miss Cash seemed like a reliable witness, no shilly-shallying, firm about what she saw. He had underrated her, and who else? And then the thought intruded that she, as well as some of the others, might have secrets to hide. There was only her word for it that she'd heard someone running away. There could have been just two people at the lake – Jocasta Keith, and herself. He soon rejected the idea. If there had been only the two of them, why had she saved her? Unless it had been, like Josie's attack, a warning? Then he thought about those shoes.

'What do you know about Miss Keith?'

She finished off her tea and put the cup and saucer down on the table beside her. 'Nothing, except that she doesn't mix much.' After a minute, she added, 'And she does splash her money about a bit. She goes up to London sometimes, just to get her hair cut.'

That was quite a dig. The standard of hairdressing among the women here was not high, probably catered for by Folbury's hairdressers. Miss Cash's own short, curly locks were drying quickly after her immersion and springing natur- ally back into place, clearly needing nothing in the way of expert styling. 'All the same,' she went on, endeavouring to be honest, 'I can't see her doing anything that justified someone trying to drown her. And I know she says she can swim, but she wasn't making a very good show of it when I turned up.'

Kay Dysart was just leaving the cottage hospital when Reardon arrived to see Jocasta Keith. They met on the steps. 'How is she?'

'Nothing to worry about, but they're keeping her in for obser-vation.' She hesitated. 'I'd like a word with you before I leave, Inspector.' She turned back into the hospital, expecting him to follow, and led the way into a small room off the reception area, with chairs pushed against the notice-plastered walls, eight of them surrounding a table piled with tired-looking magazines. She waved him to a seat and took one herself.

It was part of Dysart's persona, as well as a professional require-ment, not to waste time. She was known for speaking her mind. She sat down, pushed her short dark hair to one side and asked bluntly, 'What's going on out there, at Maxstead?' He didn't immediately reply. She knew about Isabelle Blanchard, of course, but not about Josie, he thought. It hadn't been deemed necessary to get a doctor to her, Matron's experience being enough. 'The last time I was called there,' she went on, 'it was to a murder, and now this. Another thing there's something fishy about.'

He thought again of the shoes. Fashionable, lizard-skin, neatly put together. He thought of 'falling' into the water when you couldn't swim.

'You're saying you think it was a suicide attempt?' He wouldn't have put Miss Keith down as a candidate for that, but weren't artists reputedly that way inclined? Beethoven was supposed to have been mad as well as alcoholic. Van Gogh had cut off his own ear and you couldn't get much madder than that. 'Is that what you think, Doctor?'

'I could speculate, but I'll leave that to you.'

'Speculate away, please.'

Still she hesitated, and he could understand why. She knew as well as he did that suicide was still a criminal offence, regarded by the church as a mortal sin and by the law as 'self-murder'. Those who succeeded were indeed beyond the law, but those who did not faced prosecution, if the act was reported. It was an outdated law which took no account of compassion and increasingly outraged public opinion, including those like himself and, he suspected, Kay Dysart, who necessarily came into contact with those in despair, who could see no way out other than by ending their life.

'Suicide? No,' she said at last, 'you can put that out of your mind.'

'That sounds pretty uncompromising.'

'It is,' she said flatly. 'If she said she fell in, there's no reason to disbelieve her.'

He was willing to go along with it, regardless of those shoes she had removed, especially when he remembered Daphne Cash's firm assertion that someone else had been there before she had arrived. He smiled at Dysart. 'We won't pursue that idea any further then, Doctor. Agreed?'

'That's right.' She smiled back and stood up. 'We won't.'

She had been given a bed in a small ward with five other women in various stages of recovery, all of them agog with curiosity about the new arrival and her visitor. Jocasta Keith wasn't in bed, however, but sitting on a chair by the side of it, looking woebegone, a total stranger to the Jocasta he had previously met. Hair in rats' tails, face free of make-up, feet in large, borrowed slippers, and wrapped in a dressing gown miles too big for her, taken from the hospital's store of garments kept for emergencies and drawn up tight under her chin. He hoped it hadn't occurred to her that it might once have belonged to someone who'd gone where they didn't need dressing gowns any more. And, for her own sake, he hoped it would soon occur to someone from the school to bring her what she needed.

He looked around the ward, at the other women, flicking magazines or dipping into convalescent-gift chocolate boxes, their eyes on stalks and their ears no doubt attuned. 'I can't talk to Miss Keith here,' he said to the nurse who had accompanied him. 'We need to be private.'

She looked doubtful. 'I must ask Sister.' She came back within a minute and told him they would have to sit in the corridor. 'It's that or the sluice,' she added with a cheerful grin. 'We're pretty full up at the moment.'

This was a small cottage hospital with not many beds, used

mainly for emergencies and to avoid journeys, for both patients and their families, to bigger hospitals in Birmingham. It was always busy. But just now the corridor outside the ward – wide, warm, and with chairs for those waiting before visiting time – was empty, apart from the odd nurse or ward orderly passing through. 'It'll do,' Reardon said.

Miss Keith hadn't so far said a word. She didn't in fact look at all pleased to see her visitor. Finally, when they were seated outside the ward, she decided to speak. 'Get me out of here, for pity's sake. There's nothing wrong with me, I'm perfectly all right and I'm taking up a bed they can ill afford.'

She looked far from all right and – without make-up – defenceless, her face oddly vulnerable.

'I don't think they'll let you go. I've just seen Dr Dysart and she tells me they need to do some tests for that bump on your head.' He paused, judging how she might respond to what he had to say next.

'It's gone down already, and no harm done. I don't know what all the fuss is about. I could quite easily have got myself out of the water.'

'Miss Cash thinks you can't swim.'

'Then Miss Cash thinks wrong.'

He said gently, 'Your shoes were on the bank.'

A heavily built nurse approached, carrying a metal dish covered with a cloth. The polished boards moved like a sprung dance floor as she passed by, giving them a curious glance. Jocasta waited until she'd disappeared. She said deliberately, 'You think I tried to kill myself? Well, you're half right. I was feeling bad, and at that moment there didn't seem anything else for it. I'd decided I couldn't live with myself any longer, but . . .' Her dark eyes had become pools of misery and she laughed bitterly. 'I suppose I'll never know whether I would actually have had the guts to do it, because all I can say is, one minute I was on the bank and the next I was in the water.'

This wasn't the time to press her as to why she'd had cause to feel so bleak. 'Someone else was there with you,' he said. 'Someone who pushed you in.' She didn't answer. 'You do know that's true, don't you?'

'Maybe they did. Or maybe I did fall in.'

The sludgy brown and green check of the dressing gown didn't help a complexion that was drained of all colour.

'Do you have any idea who it might have been?'

'I don't know that anyone did,' she insisted, tracing the wood-block pattern of the floor with a flapping slipper.

This wasn't getting them very far. 'I have to ask you this, Miss Keith. I appreciate there may be things too painful for you to talk about, but—'

The unadorned face she raised said he'd spoken the truth. Before he could go on, however, she interrupted. 'Look, I know why you're here, and I'm not being obstructive. I want to help. I'm going to tell you everything, because it's gone too far. But you'll have to let me tell it in my own way.'

'Fair enough.'

Silence followed. 'I don't know where to start.'

At the beginning was never a useful answer. Who knew where anything really started? Go along that route and you could end up at the dawn of time. 'You might begin with how you came to be working at Maxstead.'

After a moment she said, 'Yes, I suppose that was partly where it started. But it was that child, Josie, being left all night in the dark, alone. That was what finished it as far as I was concerned.'

It was time for him to sit back and let her take her time. And, gradually, some of the tension dropped away from her as she tried to focus on what she had to say. She began by telling him how she had been recruited to work at Maxstead by a man from her home town, whom she had met in London.

'Your home town being Stoke-on-Trent,' he hazarded.

'Burslem,' she said. 'But it's all the same.'

'And the man was Liptrott, Newman Liptrott? Was he from there as well?'

'Nol,' she corrected, accepting without surprise that he knew who she was talking about. 'Everyone calls him that. Ever since we were at school together. Because of his middle name, Oliver.'

Once started, she was gradually able to speak almost calmly about how she'd met Liptrott by chance in the street, in London, and how she'd agreed to his suggestions. Twisting her hands tightly, she said, 'It seems incredible to me now that I ever went along with what he asked, but I didn't feel I'd any choice, you know? I felt trapped; I was down to my last few shillings, hadn't eaten properly for days, and I wasn't getting anywhere with my work. I knew by then that I'd made a mistake, thinking everything would be different if I was in London, mixing with like-minded people who wanted to do something with their lives other than just . . . but I never met any.' She stopped and swallowed, dry-mouthed, as if it was too painful to speak.

'Wait,' he said. 'I'll be back.'

He went in search of a nurse and found the same cheerful woman who had taken him up to the ward. She gave him a glass of water and made him promise not to keep the patient talking too long. 'She's had a shock. Talking too much won't help her.'

He thought, however, when he returned with the water, that she was already looking better, and probably feeling it, too, having begun to release so much that had been bottled up inside her.

She sipped the water gratefully and immediately continued from where she'd left off. 'He told me everything, you know. He wanted someone to talk to and it all came out as if a dam had burst, or something. He wanted someone to tell his grievances to, I suppose, and I was a captive audience, after all. Well, the gist of it was he wanted me to apply for the job of art teacher at Maxstead. Miss Hillyard was still advertising for staff, he said, and I should apply for the position, on the off chance. I did, and I got the job. And no,' she added, anticipating his scepticism, 'it wasn't such an off chance as you might think. No one was exactly clamouring for a job there – Maxstead's a new venture that still might not succeed, the way things are at the moment. Besides, it's cut off, out of the way, no shops, picture houses or anything, so candidates aren't queueing up. I was far from keen myself, but I needed the money; not only the salary, but what Nol was supposed to be paying me. I didn't have any qualifications, as I've told you, but Miss Hillyard didn't seem to mind and I've done my best. I don't think I've been a bad teacher.'

'No,' he agreed, thinking of that drawing he had seen, and the way she'd encouraged Antonia, the girl who'd drawn it. He thought he could better understand her passionate support of the girl now. 'You say Liptrott offered to pay you, over and above your salary?'

'Offer is all it was, it seems,' she came back sharply. 'I've yet to see any of it.' Then she gave a 'what-does-that-matter-now?' shrug. 'I had to sing for my supper, after all, and it didn't seem wrong, you know, he only wanted . . .' All at once her courage evaporated. Her voice broke and she couldn't go on.

'He wanted you to find out what you could about Edith Hillyard.'

'Spying, for want of a better word,' she came back wryly. 'How did you guess?'

Her hand was shaking and, gently, he took the empty glass from her. 'Adding two and two is safer than guesswork. We've reached a point where it's become fairly obvious that someone is wanting to discredit Miss Hillyard and, by implication, the school.' Not until he said it did he realize how far he'd been gravitating towards the inevitable conclusion that had been staring him in the face all along – that someone might have it in for Miss Hillyard, or the school. If they were trying to ruin her, they seemed to be going the right way about it. Even so, such extreme lengths took some crediting. Yet, for the first time in this enquiry he was getting a buzz that signalled things might be coming together, ready to fall into place. He had found it increasingly difficult to accept that the two previous occurrences – Josie's imprisonment and the murder of Isabelle Blanchard – could have been coincidental. Now, with what had just happened to Jocasta Keith herself, he was certain they were not. They had been aimed specifically.

'All this was because Liptrott wanted to scupper the enterprise?'

Her lips twisted. 'Hardly that. Not at all, in fact. That would have defeated his object.'

He folded his arms and leant back. 'I'm sorry, I interrupted you. You said you wanted to tell me everything about him. Please go on.'

After a minute, she did. 'Well, what it was, you see, Miss Hillyard had come into some money. A fortune, Nol said it was, and it had really got him on the raw, because it had actually

come from his own stepfather and he was convinced *he* was
the one who was entitled to it. His mother had died and the old
man hadn't left him anything at all in his will, not a penny. It
shouldn't have been any surprise to him, because they'd never
seen eye to eye, and in fact he'd hated his stepfather for what
he called his meanness to him; but it was a shock, and it's been
eating him up ever since. He's been determined to get his hands
on that money, by hook or by crook. I know he'd tried pleading,
appealing to Edith Hillyard's fairness, threatening her even.'

Which would have got him nowhere, Reardon thought, if it
had ended in the encounter Ellen had witnessed.

'Who was he, the person who left the money to Miss
Hillyard?'

'Oh, he didn't leave it to her directly. It was left to her mother,
and Edith inherited it when she died. His name was Thomas
Pryde. Ever heard of Prydeware? Tea sets, dinner sets, cups and
saucers?'

Yes, he had heard of it. Who hadn't? Prydeware was nearly
as well known as Wedgwood, if not as exclusive. He saw the
name stamped underneath the dinner plates every time he helped
with the washing up. He had no trouble in believing in the
fortune it had made for the manufacturers. 'You told me you
once worked at painting ceramics, Miss Keith. Was it this
Thomas Pryde you worked for?'

'Yes, though not on the Prydeware range. I was a hand pain-
tress, a ceramic artist and designer, but I never came into contact
with Thomas Pryde, I was only one of his workpeople. Just as
well I didn't, perhaps; he's caused plenty of trouble, leaving all
that money. Even though I believe Miss Hillyard did actually
offer Nol something from the legacy, he was furious, said so little
was an insult and he'd take her to court, then she'd have to give
him more. He's convinced he's quite entitled to at least half.
Well, of course, just supposing she'd wanted to, she couldn't let
him have much, could she? It's all invested in the school. Even
he had to admit that was true, and in the end he came back with
the idea that she'd have to make him a partner. She just laughed
and told him to go away and leave her alone . . . well, wouldn't
you? Wouldn't anyone? It was ridiculous, but if she'd known
Nol, she'd soon have realized what a big mistake that was. He's

quick-witted enough, but he's basically stupid, and he doesn't like being crossed. He can be vicious. I think that was when things became nasty, when he started to get this other idea. He'd nothing to lose, so he was determined to find something he could use against her, and make it public. And he could, you know. He could get it into one of the papers he writes for.'

'He's a journalist?'

'Of sorts. A freelance. He gets bits and pieces in whatever papers he can. I don't think he makes much of a living.'

Miss Ainsworth hadn't been all that much mistaken in believing him to be a writer, then, though freelance journalism wasn't likely to have been what she'd been thinking of when she'd heard him hammering away at his typewriter.

'But I never did find anything about her that I could pass on, you know,' Jocasta went on miserably. 'I must confess I didn't try all that hard, and I didn't know exactly what he wanted. Listen to the gossip, he'd said, but they don't gossip, the teachers there, even if they had found me easy to talk to, which they don't.'

'You haven't told me yet where Isabelle Blanchard came into this. Did Liptrott recruit her, as well?'

'Isabelle? Yes, I suppose he did,' she said, and went very quiet. He waited. 'But she was a very different proposition. I don't believe she was working for Liptrott, though he thought she was. She used to say he was *imbécile*. She had her own agenda, isn't that what they say? They used to argue a lot. That's why I became frightened when she died. I should have left, there and then. Or rather, I should never have gone there.' She looked at him as a thought came to her. 'You think Nol killed her, don't you?'

'I can't say that.' But if what she had been saying about the man was right, he was both resentful and dangerous. And that was quite a combination.

She shook her head. 'He wouldn't. He's a nasty customer, and he didn't like her, but he's sharp enough not to risk killing her.'

'What about Josie Pemberton? Could he have done that to her?'

'The same thing applies.'

'Did you know he was living in Folbury?'

'Yes, but I don't know where.' She frowned. 'I think Isabelle must have gone to stay with him there. After she left Maxstead, I mean.' She wasn't saying anything about Isabelle's pregnancy, or her relationship with Deegan. She hadn't known, he thought.

'A place called Melia Street, but he isn't there now. He's done a disappearing act.'

She thought for a minute or two. 'Do you know, I think I can tell you where he might be – or possibly, I wouldn't bank on it. There's a hotel where he used to stay before he came to Folbury. He promised me money when his ship came in, but I doubt I shall see any now,' she said bitterly, not having lost sight of her main objective in putting herself in Liptrott's clutches. She gave him the hotel name, then stood up and turned towards the ward entrance.

'You've been very helpful, Miss Keith. Thank you for what you've told me.'

'Was it what's called "making a statement"?'

He smiled. 'Not officially, though we may need that later.' He held out his hand.

'You think I've been very naïve, don't you?'

He thought other adjectives might apply, but that too. He said, 'What I do think is, you've had a rotten experience and you should go back into that bed and try to get some rest.'

'Well,' Jocasta said. 'Thanks, anyway. Talking to you has made me feel better.'

It wasn't the usual reaction from witnesses he'd questioned.

The evening had brought no cooling breeze and it was really too hot for a walk. Had it not been for Tolly needing to be exercised, scampering ahead regardless of the heat, exploring, wriggling his whole body under hedges to see what he could find, happily scuffing about in the dust left in dried-up puddles, they wouldn't have bothered.

Ellen laughed as she watched him enjoying himself, as she and Reardon followed on behind him, arms linked, fingers interlaced. Comfortable, easy.

The thoughts Reardon had had earlier about her employment at Maxstead suddenly seemed groundless. Though not the sort of woman to swear she loved all children regardless, Ellen liked most of them, and loved certain others – one of them, her little goddaughter, Ellie, with passion. After that last miscarriage, they had both accepted the sadness that they never would have any themselves. They had mourned and adjusted, or perhaps she was still in the process. Meanwhile, she found satisfaction in teaching, and was certainly happy to be working with the girls at Maxstead.

'Tell me about Jocasta,' she said, as they skirted the perimeter of the castle ruins and turned back up the lane that led homewards.

'It'll wait until we've had supper.'

'What's wrong with now? It's nice out here.'

Because it was falling down, the wall along the edges of the lane was low enough to offer a seat, or at least a perch, and a lovely view across the town. If they climbed over the wall, which they mostly did, they would be in their own garden. It was long overdue for repair and they would miss the short cut if it was ever mended.

Ellen found a flat stone, still warmed by the day's sun, that wasn't too uncomfortable to sit on, and he found another. Through the wall, contributing to its decay, a seedling ash had pushed and grown into a majestic tree. It wasn't much cooler sitting underneath it, but it offered shade against the setting sun, which was making spectacular but blinding efforts. Later, when it had gone down and it became dark, you'd be able to see the panorama of streetlights and a distant, rosy glow that was the night sky of Birmingham.

She paid grave attention as he gave her the gist of his conversations with Daphne Cash and Jocasta.

'How's Miss Draper?' he asked her when he'd finished.

'Back on form after getting her feet up for a while. I took her back to her room and stayed with her for about half an hour.'

'Should she be working at all in that state of health?'

She laughed. 'I wouldn't like to suggest it to her. She swears it was nothing, only her dickey heart, which she's quite used to, and she's absolutely devoted to the school, and to Miss Hillyard – it's her life.' She picked up a fallen leaf and began shredding it. After a moment she said, 'Did you know Catherine Leyland is her niece?'

'Miss Hillyard's?'

'No, Eve Draper's. Her mother was Eve's sister.'

He was surprised, though not as much as he would have been had he not witnessed that little scene when Josie went missing. He told her about it. 'Miss Draper saw that I'd seen and she explained that Josie was one of Catherine's friends, that was why she'd been so upset.'

'Yes, they are chums.' She fell silent. 'I don't think it's generally known they're related, Eve and Catherine, I mean. In fact, I think it just slipped out. She keeps some brandy in her room for when she's "a bit down" as she put it, though I'm not sure she should. She drank some and it made her very flushed and loosened her tongue. Afterwards, she looked a bit sorry she'd mentioned it.'

'I can see why. Wouldn't do to let it be known that the girl had only managed to be there because of her connections. Isn't that called nepotism?'

'Oh ye of little faith! If you're doubting that's how Catherine got to Maxstead, you're wrong. She would have sailed through the exams and won the scholarship anyway. Ask any of the staff. That girl's a joy to teach. She's brilliant at most things, French included, and she was a great favourite of Mam'selle. It seems to have been mutual; in fact Catherine seemed to have developed a bit of a schoolgirl crush.' She fell silent again, watching Tolly, nosing about in the hedge, looking for something interesting.

'Go on.'

'Eve has a photo of herself and Catherine on her mantelpiece. Catherine was wearing a little brooch, exactly like that one you told me about. I remarked how pretty it was and she said she'd given it to Catherine for her birthday, but she'd lost it. She didn't say so, but she looked rather hurt that she hadn't taken more care of it.' The leaves had shredded to a pulp and she let them fall to the ground, rubbed her fingers together. 'Do you think Catherine could have given it to Mam'selle?'

'I suppose so, if she was one of her favourites, though it wouldn't seem very tactful. Brilliant, you say? The girl's beginning to sound like a paragon of virtue. Prime candidate for the other girls not to like her?'

'No, she seems popular enough, I suppose. Although, to tell you the truth, from what I've seen of her, I do find her rather odd. Oh, I don't know. She seems a bit – well, too old for her years, I suppose. Maybe too determined to get what she wants. It must be a difficult situation, for both of them, Eve as well as her.'

Tolly began a volley of barks, then came trotting briskly towards them, triumphantly bearing a trophy. 'What's that you've got? Ugh, it's a dead bird, you disgusting animal! Drop it, drop it. *Now!*'

After a chaotic few minutes, with order somewhat restored, they climbed the wall and went to the house to complete cleaning-up operations.

SEVENTEEN

Gilmour professed himself chuffed at what Reardon had learnt from Jocasta Keith. 'Looks like Liptrott's our man, then.'

He'd had Deegan in his sights as chief suspect almost from the word 'go', and didn't really want to let him off the hook. Policemen weren't supposed to have likes or dislikes, at least not to let them interfere with their judgement, but they were only human. But, disliking the man as he did (and for no justifiable reason, if he was honest, other than he just didn't), he had to admit Liptrott was probably a better bet at this stage. 'Mind you,' he added doubtfully, 'if he is, he chose a feeble way of going about getting what he wanted, didn't he? What did he hope to get from just snooping around? Folks don't leave their private lives open to anyone who wants to do a bit of random nosey-parkering. Not people like Miss Hillyard, anyway.'

'Jocasta as good as said she thought he was a fool and, for what it's worth, even Phoebe Catherall did, and she doesn't always have all her chairs at home herself, seems to me. But think about what he was doing it for. Money. And since when has there been a stronger motive to override common sense?'

Reardon was saying this as much to convince himself as Gilmour. Liptrott as their killer was by no means in the bag. Causing trouble for Edith Hillyard as a means of getting hold of her money was one thing, but murder was another. Not to mention the difficulties of him staging a murder, plus everything else, at Maxstead. Everything about the recent events implied a knowledge of the school, its surroundings, and what went on there, and that bothered him about Liptrott. 'Would he have the know-how for all that, Joe?' He shook his head. '*Jubous*, as me old Grandpa used to say. Very jubous.'

'As far as Isabelle Blanchard's concerned, he could have either followed her taxi to the school that night, or was waiting for her, having got her here under some pretext.'

'Leaving aside why he should choose *there* of all places for a meeting . . . And what about Josie?' That child's ordeal was never far from Reardon's mind, and he wasn't yet ready to abandon the gut feeling that it was connected to everything else that had been going on.

'All right, I'll admit you have me there.'

'And trying to kill Jocasta Keith? Think about it. Liptrott couldn't have *known* she would have been there by the lake so, if he did push her in, it must have been done on impulse. But why would he have been there at all? First thing of a morning? What justification could he have had for hanging around the school grounds at that hour? Why should he have wanted to kill her, anyway, as well as Isabelle?'

'Both women knew what he was up to, didn't they? Maybe he thought Miss Keith was about to split on him. Instead she decides to kill herself, so he could have saved himself the bother.'

Reardon shook his head. 'She was on the brink of doing so – literally – but she's half admitted she was actually pushed in.' He fell silent.

'What's up?' Gilmour asked after a moment.

Reardon didn't know, himself. A deeply disturbing possibility had begun worming its way into his mind since yesterday, an embryo idea too unformed as yet to be grasped, but hovering there, waiting. Something Jocasta, or even Ellen, had said, triggering a notion that had been lodged in his subconscious all along? 'I don't know, Joe. But never mind. Let's get this show on the road before the man scarpers again.'

Which was where they were now, on the road to Birmingham, where they hoped to find Liptrott at the city centre hotel Jocasta had named. And, contrary to what they'd half expected, they did indeed find he was registered there. Satisfaction diminished when they heard he had checked out.

'But he asked to leave his luggage for a while, so he'll be back to pick it up,' the young woman receptionist told them brightly. 'No more than half an hour, he said.'

'We'll wait,' Gilmour told her.

'Take a seat.' She waved to a few chairs and tables in a small bay to one side. 'Can I get you anything while you wait? Coffee, tea?'

Reardon declined with thanks. He didn't want to be caught taking tea and biscuits when Liptrott arrived.

The hotel was used mainly by visiting businessmen and, since it was mid-morning, few people passed through the foyer. Gilmour riffled through yesterday's *Evening Mail*, left on the table, and Reardon occupied himself with trying, and failing, to grasp the thought that was still eluding him.

Twenty minutes later, their quarry arrived, with no prizes for guessing who he was as soon as he stepped through the swing doors. A tall man, his hair glossy with Brylcreem, combed back in regular waves, a toothy smile. Double-breasted, navy and chalk-stripe suit and white shirt. Brown shoes that shone like polished conkers. He was too good looking; he walked with a swagger and had a smirk that said anyone other than Newman Liptrott, God's gift to women, was of little account. He was everything any policeman worthy of his salt would detest in a man, and Reardon loathed him on sight.

Unaware they were waiting for him, Liptrott asked for his luggage, making a joke that caused the receptionist to laugh. Then he swung round, still smiling, as she added something and indicated where they were sitting.

'We'd like a word with you, Mr Liptrott.'

The practised smile faded ever so slightly. Reardon knew that both he and Gilmour had policeman written all over them, and that Liptrott saw it immediately, as people did. It was an uncomfortable fact of life which could be useful or not, depending on the occasion. The receptionist had probably picked it up, too, from the interested way she was looking at the three of them. But Liptrott recovered quickly and extended a manicured hand, small for a big man like him, white and soft, with half-moons and white nail tips. Could you imagine those hands resting on a woman's back, pushing her into a lake with a hard shove, or grabbing a young girl and leaving her shut up in a darkened room? Or tossing a woman out of a high doorway like so much rubbish? Well, none of these required any considerable strength, after all. No more than a combination of the victim being taken by surprise and the will to do it.

At any rate, he showed no more concern now than a shrug when Reardon showed his warrant card and told him they wanted a few words with him. Gilmour crossed to the reception desk and requested somewhere more private than this where they could speak to Mr Liptrott. This time, the woman didn't hesitate, no doubt anxious for them to remove themselves from the foyer. 'We don't really have anywhere else – but there is the dining room, if you like.' She indicated a pair of wide double doors.

'Thank you.'

Liptrott, making no protest, went with them. The tables had been set for lunch, but it was too early yet for customers. The room was large, dim, maroon-carpeted and maroon-walled. Doubtless the required warm ambience for evening dining, when the lamps in the alcoves glowed and candles were lit on the tables, but unwelcoming at half past ten in the morning. It faced north and didn't get the benefit of the bright morning sun, lights hadn't been switched on, and the only illumination came from outside. Reardon crossed the room and selected a table underneath one of the windows, and sat with his back to it, Gilmour by his side. As Liptrott seated himself opposite, Reardon told him they would like to speak to him about the murder of Isabelle Blanchard.

'Who?' The question tried to be convincing but his face had already given him away. He had known immediately why they'd sought him out. He summoned up a puzzled frown for a moment, 'Oh, I have it! The Frenchwoman who had the nasty accident at some boarding school or other? Well, sorry, I can't help you there. I didn't know her, only read about it in the papers.'

Reardon made no attempt to dispute the lie he'd been prepared for. 'That boarding school was Maxstead Court, where Miss Edith Hillyard is the principal.'

'Hillyard? The name's familiar.'

'It should be.' Gilmour, who would have been a bit of a natty dresser, given the chance and the money to do it with, couldn't look at the man sitting opposite without wincing. He took his eyes from Liptrott's blue and yellow polka-dot tie and tried not to let it influence him. 'Come on, Mr Liptrott, you know who she is,' he went on, fixing him with his eye. 'You went to see her at the school. You were seen arguing with her.'

After a while, he spread his hands. 'That headmistress? Oh, well, yes, I did visit her. I had some business with her, but I

didn't know her before then. I'm a journalist, you know, and I
went along to get a story from her. Such a courageous attempt,
to start up a new school, these days. I put it to her that the
article could stimulate some welcome publicity, but she wasn't
interested.' His face registered incredulity.

'Your stepfather was Mr Thomas Pryde,' Reardon said.

Something in the back of his eyes flickered. 'Yes, he was.
What of it?'

'He left the bulk of his estate to Miss Hillyard's mother.'

He didn't answer. Then he seemed to see further prevarica-
tion was useless, shrugged and abandoned pretence. 'Which is
how Miss Hillyard was able to put money into the school, after
her mother died. In fact, leaving the money to Mrs Hillyard
was how I came to know of their existence.'

'Your stepfather didn't leave anything to you. How did you
feel about that?'

Liptrott slid his hand into his pocket and pulled out a cheap
Bakelite cigarette case. 'Look, do you mind if I smoke?' The
flat case was a novelty. The cigarettes inside were on springs
and, when he slid back the narrow top strip just far enough,
one popped up. 'No, he didn't leave me anything, the old skinflint,' he said after he'd lit up. 'I suppose he didn't see me as
a suitable candidate. I didn't bend the knee at chapel, for one
thing, or have what he considered the right sort of job. I was
disappointed, of course, but it was his prerogative to leave his
money where he wanted.'

'You didn't get on.'

'We had our moments, I confess, but I was actually quite fond
of the old boy.' Which was a direct contradiction to what Jocasta
had said. 'And look, if that's all you have to say, I'd like to be
on my way. I have appointments, in Bradford, actually.' He shot
his cuff to consult the big silver watch on his wrist.

'I don't think so, Mr Liptrott. We need to keep in touch, so
you'd better stay around.'

'I've already checked out and I can't stay any longer; this
place isn't cheap, you know.'

'Then perhaps you can go back to Melia Street. I'm sure
Mr Shefford would be delighted to have you back as a tenant.
And he'd like his keys back.'

'Ah. Shefford.' He didn't let it show that he'd been taken aback, but clearly he was, and evidently had forgotten all about returning the keys.

The ashtray was in the middle of the table and, in reaching out towards it, he'd already scattered ash over the clean white tablecloth. He reached to stub out his present half-smoked cigarette, dropping more. Gilmour had been fidgeting with the knives and forks as they spoke. The waiters would not be pleased at having to strip everything down and start again.

Reardon studied the man as he took several drags on his cigarette, squinted narrowly through the smoke and finally stubbed it out half-smoked. He was not quite the fool he'd been presented as. Clever in his own way, a journalist used to twisting words – and he was wily.

'You admit to living in Melia Street, then?'

He shrugged. 'For a while. I rented the house when I was hoping for that article on Maxstead Court from Edith Hillyard. And then I decided maybe I could do a few others as well, after she refused. Folbury's an interesting town. A lot of history. Someone had once approached me with the idea of collaborating on a book about the place and I thought it might be worth pursuing. There's a demand for that sort of thing.'

'So how did you come to know Isabelle Blanchard?'

'I've already told you. I didn't know her.'

'And Phoebe Catherall?'

He pulled out his cigarette case and popped another one, giving himself time. The flame of the match quivered as he waved it out, leaving a smell of brimstone. 'That woman. That stupid creature!' Reardon blinked, surprised by the malice. He had not so far been over-impressed by Phoebe Catherall's basic intelligence himself, but that was coming a bit strong. 'She came looking for that other woman, Blanchard, as if I knew where she was. I'd read about the accident in the paper, but when I told her about it she wouldn't believe me, not at first, said it must be someone else. She made a bloody nuisance of herself, but she was upset. I felt sorry for her and, like a fool, I let her stay there. Where she still is, as far as I know.'

The papers – by which he must mean Folbury's local, the *Herald* – hadn't been slow to latch on to the fact that the police were regarding Isabelle Blanchard's death as suspicious, and Reardon said, 'You must know what happened to Isabelle Blanchard was no accident.'

His hand shook, very slightly, as he reached in a nervous habit for his fancy cigarette case. Realizing the last one was still only half smoked, he put the case back and began to push his chair back. 'Look here,' he said truculently, 'I don't know what you want with me. I had nothing to do with all that. And I really do have to go.'

'Don't go anywhere just yet. Here, or Melia Street, it doesn't matter, as long as we know where to find you.'

They left, still wondering if, for all his superficial, flashy appearance and cocky manner, there wasn't something deeper – nasty, even perhaps dangerous – about Liptrott.

EIGHTEEN

'**B**ut I told you everything in that letter I sent,' Phoebe Catherall protested.

'Not quite.' She might feel the explanations she had given in her letter were sufficient, but there were still many gaps that only she could fill; questions to which she alone had the answers. 'I'm afraid we need to ask you a few more things,' Reardon said. 'So I'm glad to see you're feeling better now, Miss Catherall.'

She had come into Mrs Longton's front parlour to meet them, neat and tidy, smiling, smelling of 4711, 'earphones' in place, wearing a hideous apple-green knitted silk jumper with a band of orange at the yoke, and a slightly baggy brown skirt that reached nearly to her ankles.

'Better? Oh, oh, yes, I'm feeling much better, thank you. Mrs Longton has been so kind, looking after me.'

Looking after me?

Well, it was fortunate that she felt grateful. It wouldn't be a penance for her to have to stay here longer. She had announced yesterday that she would be returning to stay with Mrs Cooper, and though Gilmour was certain her old landlady was sure to have welcomed her, Reardon had no wish for her to slip away just yet. She had been politely asked to stay where she was for the time being.

They had driven straight from the meeting with Liptrott, prepared for a difficult half-hour. Normally stoical when it came to dealing with witnesses, Reardon knew he was going to have to suppress the irritation Phoebe Catherall roused in him, but, after Liptrott, he was in no mood for evasions, and he prayed not to be faced with more floods of tears. There was no sign of them at the moment, though her eyes were suspiciously bright behind the huge glasses. 'We need some answers, Miss Catherall.'

She contrived to look hurt and innocently bewildered. 'What more is it you want to know?'

'We could start with the truth of why you agreed to let Isabelle
Blanchard step in and take a job that obviously meant a good
deal to you. Because I know, in spite of what you said to me,
that you were well aware of why she asked you to do it.'

There was a lengthy pause. The curtains, closed against the
possibility of the sun fading the furniture, had been drawn apart
a little while they talked. Dust motes danced in a narrow shaft
of sunlight, directed from the space between them, and came
to rest on Mrs Longton's best Axminster. Phoebe's foot traced
a cabbage rose. Her fingers twisted a silver ring around on her
fingers, allowing it to catch the light. It took some time before
she spoke. 'You have to understand that neither Isabelle nor I
would ever do anything to hurt Miss Hillyard. She was our
friend. We'd known her ever since the war. We only did what
we did to protect her.'

'From what?'

'Well, from that man, Liptrott.'

'What reason did you have for thinking he was any threat to
her?'

He could almost see the calculation, wondering how much
he knew, and how little she could get away with. She couldn't
answer. Or wouldn't, and went on twisting that ring around,
reminding him once more of a stubborn child.

Then, quite suddenly, without warning, she said, 'If I hadn't
agreed to let her take my place, she would have told Mathilde.'
She stopped abruptly, as if she'd gone too far.

'What? Told her what?' he prompted when she didn't go on.

'That I – that I burnt Father's manuscript.'

For a moment, he wondered what she was talking about.
Until he recalled the book about Napoleon that her father, Hugh
Catherall, had supposedly been writing. A lifetime's work that
he had never expected to finish, or be published.

A silence drifted between them all. He saw that Gilmour was
about to break it and signalled him not to with his eyes. At
length, Phoebe sighed and began again, and this time the words
came rapidly, as if she was afraid she might otherwise not say
them. 'Father was ill. Not as ill as he became later, but he'd
lost the will to summon up the energy to do any more work on
his book, so Isabelle, without telling him, took it on herself to

send the manuscript away, just as it was, to his academic friend, Henri Joubert. The two of them had been corresponding for years about the book and he knew almost as much about it as my father did. He read it and returned it, saying it was good – more than good; it was outstanding. It should be completed and sent to a publisher he knew, at once. He knew Father wasn't well enough to do the necessary work to finish it, of course, but he also knew how he had intended it should go, and he offered to complete it. Father was livid. He became so upset he refused to speak about it.'

She abandoned the ring and clutched her fingers together. 'It may sound ridiculous to anyone else, but I don't believe he'd ever *wanted* it to be published, and I understood that, though Isabelle couldn't. It was his creation, for his eyes alone; he'd given it everything and had no more to give. It was finished as far as he was concerned, over and done with. But she thought this was all nonsense, that he didn't really mean it. She was going to pack it off again to M. Joubert, regardless. So before she could, I burnt it. It meant nothing to me.' Her chin lifted, daring anyone to be shocked. 'Father knew what I'd done, but he told everyone he'd destroyed it himself. There were the most frightful scenes. Isabelle was furious. I expect she thought it would have made a lot of money. And Mathilde was not well herself, and looking after my father was a real strain. She thought he must be losing his mind, doing something like that. But Father knew if he told her the truth, if she ever knew that it was me and not him who'd destroyed his life's work, she would never have forgiven me.'

'So what happened?'

'Isabelle knew who'd really destroyed that wretched manuscript, of course. It was just possible that Father might have found the physical strength, at that time, to take it outside and burn it, but she knew he hadn't. She never said anything, she kept it to herself, to use when she could, as she always did. Which happened when I got the position with Miss Hillyard.'

'I see,' Reardon said, though he didn't. At least, he saw how it had been, but he still didn't understand why Isabelle had wanted that job so badly. Or even, perhaps, why it had been offered to Phoebe in the first place. But Phoebe still wasn't saying.

'Miss Hillyard agreed to all the subterfuge because you were blackmailing her,' he said.

'*Edith?*' The facile tears that flowed so easily were now caught in her throat, as if she had a tight, hard knot there, as she struggled against giving way. 'Don't use that word! I wouldn't have done that to Edith,' she said at last. 'Ever! She didn't see it as subterfuge – Isabelle must have left Edith with no choice but to accept the idea that I was ill. I expect she was very concerned and it worried me that she might have wondered, later perhaps. But by then it was too late.'

'You wouldn't have put pressure on her, but Mlle Blanchard would?'

She spread her hands in a Gallic shrug. 'That was the way Isabelle was. I told you before – you didn't know her. She enjoyed seeing people suffer. Watching, like she always did. She would have made a good spy.'

And there it was. The pent-up jealousy of years, boiling up and erupting on to the surface.

'Something happened, out there in France, that would have given her a hold over Miss Hillyard, if she could prove it?'

He thought she wasn't going to tell them, but then she did.

'How did Isabelle and Liptrott get into contact?' he asked when she'd finished.

'I told you: when she came over to see me, she disappeared on her own concerns. I found out later where she'd been. Edith had told me her mother had inherited money from a rich man called Pryde, in a town called Burslem, where she used to live. And, like a fool, I told Belle. She went there, found Pryde's factory was being taken over, talked to all sorts of people, and in the course of it heard about Liptrott. She sought him out and, when she discovered he was already trying to get money from Edith, she told him she had a weapon against Edith – though she hadn't, not really, not without proof. But she made him believe she could help him, if she could wheedle her way into Maxstead somehow. Which in fact she did, through me. Edith had no suspicions about my supposed illness and accepted the idea without question.'

* * *

Twenty years after that first letter from Thomas Pryde's solicitor,
which had changed my life, came another one, this time to say
he had died. For my own sake, as well as my mother's, I had
long since settled what we both regarded as my monetary
obligations to him, beginning as soon as I got my first teaching
job and was earning. There was correspondence between Mr
Pryde and myself over this. I wrote to him through his solicitor,
each time I sent a payment, because I wanted him to understand
there was no rejection of his kindness, but rather an acknow-
ledgement of it by the fact that I was now in a position to be
able to repay honourably. He had not taken offence, and always
replied with rather stiff notes, pleased but tinged with a shyness
which touched me. They had revealed him to be an upright man
who had lived a life of the utmost probity, and I was sorry I
had never known him.

But it was only after Mother died that the whole truth was
revealed, in a letter she left me. She was not an educated woman
by any means, and it was a long letter. I guessed she had written
it slowly, over time, correcting and rewriting until she was
satisfied. I was stunned at what it revealed. I had always felt
we had no secrets from each other, she and I, but now I learnt
of that other life she had lived before I was born. And even
more amazing were the details of Thomas Pryde's will.

Between the letter, and long talks with my Aunt Louisa when
she journeyed down for the funeral, I pieced the story together.
Thomas, it appeared, had once courted my mother, and a strange
courtship it must have been. He was a bachelor who was deemed
a prize catch by every marriageable woman in the district, yet
he had managed to escape the net until, at the age of forty-four,
he declared his intentions to my mother. He was not only Addie's
employer, but a man she had known as a stern and devout
chapel-goer, whom she saw every Sunday from her seat in the
choir, one who raised his hat to her and occasionally sat next
to her at Bible class. He began to court her and asked her to
be his wife, but she'd hesitated. Hesitated? Out of her mind,
everyone thought she was, said Aunt Louisa; anyone with a
grain of sense would have jumped at it. None of the other girls
at the factory, Louisa especially, could understand her, and
neither could Addie herself at times, she had once confessed to

her sister in a rare moment. She couldn't have been unaware of the secure future a man like him could provide, the freedom from day-to-day drudgery in the factory, and everything else that went with marriage to him, but as no one knew better than I, she was also a romantic, and Thomas Pryde, though he was such a good man, was not only twenty-five years older than she was, but also a quiet, teetotal, dyed-in-the-wool Methodist lay preacher, kind and shrewd but with little sense of humour.

A man of business, unaccustomed to taking no for an answer, however, he'd even offered to build and furnish a new house for her when they married, rather than take her home to the old one fifty yards from his factory, which had been in his family for generations. And he went so far as to take advice, putting his lifelong thriftiness aside and investing in some expensive jewellery which, if he had understood my mother, he would have known she would never accept. She was not avaricious and had no interest in brash new houses and furniture, and certainly not in the emeralds he bought, which she considered gaudy.

No wonder she had fallen in love with Jamie when he appeared on the scene.

It was years after she had married him, after I was born and they had moved to London, that Thomas himself had taken a wife, a woman called Jane Liptrott, a widow with an adolescent son. The marriage had not been happy: the widow was only interested in spending his money, and her spoilt son hadn't the wit to see that if he had been more receptive to Thomas's wishes, he might have followed him into the business and inherited it.

The widow had died early, and Thomas and her son could agree over nothing. He considered the boy a spendthrift, an idler and a bit of a gambler. And, worse than any of that, a non-believer. And that was why he had not left him a penny in his will. A large amount of what he had amassed was to be distributed between various charities and his church. And the rest, which was still a staggering amount, had been left to my mother.

No one could have been more astounded than she was. Except perhaps Thomas's solicitor, when she announced that she did not want and would not accept the legacy she had been left. She wouldn't have the first idea to know what to do with all that money, she said. In the end, they persuaded her to accept, Aunt Louisa and Mr Gringold between them. Gringold because he told her she would be insulting Thomas's memory by refusing, my aunt because she saw every reason not to. If I had been told about it, which I was not, I would have tried to persuade her as they did, and I make no excuses for it. I would have known, even then, how Thomas Pryde's hard-earned money should be used, in a way far better than some ne'er-do-well who would no doubt let it slip through his fingers like water.

Mother died not long after the money had been made over to her. She had never touched a single penny.

NINETEEN

It had been another sticky night, making sleep difficult, except in snatches. Reardon gave it up just before five and slipped out of bed so as not to wake Ellen, who had managed to drop off uneasily. He made tea and wandered out into the garden, mug in hand. It was no fresher outside, the atmosphere thick and heavy, airless. He watched a few desultory flashes of lightning, somewhere towards Kidderminster, and waited for the thunder, then the rain and the storm that had been hanging on for the last couple of days. Neither happened. Rather as nothing more was happening in the Blanchard case.

Nearly two weeks since it had begun. Sunday morning, and the church bells ringing. He stared across the hoped-for, still-weedy garden, stirring to life with birdsong. Even that sounded muted, as if the birds had had a weary night of it, too.

As he made breakfast, the local wireless crackled with electricity and told an unsurprised world they were having a heatwave. Reservoirs were dangerously low and people should not waste water. A carthorse had died of heatstroke while dragging a coal-cart up Emscott Hill.

The newspaper landed on the mat, headlines uppermost. 'What a sizzler!'

At Market Street, the day was getting under way. All the doors were propped open and Longton, in shirtsleeves and to hell with protocol, was reading the occurrence book. Nothing more exciting had happened than the usual Saturday-night pub brawl at the *George and Dragon*, two drunk and disorderlies brought in. 'Bloody hot, sir, isn't it?' he offered as Reardon came in.'

'Too right.'

Gilmour was already there. 'In my office, Joe, all right?' Reardon said. 'And bring some tea in with you, please.'

Five minutes later, Gilmour shouldered the door open wider, two mugs in his hand, and kicked it to behind him.

'For God's sake leave it open.' The window opposite was wide to allow for a notional passage of air, and it wasn't making much difference, but anything helped. 'Sit down, Joe.'

They drank their tea. Phoebe's letter was on the desk. Reardon picked it up and scanned it before handing it over to Gilmour. He walked to the window and stared out, hands in pockets, while he thought about what she'd told them the last time they'd seen her. Thought about Maxstead Court school, the teachers and the few pupils he'd spoken to. Watched a cat strolling slowly across Town Hall Square below, luxuriating in the heat, its tail in the air. A pigeon ventured too close. The cat stopped, arched its back, but then decided it couldn't be bothered and stalked away.

And it came to Reardon, just like that. That elusive idea he'd been chasing for days. He reached out and grasped it and things began to move into focus. The truth of what had happened had been there, in front of him, all the time. And as he realized the sickening import, he could have wished with all his heart that it had not.

The school, Eve Draper thought. What my life has meant. Edith. Everything I've done, always for her. Has she ever realized how much? She has never said so, nor ever thanked me in so many words, not after that first time, but that's Edith. She thinks because she said it once, it has never needed saying again, and of course that's true. Everything she is and does proves that she knows I don't need to be told that I am the rock she has leant against, always, just as she is mine. Until now.

She held the photograph of herself and Catherine. My Catherine. The moment I held you in my arms and saw the small, red face, crumpled like a new butterfly's wings, saw with wonder the little starfish hands with their tiny, perfect nails, looked into the eyes that as yet knew nothing of the cold world you had been born into, we knew each other, you and I. Love. Perfect love. You smiled, or what I fondly imagined was a smile. And all the way from France, when I carried you close to me, wrapped in a blanket, you only cried a little, when you were hungry. I've scarcely seen you cry at all since then. You were such a good child, and I used to be afraid you were bottling things up and tried to comfort you with a cuddle, but you always wriggled away from any contact. I had to content myself with the assurance that some people are born not able to let their feelings show.

We are bound, inextricably, the three of us: you, Edith and myself. Like you, Edith is not one for tears, or regrets. I am the one for that, the one whose heart rules her head in every way. My heart, that unreliable organ, jumping now like a caged bird at the very thought of what is to come. I must not allow myself to be afraid, so terribly afraid, that the shock of what I have just realized is the truth is going to be more than it can sustain.

But no, let's not prevaricate, I have known – or at the very least suspected – the truth from the first, but refused to admit it because it is more deeply painful than anyone can be expected to endure.

The weather had broken at last, and they drove to Maxstead in a thunderstorm of epic proportions. The rain hammered on the roof of the car, slid like a river down the windscreen, making the wipers virtually useless, visibility practically nil. Gilmour drove by instinct, thanking God they were the only madmen out on the road.

Grey old Maxstead could look forbidding even in the sunshine. Now, with the storm beating down upon it, it stood inimical and impervious to the elements as it had stood for centuries. By the time they had dashed the few yards to the massive front door, they were soaked. Inside, they shook themselves like terriers.

The school had remained blessedly cool all through the last enervating days of heat, its thick walls acting as insulation, and the air still struck chill on their dampness. No one had bothered to switch on the lights as the morning had darkened, and they made their way through dim, cool corridors that the storm had made even darker, while the rain continued to lash against the windows. Classes had started and murmurs came through the doors as they passed – a mere thunderstorm wouldn't be allowed to stop the march of lessons. No crocodile to church today, not in this weather, so lessons instead? Poor girls. When they reached the small anteroom to Miss Hillyard's study, the door was wide open, as was the study door. She wasn't there. Gilmour raised his shoulders and they went back to the entrance hall, just as she appeared at the top of the steps, Matron beside her.

Immediately she saw them standing below, Matron said, 'Not now, Inspector. Miss Hillyard can't talk to you. Something very sad has happened. It's Miss Draper. I'm afraid she has just died.'

Miss Hillyard was almost unrecognizable, tight-faced with grief. But she pulled herself together with an enormous effort of will, enough to say, with authority, 'It's all right, Matron. Perhaps you'd kindly find Catherine Leyland and send her to me? She's with Miss Golding, I believe, just now, Room Seven. Meanwhile, what did you want, Mr Reardon?'

I had wanted to speak to Miss Draper, Reardon thought, while Matron repeated, her eyes bright with astonishment and curiosity, 'Catherine, Miss Hillyard?'

'If you please. I'll wait for her here. We'll speak later, you and I, about – what's to be done.' Matron gave her a concerned glance, but hurried away.

Another crack of thunder rumbled away into the distance and left the hall oddly silent. The lofty, echoing spaces soared above them as they waited, no one speaking. The bowls of fresh flowers and small groups of easy chairs which had been introduced helped to make it slightly less empty and cavernous than when it had still been the Scroopes's gloomy ancestral home, but the walls where once forebears had hung looked oddly denuded, washed in a pale stone colour. No doubt awaiting a portrait of Miss Hillyard as founder of the school, and honours boards to record the achievements of past pupils.

Then, as suddenly as it had begun, the rain stopped. Almost at once the sun burst through and rays of sunlight poured though the great stained-glass window halfway up the stairs, staining the walls with splashes of vivid colour. Still no one spoke. Miss Hillyard, motionless and stunned-looking at the shock she had just received, was evidently waiting for them either to state their business or, more probably in the circumstances, to take their leave politely. But it hadn't taken Matron long to find Catherine, and now she too stood at the top of the stairs, a dreadful

awareness on her face. Miss Hillyard briefly closed her eyes.
Matron, no doubt with the best of intentions, had already broken
the news.

The huge staircase was wide and its stairs shallow, rising
fifty or sixty feet above the cold encaustic tiles beneath.
Catherine walked down quietly, sedately, each foot precisely
on each tread until she reached the foot and faced them.

'She's dead,' she said tonelessly. 'Aunt Evie's dead.' The
coloured light shone on her smoothly combed, fair hair. Her
beautiful eyes were gold flecked with green. They were wide,
blank, tearless.

'Catherine, my dear,' the headmistress said. She turned to
Reardon. 'I must ask you to leave us alone for a while, Inspector.
I need to speak with Catherine.'

'I understand, but I can't do that yet, I'm afraid. We need to
talk to you, you and Catherine.'

She drew herself up. 'At a time like this? No, I'm sorry, it's
not possible, not at this moment.'

'Miss Hillyard, it's not an option. I must insist.'

A bell rang and almost at once there were sounds of activity.
The girls would soon be in full flow, emerging from their classrooms. Wordlessly, Edith Hillyard turned away, her arm around
Catherine's shoulders, and led them into a small room off the
hall. Reardon remembered it had been used as the estate office
before Maxstead's existence as a school; a functional room,
then all Victorian sombreness. Like the rest of the school, it
had been redecorated. The walls were now a pale biscuit colour
and there were roses on the table, crimson and shell-pink. There
seemed to be roses everywhere at Maxstead now.

'Please say what you have to say as quickly as you can.'
Miss Hillyard took a chair for herself and waved a hand towards
others. Reardon took one with his back to the window, Gilmour
next to him, his role to listen and take notes. 'I don't wish
Catherine to be any more upset.'

'That's not my intention.' Reardon had scarcely ever been in
more of a dilemma as to how to carry out what he had to do
– or rarely felt so ill-equipped. He began by saying, 'We've
recently spoken to a man called Liptrott, Newman Liptrott.'

Her lip curled. 'Liptrott. Is that all you've come to talk about?

If so, you're wasting your time as well as my own. I've nothing to say about that man.' Her glance went again to Catherine, as if all this was an irrelevance in the face of what had just happened. 'I'll say again, it's not at all a convenient time to discuss such an unpleasant subject. Please say what you have to say, and leave. Catherine and I need time alone.'

'It's all right, I don't mind, Miss Hillyard,' Catherine said politely. She was white as milk and she had chosen to sit in a slightly uncomfortable-looking upright chair, ankles neatly crossed, her hands folded on her lap, keeping her thoughts, and her tears, to herself. For a girl her age, she was taking this in an extraordinarily self-contained way. 'Should I go?' she asked.

'I think not, Catherine,' said Reardon. 'What I have to say concerns you both.'

'Oh.'

Gilmour found his place in his notebook and licked his pencil. A bee blundered aimlessly around the room. Miss Hillyard drew in her breath and consulted her watch.

'Mr Liptrott is by no means all I want to speak about,' Reardon said at last, knowing the man would soon be the least of her worries. 'I'm aware the timing is unfortunate and very distressing for you. Murder is rather more than "unpleasant", however, which is why we are here. No, please listen to me. You know we have been looking for the person who was responsible for Isabelle Blanchard's murder, for terrifying young Josie and for attempting to kill Miss Keith. Yes, kill. She was pushed into the lake, and nearly died, and would have, if it hadn't been for Miss Cash.'

'Pushed? More mischief by some person trying to ruin the school, then.'

'No one has been trying to do that, Miss Hillyard. There's been no vendetta. That would have been in no one's interest, as someone recently pointed out to me. No one wanted your school to fail. Indeed, there was at least one person who was determined it should not.'

She didn't answer. The bee was now banging itself frantically against the windowpanes. Gilmour stood up and opened the window, wafted the creature to freedom with his notebook, and closed it again. He'd have done better to leave it open and let the cooler air from the thunderstorm's aftermath clear its stuffiness.

'Are you by any chance suggesting,' Miss Hillyard said incredulously, at last, 'that I, or any of my staff, had anything at all to do with any of that?'

'All of you were concerned with the school's welfare, especially yourself and Miss Draper.'

Catherine shifted on her chair and smoothed her skirt across her knees.

'And you think that means . . . How utterly ridiculous! I can't believe what I'm hearing. Myself? Miss Draper?'

Reardon himself was struggling to believe what he now knew.

Catherine suddenly spoke. 'Did you know Miss Draper was my aunt?'

'Yes, she told Mrs Reardon she was. I'm very sorry, Miss Catherine, about what's happened to her.'

'Thank you. But I must tell you,' she said, 'you're quite mistaken if you think she would do anything wrong. She was a good person and she'd never do a bad thing. Not possible.'

'I believe you. And from what I have gathered, she had the interests of the school very much at heart.'

She nodded. 'That's what she was like, always.'

'You were very close to her?'

'Yes. She brought me up after my parents died together in a motorcar accident when I was little. It was really hard for her, teaching all day and coming home at night to look after me, but she never complained. Evie would never do a bad thing,' she repeated, and then, having said her piece, she fell silent and began to smooth her dress again.

Miss Hillyard intervened. 'Catherine, my dear, this has been a great shock. Please don't upset yourself.'

'I'm not upset, Miss Hillyard, I knew about her heart, so it's not *such* a great shock. I don't mind talking about her. Honestly.'

'Well, for the moment, it's Mlle Blanchard I want to talk to you about,' Reardon said. 'I gather you were quite a favourite of hers.'

'Only because I was good at French.'

'But you and she had a friendly relationship.'

'No, not really.' After a pause, she added, 'Actually, I didn't like her at all.'

'Was there any particular reason for that?'

She considered. 'Well, for one thing, she was making Aunt Evie very miserable.'

'In what way?'

'Just that she was forever wanting her to talk about the time when they knew each other in France, years ago. Evie didn't want to; she said what was past was past. In fact it was upsetting her very much for some reason. I begged her to tell me what it was but she wouldn't. But I thought I knew, and in the end, I did find out.'

'Find out what, exactly?'

She was quiet for a long time and he thought she might be going to refuse to say, but in the end she began to speak, flatly and without expression, almost as if she were reciting something she'd been given to commit to memory. 'I don't see why I shouldn't tell you, not now. You see, Mummy and Daddy were lovely parents from what I remember of them, but I always knew I was adopted. They told me I was born in France during the war, on St Catherine's Day, just after that big battle on the Somme had finally finished, where my father had been killed. And Evie left off driving ambulances and brought me home to England because she knew her sister longed for a baby. She used to tell me how she carried me all the way, wrapped in a blanket. It was nearly Christmas, and it was a rough crossing, but she took good care of me. Of course, as I grew older, when I was living with her after my parents' accident, I came to realize that was just a story they'd all made up and that it was Evie who must be my real mother. It was the only logical explanation, wasn't it? She could never have carried on with her career as a single woman with a baby, but if her sister adopted me, she could be near me always. After they'd died and I was living with her, it was different. Everyone thought she was wonderful, taking me on. And she was. She wouldn't even have taken the job here if she'd had to make other arrangements for me. Abandoning me, she called it. So I determined to work for the scholarship, so we could still be together.'

He could well believe this of her. You didn't have to be long in her presence to believe this girl capable of such single-minded resolve, setting herself a goal, a purpose, letting nothing stop her until she achieved it. If Catherine decided to do something, she would.

'So, what was it you found out about Mlle Blanchard and your aunt?'

She frowned, as if weighing up how much she ought to say. But then she said, very matter-of-fact, 'Well, I think you've guessed, haven't you?'

He was taken aback. Something about her was beginning to unnerve him. 'Let's see if my guess is right, then: you found out that Isabelle Blanchard knew what you thought was the truth about your birth, that Miss Draper was your mother, and she was threatening her with it?'

'I thought so at first.' She frowned again. 'It didn't quite fit though. Evie had never admitted to being my mother. But I couldn't see it would have mattered all that much, anyway, when she was settled here at Maxstead. It seemed to me she believed it would, though, and it was making her ill. That woman was worrying her into her grave, and what was I to do without her?'

'So you struck up a friendship with Mam'selle in order to find out if what you thought was correct?'

'I couldn't do that, could I? You can't be friends with the teachers, but we did talk sometimes, after class. I suppose she thought she could find out what she wanted through me, because somehow she knew we were related, though I've no idea how she found out. She must have eavesdropped on us some time or other when we were talking.'

That was more than possible, he supposed, given Phoebe Catherall's assertion that Isabelle always managed to find out things, one way or another.

'All right, Catherine – you say you didn't like Mlle Blanchard, yet you gave her a brooch, didn't you? A little diamanté cat with red glass eyes.'

'No.'

However good she was at not showing her feelings, she was fibbing now. He sighed. 'I think you gave it to her to gain her favour, to stop her pestering your aunt.'

'I didn't give it to her. In any case, it was *me* she'd begun pestering. If she couldn't get what she wanted from Evie herself, she obviously thought I could, and would pass it on. I let her go on thinking that. I wanted to keep her away from Evie, yes, but I wanted to find out the truth more. And in the end I did.'

Reardon, who knew which truth she meant, waited. She didn't elaborate. 'Would you like to tell us what that was?'

'Well, she told me what had really happened when she and Evie had known each other in France, in the war. My father *had* been killed at the Somme, that was true, but Evie wasn't my mother. The woman who gave birth to me wasn't married to him and didn't want me.'

'Catherine,' Miss Hillyard said.

Something flickered in the strange green eyes. The girl turned and looked at her. Edith Hillyard sat as if turned to stone. Neither said a word.

'How did she know that, Catherine?' Reardon asked.

She shook her head.

He sighed. 'Then I'll tell you. She knew because she was there when you were born, fourteen years ago, and that knowledge could still make trouble. Sadly, however unfair, a shameful pregnancy and its concealment can follow a woman for the rest of her life. It can spell ruin if that woman has subsequently made a good marriage – or become successful in her own right. It's a motive for blackmail, serious blackmail in this case. But who would have taken Isabelle Blanchard's word alone for what she knew? She needed someone to back her up. She seriously miscalculated, however, if she had hoped to bribe your aunt, which was what she was trying to do.'

'Yes.'

'Because although there were other people who had been there when you were born, her mother and her stepsister, she knew they would never have agreed to help her in what she was trying to do. Her plans were not going as she wanted, and I think she told you the truth about your birth because she knew you'd hate your birth mother and hoped it would make you try to persuade your aunt against her. But it was Isabelle Blanchard you hated, for telling you that, wasn't it, Catherine?'

Still she kept silent.

It had come to the point where he couldn't put it off any longer, a duty that had to be accepted. This time, in circumstances he could never have envisaged, he had to brace himself for it. 'What she'd told you was enough cause for you to push her from that door.'

Miss Hillyard came to life, making an odd, strangled sort of sound. Gilmour raised his eyes from his notes, and his look cautioned her to silence.

Catherine, however, was quite unfazed. 'It didn't matter what I thought, not really, but she couldn't be allowed to ruin the school, could she? What would Evie and I have done then?'

He had questioned many murderers, but he had never been so flummoxed. Someone so young, a suspect in such a terrible crime, was outside his experience. But he realized he had ceased to think of her as a schoolgirl, even while he was struggling with what he knew was still to come. Catherine herself was not, however. She was almost smiling, as if what he'd said was quite reasonable, and she was prepared to give an equally reasonable explanation. And Edith Hillyard? She had known the truth, too, he thought. Instinctively, perhaps, or perhaps she had just suspected and been unwilling to believe it would ever come to this. She, too, was rigidly silent now, imprisoned in her own thoughts. Then she said, white to the lips, 'It must have been an accident. Catherine?'

'No, Miss Hillyard,' Reardon said, 'it was planned. Very cleverly planned, wasn't it, Catherine?'

She returned his gaze steadily, even smiling very slightly. 'Well, it seemed impossible at first, but nothing is, is it? I didn't mean to kill her, just to scare her – but the idea grew.'

'How did it happen?'

She was still sitting upright on her chair, ankles crossed, her hands folded together in her lap. 'Well, you see,' she said conversationally, 'she left Maxstead quite suddenly and I thought it was all finished. Until she sent Evie a letter. She hadn't given up at all. Evie said to ignore it, but I couldn't do that, because I knew that wouldn't stop her. So I answered it myself, telling her I'd found out what it was she wanted from Evie, and we had to talk.'

'And she agreed?'

'Oh yes, I knew she would. I'd worked it all out. It had to be here, at Maxstead, of course, I couldn't get away from here to meet her anywhere else, could I? I knew she could get here by taxi, and she wouldn't keep it waiting – too expensive. She would have meant to do what she'd always done before – walk along to the village and ring from the callbox there, either for another taxi or for that man, Mr Deegan, to take her home.'

'Mr Deegan?'

'She used to meet him in the east wing. She thought nobody knew, but we did. She didn't even suspect anything when I suggested the room where they used to meet. It was quite near that door that came to light when that last bit was knocked down. Avis had said what a hoot it would be if someone opened it and stepped out, not knowing, like one of those silly tricks she played. I went to have a look. It was boarded up, but the nails were quite easy to remove, as it happened.'

'And replace, afterwards?'

'Well, not really. I had to use a brick to hammer them in and they wouldn't go back properly. But it didn't matter. I knew when she was found, they'd soon work out what had happened.' She stopped and smiled into their stunned silence, then frowned. 'So long afterwards, how did you know it was me?'

'For one thing, the brooch, Catherine,' Reardon said at last. 'It was a complete giveaway.'

She shrugged. 'That's not important.'

'I'm afraid it is. She was wearing it when she was found. You did give it to her.'

'No, I would never have done that! I was wearing it that night, for luck, but when I tried to move that canvas to cover her – you wouldn't believe how awfully heavy it was – it caught the brooch and pulled it off. The clasp wasn't very strong, anyway, and it fell, right on to her face.' For a moment, she looked outraged. 'I loved it, Evie had given it to me. I couldn't leave it there – but I could never wear it after that, could I? It wasn't very expensive, *she* would have despised it, so I pinned it on her dress. She was mad on cats, so it seemed right.'

All this was quite outside the normal conventions he and everyone else understood. It was against nature, but it wasn't over yet. 'That wasn't all though, Catherine, was it? What about

Josie? Did she know something that made you shut her up in
that room?'

'Poor Josie, I'm sorry about that. No, of course she didn't
know anything, but she'd seen Mam'selle having words with
me. We were actually talking about Aunt Evie. I was very cross
and telling her she must leave Evie alone, but maybe Josie just
thought I was being told off for something – we were both
really angry, and I think she saw that. And afterwards, well, I
knew you'd be questioning everyone and she would feel she
had to tell, sooner or later, unless she was too frightened in
some way. She still might, of course, but it doesn't matter now.
I don't care what happens, now Evie's dead.'

The way she said it, it was as if a trickle of icy water was
making its way down his spine. Especially since he knew it
was very likely to be true. She seemed to be quite unafraid
of what must follow from her admissions. 'Anyway,' she went
on, 'the others, those silly Elites, had forced her to agree to
clear all that rubbish they'd left behind that night, so I followed
her.'

'Followed her through the pantry window?'

'There was no need. Josie needn't have climbed through,
either. If she'd thought it through, she would have seen there's
only one place the staff would keep the keys where they can
be got at easily – in the little wall cupboard by the main door.
I share a room with Selina Bright and Antonia Freeman. Antonia
was in the sick bay with a cold that night, and as soon as
Selina's said her prayers and got into bed, she wouldn't know
if a herd of elephants was in the room, so it was easy for me
to slip out, just as I had the first time.'

'And Miss Keith?'

She blinked as if she'd forgotten who Miss Keith was. 'Oh,
yes. Well, there's a wild orchid grows down by the lake that I
wanted for my botany project and I went to look for it after
breakfast. She was standing there by the water's edge, without
her shoes. Aunt Evie seemed to have had some idea she was
somehow mixed up with Mam'selle, that they were much friend-
lier than everyone thought, so . . . It was easy.'

There was nothing anyone could say.

'I had to do it, don't you see, for Evie?' she said after several minutes, as if that was more than justification, staring into the distance, beyond them all. Beyond remorse, or self-reproach. Was it possible she didn't understand the enormity of what she had done? To say that it had been done for Eve's sake didn't go anywhere near enough to explain it. Her love for her aunt seemed genuine – yet, did she even know what love was? Had the grief of knowing she had not been wanted by her own mother – that she'd been given away as an unwanted baby – destroyed it, or had she ever known it?

Gilmour closed his notebook. He still didn't look as though he believed what he'd heard. It was taking an effort of will for Reardon to remind himself sharply that she had cold-bloodedly planned and killed. He stood up, feeling bone weary. There were questions still to be answered, but for the present Catherine had to be cautioned and told she would have to come with them.

'You can't take her away!' Edith Hillyard was grief-stricken. 'She's just a child!'

'It doesn't matter,' Catherine repeated, with that bright, blank, unnerving look that made the hairs on Reardon's arms stand on end, and asked if she might take some books with her. She really didn't seem to care what was happening. Or perhaps it was just failure to comprehend what lay ahead. She was fourteen. They didn't hang children, even if they were killers. But he'd already discovered that he could no longer think of her as a child, not in any sense.

He did a surprising, and perhaps inadmissible, thing. It surprised him, most of all. He put his hand out and took hers, held it pressed between both his large ones. She let it stay there. She was a child after all, he thought, in need of comfort. Until it came to him that she was not allowing it to stay there because she was in need of sympathy. It was simply indifference.

As Gilmore guided her out to the car, Edith Hillyard said, 'I must tell you the whole truth, Inspector.'

Reardon, who had, consciously or not, known the truth ever since his last talk with Phoebe Catherall, shook his head. 'Not now.'

But she ignored this and with some desperation, she said, 'I was never meant to be a mother, you must understand. I had my career to make. I had nothing but what I earned. It was long before—'

Long before she had inherited money. Perhaps she was right; she wasn't meant to be a mother, if she still thought money would have made a difference.

EPILOGUE

A new term, the school coming to life again after the summer holidays. Taxis and cars arriving with girls and parents, and one of Folbury's Countrywide buses pressed into service, disgorging a group of girls who have been met in London by Miss Golding and brought by train.

Trunks, suitcases and bags litter the corridors as girls try to find their new rooms, screaming with delight as they greet friends they haven't seen for eight whole weeks.

Edith walks to the window and watches as Antonia Freeman drags her suitcase from the bus. A different Antonia, looking scarcely able to believe she's back here, or what has happened. A letter clutched in her hand, she flies across to Josie Pemberton. They've been writing to each other during the holidays and have asked to share a room this year. Edith smiles. She knows about the situation with Antonia's grandfather and his offer of money for her keep while she's at art college – if she can get herself accepted, which Miss Keith had been sure will pose no problem whatever. Edith knows this because she has brokered it, and persuaded the girl's mother to accept what she had hitherto insisted on seeing as charity, even from her own father.

She turns from the window and tidies herself with a touch of powder, a discreet dab of fresh scent, readying herself to have a word with parents who have brought their children and would like to see her. There are always those who need reassurance. Yes, she'll make sure Lilian wears her winter liberty bodices, that Margaret writes her Sunday letter home, that little Maureen can take her teddy bear to bed with her.

She flicks a comb through her hair and has a fleeting thought that perhaps she ought to have it cut off as so many women are doing, though she doesn't linger on the idea. She likes to think she is not a vain woman by any means. There's nothing else in her appearance to be especially proud of, except maybe that, her one asset, especially when she lets it down, at night, when it falls, still dark brown and glossy, to her waist.

Like treacle toffee, he'd said, lifting off that hideous uniform hat and removing her hairpins gently so that it cascaded around her shoulders.

She can't think of that now. But the thought remains, without her consent.

She has never been the sort of person who makes friends easily or quickly, but he was different, disarming, refusing to be held at arm's length. She had found herself agreeing to meet him, whenever they could snatch an hour. Totally out of character for her, but they were all different, less inhibited out there in wartime, in that unreal world where life was uncertain from one hour to the next, amid that unspeakable chaos of mud, blood, mutilation and death. The Great War, they were calling it now. What was great about it, except the scale of that obscene, wanton destruction of human life?

He had been an Oxford don before he was sent over to France, classified as a non-combatant since he refused to abandon his pacifist beliefs and fight, and was therefore thrown straight into the seventh circle of Hell, working as a stretcher-bearer, sent out into the front line under shellfire, unarmed, to bring in the casualties.

The school drive ends just below Edith's bedroom and one of the taxi drivers does a noisy three-point turn on the gravel, grinding his gears, setting her teeth on edge at the incompetence. Being taught how to drive an ambulance was how she and Eve had learnt to drive – properly. Eager to do their bit, never dreaming of the unspeakable awfulness they would have to face.

She should go down, do her duty. But still she sits, looking at her face in the mirror, seeing another.

He was young, a year or two younger than she was, only just installed as a don at Oxford University. He'd had a love of life, somewhat in the way of her father Jamie, but behind his laughing eyes, the joke on his lips, were the unimaginable horrors that he – that everyone – saw every day, that his quiet academic life could never have prepared him for.

He once brought Edith roses – where he'd got them from, God knows. Roses of Picardy.

Goldie senses something and comes to put her paws on Edith's knees, gazing soulfully up at her. She picks the little dog up, nuzzling her warm fur, feeling her vibrant little body. Goldie licks her face affectionately, then settles back in her arms.

Afterwards, after it was all over for her and she lay in the small house where Mathilde had tended her so well, assisted by Phoebe, and he was long dead – as by then he was bound to be, caught in crossfire as he and his companions struggled to bring yet another wounded or dying man from the trenches – she couldn't believe any of it was real. Had it been love they had experienced, or only the tomorrow-we-die disease that gripped everyone out there? The madness that said nothing mattered because nothing was real in that manic world where men were ordered to maim and slaughter one another without knowing why they were doing it. In truth they had barely known each other. There hadn't been time for love to develop gradually, as it should, but there was an undeniable attraction between them, which might, who knew now, have turned into the real thing. As it was, they had escaped when they could, where they could, and made love to the ceaseless battering of artillery fire and the nightmare of what they daily witnessed.

Why had it been such a shock when it happened? She was no innocent young girl, after all; she was twenty-six and knew the possible consequences, yet innocent in the sense that what they had done had been a new experience for her. We were all under intolerable strain, she thinks, and he was a man with the look in his eye of one faced with his inevitable doom. What was then between them might never have come to anything. Except that it had. A child had been brought into the world. A child, Edith is still profoundly, deeply ashamed to admit, even to herself, especially now, that she did not want. Addie would have called that a sin and she would have been right.

Catherine.

They are taking care of her now, where she is. Edith has not seen her. She has written to her but Catherine has not replied. Edith has been told that she is happy, and is still having some form of schooling, which seems to be all she cares about. Happy? That seems incredible, but no more incredible than what she did. Edith closes her eyes. Catherine, that lovely child with those green-gold eyes.

That other young girl had green eyes, too, but of a different kind. Mathilde's daughter – Edith's Nemesis, had she but known it. She watched us all, watched and stored up what she saw and then, years later, tried to use it.

I was alone, Edith justifies herself. Unmarried, penniless, a woman with a child, with the career I had hoped to take up again after the war fast receding towards the horizon. Had it not been for Phoebe and her aunt – and, of course, dearest Eve – I would have had to go back to London, in disgrace with nowhere to go. I could not have gone home to my mother. I was right to let Eve take the child to someone who would give her a good home and love her as their own.

How was I to know how drastically my circumstances would change? How soon I would have the chance of my own school, to make up for my mistake, hopefully, by steering generations of children through my hands? But I was right when I told Inspector Reardon that I was never meant to be a mother, in that sense.

Before she goes downstairs, Edith leans from her open window and with her nail scissors cuts off a rose. Against all expectations, the 'Zéphirine Drouhin' she got Heaviside to plant there has already reached the first floor. She buries her nose in its frilled, carmine-pink perfection, breathes in its heavy scent and fastens it to her dress.

It's not right that I should show too much grief for Catherine. I cannot. I never really knew her.

She goes downstairs to the front steps of her school, a smile on her face.